PYTHON

PYTHON

PYTHON

Hell Slithers, Lust Simmers

CARINA NOLAN

PYTHON
HELL SLITHERS, LUST SIMMERS

All publishers, movie producers, and directors are welcome to email the author at:
pythonthriller@yahoo.com
Facebook Python by Carina Nolan
Twitter Pythonthriller

This book "PYTHON" in its entirety is one hundred percent fictional.

All characters, places, people's names, things, information, descriptions, locations are purely fictional and do not exist in any shape or form at all in real life. Any individual known or unknown to the author or co-author does not even distantly inspire them. All incidents and this whole story "PYTHON" is pure invention by the authors. This entire story is totally from the imagination of the author and co-author and no part of this story has ever happened in real life.

Any similarities of people, places, things or any of the content in this book is purely coincidental and there is no relationship whatsoever to any existing person alive or dead.

iUniverse books may be ordered through booksellers or by contacting:

iUniverse
1663 Liberty Drive
Bloomington, IN 47403
www.iuniverse.com
1-800-Authors (1-800-288-4677)

ISBN: 978-1-4917-7016-0 (sc)
ISBN: 978-1-4917-7015-3 (e)

Library of Congress Control Number: 2015909343

Print information available on the last page.

iUniverse rev. date: 08/25/2015

PREVIEW

The African Rock Python lives in the tropical African Savannas and now, unfortunately, in the U.S. state of Florida. In the Savannas, winter begins in December and ends in February; summer starts in May and ends in December. In the summer, the Savannas have six to eight months of heavy rainfall, and very dry months in the winter. It has a constant, warm climate and is mostly seventy degrees Fahrenheit. This python likes to live near water and the edges of forests.

It is the third largest snake in the world. It is very bulky and has a dark arrowhead shape on its head. They can get to be over two hundred and fifty pounds and thirty feet in length. They look slimy, but they're dry and smooth to the touch. Like all snakes, the African Rock Python moves by slithering its body over the ground.

All pythons kill by constricting their prey. The African Rock Python can live for up to a year without food if they eat a creature large enough to sustain it - such as a human. Starch ligaments hold the jaw together, which stretches out like a rubber band allowing it to eat prey with awkward shaped protruding limbs such as an antelope. They have sharp inverted fangs on the upper jaw and small teeth surround the lower jaw. They sometimes use their teeth to hold prey as the python coils its body around it.

The African Rock Python is dependent on fresh water and becomes dormant during the dry season. The female can lay up to one hundred eggs and incubates them for approximately three months. She aggressively defends her eggs. The hatchlings grow between eighteen and twenty four inches in length. Their life span can be up to thirty years.

This python lives alone and hunts alone. It is a carnivore, which means it only eats meat. They eat crocodiles, alligators, birds, cats, dogs, and whatever meat is available when they're hungry. They don't chew their food but have strong acids in their stomach that digests their food well. When the snake is small, predators, such as large lizards, crocodiles, birds of prey, cats, and pigs hunt and eat the python. However, when the python is fully-grown it hunts these same animals for food.

Because of its extremely vicious and strong capability to capture and strangle most animals of any size, it has few predators as an adult, except for man. Their skin is very valuable for women's accessories. Snake accessories of all kinds are a sign of classy sexiness and good luck.

Ironically, the python is a terrorizing predator of man when the situation is right.

Recently, the African Rock Python has been discovered in Florida's everglades. This brings an additional eerie element to the already Burmese python infested everglades. Scientists have theories that the African Rock Python could mate with the Burmese python and create a vicious man-eating monster python. Is the African Rock limited to the everglades, or has it made its way to other parts of the sunshine state, unknowingly to authorities, but strikingly to an innocent community.

PROLOGUE

------- At the end of a long pier connected to his Palm Harbour lake front property, Adam Stanford sat in the shade of his umbrella table, swirling the ice cubes in his cocktail. The sound of the ice cubes tinkling against the glass came as a blessed relief from the whining phone calls he received from confused elderly customers who knew little about on-line banking. Ruffling his hair, he felt a slight breeze, which seemed to blow away the day's tension from working in a tiny cubicle where he spent grueling days as an online customer service representative at the local bank. Sudden movement in a distant tree caught his eye. Focusing, he glanced up into the eyes of a large wild bobcat looking his way. His hand stopped swirling his cocktail. Adrenaline readied his body for a fast run to the house. The bobcat had him in site and the only weapon he had was the glass in his hand. He threw it at the animal as hard as he could. The projectile hit the tree limb and shattered. The animal bounded off and away from him, disappearing into a grove of mango trees. The tranquility of the evening had ended. He felt his heart pounding in his ears. Looking around for a possible mate to the animal, he saw none but didn't feel like sticking around if one decided to show up. Therefore, he quickly went back to his condominium. He never imagined a bobcat to be that large. Little did Adam know that this was only the first and the least of many terrifying physical violations and mental horrors waiting within this tranquil sub-tropical environment he and his wife Stella now called home.

CHAPTER ONE

With her face upward, Stella closed her eyes. She took a gentle breath, inhaling the warm, soothing aroma coming from homemade bread that was baking in the oven. Her body felt a sense of calmness as her beautiful, dreamy eyes slowly opened.

Flowers and candlelight already on the table, she then drew the dining room shades, the final touch in setting the evening for dinner with her husband Adam, with whom she was lucky to have a treasured romantic relationship.

Moving into the kitchen, she put oven mitts on her hands and stood patiently against the counter, waiting for her bread with her arms folded. With a slight turn of her head, she was able to capture sight of the glowing candles in the darkness. As she stared and admired the gently moving, yellow and orange flames, her mind drifted in the peacefulness of the afternoon. Daydreaming, she found her thoughts seductively soaked in a pool of passion. The timer bell went off. She snapped out of her trance and removed the hot bread.

Stella felt fortunate to have a comforting sense of security deep in her heart that was rare with women.

She placed the bread on a wooden slab along with fresh creamy butter and took it to the table. The romantic dinner was ready. If Adam showed up soon, it would be perfect. She walked to the kitchen window to see if he was on his way back from the pier. There was a warm summer breeze, and the soft cotton curtain swept her face. Standing on her toes, leaning over the sink, she glanced out and looked around. Suddenly, all the calmness zapped out from under her, faster than a lightning strike. She noticed a look of fear on her husband's face as she watched him scurrying and tripping on the walkway back to their home. Her eyes flickered all over, wondering what could be happening.

Suddenly, she saw movement in a nearby tree. "Holy crap! It's a big bobcat." The bobcat gave a long content yawn while its eyes closed and opened and then opened wider. It was fully awake and looked prepared for its next primitive endeavor. Stella's body froze. Her eyes bulged in shock - its fangs seemed as long as elephant tusks and its head looked gargantuan. It stood up, moved its nostrils up and down with a look of curiosity, and began its famous catwalk on a long branch leading to their front balcony.

Adam rushed in through the front door in a steaming rage. He kicked his shoes off with such force they hit the ceiling. Pieces of the old popcorn paint fell to the floor. "Damn it! Make me a drink fast! Make it strong!" He glanced down and noticed spots of blood on his wife's feet. "I saw the bobcat through the kitchen window. Try to sit and relax, honey." Stella was nervous but tried hard to appear calm. Adam walked anxiously into the living room and plopped on the couch. "Why is there blood on your feet?" "I'm okay, the kitchen window shattered when I slammed it shut."

She felt his high voltage fright and frustration emit from across the room while she fixed his drink. Her stomach flipped over in a jolt of anxiety and fear. She remembered that she had left a bowl of fresh cat food by the front door that morning for a stray. She did not feel safe enough to open her front door and retrieve the bowl of cat food.

She handed Adam a double scotch and milk, his favorite, sat next to him and gave him a hug. She could feel that her comforting embrace helped her husband to relax. He took a deep breath and calmed a bit down.

"You always know how to handle me, honey," he told her. She whispered in his ear, I've handled you a lot better than this, calm down and wait a little while, the cat will go away - hopefully far away. Adam could not help but take another deep breath. Suddenly they heard a loud vicious growl outside their front door. They ran to a window and saw the mean faced bobcat walking along their front railing.

"This bobcat looks unusually big. It might be a different species. I have to shoot the bastard. He's too close and too hungry. Look at him, he wants dinner," said Adam. Stella grabbed Adam's arms, "*No, you can't*, it's not self-defense. Leave him alone. He'll go away."

"When will it be self-defense, Stella? When his fangs are sticking deep in your throat, out the other side. With your tonsils and thyroid like a kabob, and your flesh scraping against the cement - as he slowly drags your petite body down the rough stairs. Will you let me shoot him then or *will you have trouble speaking?*"

Bang!

Stella jumped from fright. "What the heck was that?" Adam ran into the kitchen and quickly drew his head through the sharp points of glass on the frame of the kitchen window. "Watch your face and feet, honey!" She grabbed a broom and hurriedly moved as much glass as possible out of his way.

"Where the hell is he?" Adam scoped all around and brought his head in. "Oh God! A sharp point of glass just missed your eyeball." Stella panicked. "Don't put your head through that window again!" Stella suspiciously walked out of the kitchen and opened the front door. She screamed, *"Oh My God!* She slammed the door shut and stood with her head, back, and arms against the door in horror. Her eyes looked ready to explode....*"Hurry, get your rifle!"* Adam bolted upstairs to get his rifle. "He's swinging back and forth on our wrought iron door. He ripped the screen. He's going to kill us!" screamed Stella.

A deafening gunshot came from outside. A crumbling sound ran down the front door and then there was a heavy thump. A shivering chill ran up Stella's spine. "What the fuck!" said Adam, holding his rifle.

"Are you alright in there?" They heard their neighbor Harry ask, as he held his rifle in front of his condominium next door, out of sight.

Adam opened the front door. The bobcat was laid out with the whole screen and frame entwined in its long nailed claws and fangs. "Yes, we're fine," yelled Adam. That was horrifying. He was over on a branch and suddenly we saw him walking on our railing. Good thing you were home, Harry."

Harry's voice was hoarse and scratchy from tobacco damage. All those years of smoking cigarettes ate away at his vocal cords and rotted his lungs. He quit the poison chemical sticks a few years back but his symptoms haven't changed. He still hacks green and yellow bloody mucous every morning. On some of his real bad mornings, Stella and Adam can hear him through the walls and they picture his black bloody lungs in the toilet. It's a terrible thing to listen to and a very painful thing for Harry to suffer through.

"Yeah, I heard him growl, said Harry. I looked out my kitchen window and said to myself, this wild cat is much too close for comfort. It gave me a chance to challenge my old skills."

"Well, you surely still have it."

A few residents spilled out onto the parking lot and asked, "What is going on?" Harry leaned over the balcony railing and tried his best to yell out in between his coughs, "Don't worry, it was just a bobcat that smelled my chicken cooking. I'll get a shovel and bag, and bury him in the woods. It's very rare that one comes around. Nothing to be scared about," he yelled in a scratchy hoarse voice to the residents. "He does look a little bigger than the ones that sometimes are seen lying on a branch and minding their own business. This one might have escaped from a zoo a long time ago. I haven't heard any news about an escape recently."

Adam stood with his rifle pointed at the laid out cat through the wrought iron bars. "I'll help you Harry," Adam offered.

"No, I think your nerves have had enough. I'll have my roommate Sam help me carry this meaty cat to the woods."

"Are you sure he's dead?" asked Adam.

"He's deader than a doornail. Shot him straight through the head. I'm a hunter from way back, up in Vermont. Now you go ahead and take care of your little woman."

"Thanks so much, Harry, we are so grateful. We owe you one," Stella told him.

"Yeah, a big one," said Adam.

Adam slammed the front door shut. We'll have the screen door replaced next week, he told his wife.

"Are you still nervous, Stella."

"Just a little. I'll be okay. Though I did lose my appetite."

"I did too, said Adam."

"Let's forget dinner. Besides, I don't trust having any of the food I made. You know how broken glass flies."

She gently grabbed Adam's hand and led him to the sofa. Sitting close to each other, Adam held his drink in his right hand and put his left arm around her shoulders. He lovingly pushed her head toward his lips and kissed her gently on the forehead. In a tired worn out voice he said, "I don't know what I'd do without you sweetheart, *or Harry!*" They laughed. She sensuously brushed her nose and lips against his cheek and gently said, "I think I know how to make up for our unfortunate evening, honey. I'll call our friends in the morning and plan a fun get together by the pool this weekend."

Stella wiped her feet with a dishtowel and picked at the splints of glass with tweezers. "They're very small cuts, nothing to worry about." The slight bleeding stopped. With a seductive stare that could melt a stick of butter, she held Adam's hand and gently led him up from the sofa. She felt a slight sting on one foot and a tingle between her legs. She turned, stood still, and stared into his eyes with depth as the deepest ocean. Adam's mouth loosened up as he gazed back into her ever so rare bright baby blues lined with natural dark lashes. He grabbed her shoulders fast and strong with fierce love. He hesitated for a second, still looking into her eyes, and then began kissing the side of her neck with great passion as her head fell back and a beautiful sensation ran through her. She lifted her head and looked at him with a mysterious glow that told a story. His tongue was about to fall out any second. He grabbed his drink, took a fast swig like a tough cowboy, attempted to place the glass back down on the end table, and missed. Neither of them reacted to the mess. After all, what's a spilled drink after a bobcat invasion. Adam slowly followed his wife's mysterious dainty steps up to their bedroom, with his eyes glued to the two beautiful smiles hanging from under the back of her skimpy shorts.

After an intense exchange of the love they had for each other - they laid in bed and talked. Adam grumbled, "I can't sit and relax on my own property without some wild animal getting in the way." Stella rolled over, gently placed her head on his comfortable broad chest, and sweetly whispered, "Honey, there were compromises we made before we agreed to move to Florida." "I know," said Adam. "The frigid temps, sleet, snow, and gusty winds at our cozy colonial home in Massachusetts for the warm tropical climate and wild bobcats at this beautiful Holly Meadow Village on Emerald Lake."

She smirked, "Oh, we'll probably never see another one." She saw his eyes were closing and as he began to fall asleep, he mumbled, "I'm glad we're in Florida, honey." Her eyes became dreamy and she fell asleep on his furry chest.

CHAPTER TWO

Stella knew when Adam became vice president of the Holly Meadow Condominium Board, while he was still working full time at the bank, it would cause more stress than he could handle. However, retirement was not in the near future and Adam enjoyed his board work more than his regular job.

The next morning Stella woke a bit earlier than Adam. The sun shone brightly through the side of the blinds. Adam yawned and peeked over to her with a smile, "Good morning sweetheart." She returned a sweet smile and rolled onto his body. She swept his graying black hair off his face and played her fingers through it. They felt the same level of contentment as they did ten years ago, as newlyweds. This was a second marriage for both.

He loved the hourglass shape he felt when he ran his hands along the sides of her full breasts, into her curved waist, around her hips and over her buttocks. At middle age, she still astounded him.

Stella always knew the hourglass look and feel of a woman's body is an innate uncontrollable turn on for men. She maintained her weight and felt fortunate that she inherited her mother's natural proportionate figure.

She turned her head, glanced at the strong ray of sunlit cotton dust dancing over the snow-white sheets, and softly spoke in her sensuous tone, "It looks like a perfect day to gather our Holly

Meadow friends and embrace the beautiful sun by the pool, don't you think so my love."

"Sounds fine with me," he responded.

She knew he would enjoy being with his friends and having a few beers after a hard workweek.

Stella turned onto her back and gave her body a seductive twist and stretch. She threw the sheet over him and arched her upper back with a slight moan in her exhale, so he could not help notice her still firm breasts and pink nipples. Desire seeped through her body.

"Good genes, Wow, did I hit it lucky, and her mother still looks good at seventy-five." He thought with a big smile.

She hoped for a romantic session like the one the afternoon before, but the outline of his magic wand looked limp under the sheet. Therefore, she felt he was not thinking the same way.

She hopped out of bed and grabbed her bathrobe off the chair. As she walked out of the bedroom, she told him, "Honey, I'll be in the next room making calls."

Stella called her friend Bernice. "Hey woman, are you and Nick busy today? Do you feel like having a relaxing day at the pool with no cell phones?" She heard Bernice yell to her husband Nick and ask him what he thought.

Stella could hear Nick in the background.

"Tell her sure, I'll bring some beer."

"Did you hear him, Stella?"

"I sure did. How about one o'clock?" Stella asked.

"See you then," replied Bernice.

"Adam, who should I call next?"

"Maryann and Abe, honey."

Maryann's response was warm and happy. "Abe and I were just wondering what we should do today, we will be happy to be there."

"Adam and I thought we could all make it an old fashion day of just plain fun and ask everyone not to bring their cell phones. Will that be a problem?"

"Not at all, that's a great idea! I'll enjoy the peace of no cell phones. Actually, it's such a good idea, we should practice having "no cell phone" parties every once in awhile. It would be quite a challenge for some. See you then," Maryann responded.

Maryann's husband Abe, now retired, worked hard all his life as a CPA. His many years of long hours at the office - often tested his marriage. Maryann being an old fashion country girl was very understanding. She spent many nights feeling lonely, but Abe was a good provider and a good family man, whenever he did have the time.

Stella thought about calling others, but knew that Maryann would spread the word for her. The people Stella did call were some of her closest friends in the complex and they socialized often. They shared their dreams, hopes, desires, happiness, sadness, and everything else that went along with life. There are always a few people that meet and fit together a little more comfortable than others fit. However, all Holly Meadow residents were always more than welcome to join any gatherings or parties at the pool.

Stella returned to the bedroom and found Adam snoring away as if he had the trunk of an elephant. With her hands on her waist, she stared at him and thought, "Well, *that* didn't take him long. I'll use my ear plugs and join him for a morning nap so we'll both be well rested this afternoon."

After a couple of hours, they both awoke. Adam's well-endowed wand stood up with great posture, draped with a corner of the soft white sheet. "I see we have a visitor who stands tall and likes to poke around" said Stella. Adam smiled, "He's lost, direct him to the right place"

"He can use his GPS later on tonight," she responded.

Stella explained she felt too preoccupied thinking about getting prepared for the pool and seeing their friends. They hopped out of bed and got themselves ready for an enjoyable afternoon.

As they stepped onto the long pier that led to their pool on the lake, Stella admired the stunning flowers that crept over the border of the walkway. "Look Adam!" She swung her arm across his chest. They stopped walking. Three adorable tiny baby alligators scooted out from the flowers, ran across their way and into the water. "All of God's babies are irresistibly cute, even those of the most vicious animals. Maybe it's nature's way of programming the mind to channel the greatest desire to nurture and love all offspring," she thought.

The sky was turquoise blue and a few cotton candy clouds floated by. "I can't say it enough times, this is paradise," Stella told her husband.

As they approached the pool gate, they heard laughter in the short distance. "Sounds like some friends are already here," remarked Stella.

They walked through the gate and noticed Bernice relaxing on a lounge chair. Bernice looked at Stella and Adam. "Hi guys, glad you could make it," she said with a sarcastic smile. "Would you like one of my home-made wine coolers, Stella." Stella looked at Bernice's heat catching black pants and got a hot flash. Bernice always wore black capri style pants at the pool, or pedal pushers as they use to call them in her old home town of Hampton, New Hampshire. She was self-conscious about her legs - but not her large breasts. She was always sure to show off her bosom with a low cut bright colored bikini top. For forty, she looked great.

"I'd love a wine cooler," Stella responded. "Adam brought plenty of beer and wine in his cooler. Everyone is welcome to help themselves."

While Bernice prepared her drink, Stella looked around and took in the beautiful scenery. The forest around them was afire with rich warm golden sun light and a misty glow hung over the rich deep green leaves that dressed the trees along the canal. "It's a perfect day," she said.

"Yes, it is," said Bernice. She handed Stella her drink and lay back down on her chair. Bernice gazed at the long legged Herons as they walked elegantly among the thick grass carpet that lined the water near the pool. She loved the interesting wild life that surrounded her home.

In the distance, Emerald Lake shimmered like diamonds.

"This is a million dollar view. I'm glad Adam and I was lucky enough, at the time, to buy the only condominium for sale here at Holly Meadow," Stella told Bernice. "I find myself mentally and spiritually in the midst of glorious beauty and sense deeply the grandeur in nature's production when I gaze at this spectacular landscape." Stella expressed with a smile.

"Now you can't give these beautiful condos away," said Bernice.

"It's a tough market everywhere, especially here in Florida," Stella commented.

Adam grabbed a cold beer and sat with Bernice's husband, Nick, at an umbrella table by the pool. "How's it going my big man?" Nick asked.

"Late yesterday afternoon I came down here to relax and enjoy a drink and I was interrupted by a large hungry bobcat."

"That must have sucked," said Nick. "One will show up around here every couple of years, but for the most part we never see them. I think once in a great while one strays away from the deep dense forest areas where they prefer to stay."

Nick and Bernice had owned a vegetable stand a few miles inland for many years. Customers in the neighborhood kept them updated on the local news. Nick now works part time in the retail business while Bernice stays home and enjoys her early retirement.

Maryann and Abe arrived a little while later and stood in the pool sipping their summer cocktails. "I'm glad you thought of this Stella, I was long overdue for a relaxing day at the pool," said Abe. "Yeah, I know, being retired is tough," Nick told Abe. Abe maintained a jolly disposition. He responded, with his signature jolly smile, "Maryann and I have to get out on our boat more often. If any of you ever feel like going out on the lake, give us a call, sometimes we need a few good friends to give us an incentive or even remind us that we own a boat. The excitement and novelty of having a boat wears off fast."

Stella glanced through the pool gate and noticed Carolyn walking down the pier. "Looks like we have a surprise guest."

As Carolyn walked through the gate, her face was glowing. She held a bottle of Merlot.

"Hey guys, mind if I join you?"

"Of course not," said Stella. "You are most welcome; it's your pool too."

"Condo living is so luxurious," said Carolyn. "Yes, it's nice not to have to worry about the grass being cut and all the maintenance that a house requires over time," said Stella. "Especially since my husband never owned a tool box. My dear Adam can't even put a nail in the wall; unless he's faking he can't, because he hates maintenance work."

"Honey, the only tool a man needs is a snake, and not the one that's used to unclog a pipe," said Adam. "Oh, Adam, stop it with the silly talk. That's definitely *not* the only tool a man needs." Stella told her husband in a harsh tone.

Carolyn, a schoolteacher - off for the summer, is sometimes envied by her friends for being single and free. She poured herself a glass of wine and lay on a lounge chair on the opposite side of the pool to face the sun.

"I wish I could just plop myself on a chair with a glass of wine so easily. It takes me a while to relax," said Stella. "I become preoccupied with being my usual vane self." She stood and threw her towel onto a chair, spread her legs and pulled her bikini bottom away from her self-proclaimed luscious bottom. She rubbed tanning oil in slow circles all over her breasts and tummy and between the sides of her thighs, down to her ankles.

Bernice flashed a brief look of shock. Stella's movements were like those of a dancer in a strip club.

Being together with her closest friends, Stella figured it was a good time to mention the ape screech she has been hearing.

"Excuse me everyone. I have to explain what I have been experiencing here at Holly Meadow. Some of you may already know about this."

"I hope it's not bad," Bernice commented, with a look of fear on her face.

"No, it's not bad, just strange.

Bernice interrupted, "How strange?"

In the morning when I go food shopping, it's sometimes just when the sun is about to rise, and as I reach the bottom few steps outside of my condo and head for my car, I sometimes hear a loud ape or monkey-like groan or scream. I never can decipher exactly where it's coming from, she told, as she sprayed lemon juice on her blonde silky hair, but it always sounds very close by." "Are you sure it's not coming from one of the bedrooms in your building?" asked Nick - trying to keep a straight face.

Stella noticed Bernice's eyes open wide with surprise. "What's wrong?" she asked Bernice.

This is getting freaky! I had a similar experience. I was standing in the pool when all of a sudden I heard a loud monkey-like screech coming from behind me. I glanced behind quickly, looked around, but didn't see anything. I ran to my condominium to tell Nick. I thought he and his friends could look further. I ran down the pier so fast I stubbed my foot on a plank and fell. I slid partially off the pier with one leg hanging off in the low marsh area and an alligator staring at my foot. My heart was racing so fast, I swear the adrenaline almost killed me.

"I did manage to make it to my condominium and look for Nick and his friends but no one was around. *Apes or monkeys can be very dangerous.*"

Abe and Maryann gave each other a wide-eyed look. Abe turned to Adam and told him, "One day last week we heard an ape-like screech when we were on our boat heading into our slip. It was more of a weakened screech, as if it was slowly dying. Maybe there is some type of primate lost in the woods. It does happen every once in a while here in Florida."

"Ape! Monkey! Come on now guys, you all know that we're the only primates around here. My wife is always complaining about finding my gorilla hairs all over the place," said Adam.

It's probably Noah after he has a few beers," Nick joked. "By the way, where is Noah?"

"I didn't call him, said Stella, because he doesn't have much time alone with his wife. He once told me, with Cindy working the late shift all week; they hardly ever have private time together and he sometimes feels very lonely."

"I wouldn't tolerate that," said Adam. I enjoy my wife home in the evening."

"By the way, if you guys think it's scary that we might have a primate animal in the woods, you haven't heard anything yet," said Nick. "Last week I saw in the news that a new giant species of python was recently discovered in the already Burmese python infested everglades. It's native to Africa and it's an extremely aggressive species. It eats creatures as small as rats and as large as crocodiles and humans. They usually eat their prey head first to make the ride in smoother." "Scientists have theorized that if the African Rock python mates with the Burmese python, it could create a giant man-eating python."

"Imagine if one got under a vehicle and traveled to another part of the state," said Abe.

"I haven't heard anything about it," said Adam, as he rudely stared at Bernice's smooth plump cleavage. "But the other day I did overhear a conversation in a gas station down the road, between two men, about a large snake they saw down the road. I thought nothing of it, except for the fact that when one guy said, "down the road," he was pointing toward this complex.

Stella noticed her husband's roaming eyes and began to massage his broad shoulders and back in a slow circular motion.

Bernice could not help but watch Stella's talented hands. She gradually could feel a delightful stimulating sensation flow through her body. It was getting so intense she took a deep breath. To distract herself she commented, "It feels good not to hear any cell phones ringing those crazy fancy tunes, and all that loud talking as if no one else is around. It's so disrespectful to others."

"Yes, but it's part of the new era we're in so we have to get used to it," said Stella.

"*This massage feels so good,* said Adam, as his head fell forward. Nothing could bother me *under these circumstances.*" A shiver flew through him, and a few others, as they watched the sexy movements of Stella's hands. "It feels *so* good honey, keep going." "Oh come on, Stella, that's enough, unless you want to give us all a massage. I'm playing some disco music," said Bernice. Stella's hands softly squeezed Adam's skin and then left his shoulders.

Adam's mind was saturated in pure bliss. The front of his bathing suit stood out like a table umbrella. He continued to finish what he had heard at the gas station. "The two men at the gas station were discussing its long jaws and wide body and said it was about ten feet long. I figured it was just someone's pet. "Oh come on, Adam! What crazy person would have a ten-foot snake in their house? That sounds too bizarre to me," said Nick. "I meant, they buy them when their small and let them loose when they grow big. It happens all the time," explained Adam. "They probably were a couple of drunken red necks that couldn't see straight. It was probably a wooden log" said Abe. "I bet they see those river monsters too."

After a few drinks, everyone but Carolyn decided to cool off in the pool. Bernice turned up the volume to the old tunes of the seventies. "Turn the beat around" she sang as she moved her hips and stepped into the pool. The fun was starting. Bernice stood next to Stella in the water and they laughed as they watched Carolyn put her head back on her chair and close her eyes with a smile. Look at her, she's glistening from head to toe, said Bernice.

"Carolyn called me this morning in pure ecstasy," Bernice told Stella. "Her smile must be from the date she had last night with a new man named Dean. She said Dean's eyes were gleaming when he saw her in her little black dress with silky strands of platinum blonde hair falling over her golden tanned pillows with cleavage deep enough to hide his head.

When he looked up and down her legs and then up into her eyes, she could sense the intense movement that was going on in his pants and it turned her on." She began to get palpitations and was becoming aroused. She wanted to grab his muscular chest and press hard up against him. She said her body was quivering with a fierce urge. Carolyn told me she just wanted him to plunge her right then and there. She then told me she controlled her feelings and gave him a light kiss on the cheek as they left for dinner. Ya sure, their feelings probably weakened on the way to the front door and they wore the hallway rug to shreds, said Stella. Their butt's were burning from the old hard threads as they tried to sit elegantly in that classy restaurant she likes.

"Being single does have its teen-like heart-throbbing exciting moments," smiled Stella with a look of reminiscing. "If we stay healthy we can be romantic until we're ninety, and I bet it can still be just as exciting."

"How can it be exciting if you have to worry about your spouse dropping dead on your body? Imagine the shock of his penis still inside you with the dead weight of his body suffocating you. You would have to pull it out and wiggle out from under him," said Bernice.

"Well at least you can live knowing you made your man happy until the last minute of his life," laughed Stella.

You're not fooling me," Stella said as she pointed and shook her finger toward Bernice. "You and Nick will still do it until you're both drooling and can't remember you did it. I pick up when you sneak your hand on his crotch under the dinner table."

"Oh Stella, you ruined the fun. I thought no one noticed."

Adam and Nick snuck up behind Stella and Bernice and poured beer on their heads.

Adam commented to Bernice, "What is it with the black pants, even in the pool!"

Abe, a few feet behind, gave a whisper to Nick. Suddenly, Abe and Nick grabbed Adam and held his arms behind his back. They then looked at Stella while Nick said, Bernice-honey, don't you want to see Adam's snake?

Stella winked and nodded at Bernice for the okay to say yes.

Adam tried to pull away while they pulled off his bathing suit and threw it in the lake. Everyone broke out in a belly laugh so hard they could barely catch their breath. "I feel young again," said Stella.

Adam faced the wall of the pool. "*Ouch, Ahhh!* This rough cement hurts." Oh come on my man, you can afford to scrape off a few layers, said Nick. "Don't worry Adam, you can turn around, we won't focus on anything personal," Maryann giggled.

"You wouldn't be able to help it." Adam smiled proudly. "You could turn your back toward me and you would still be able to see it".

"Get over yourself," said Stella.

Adam yelled, "Stella, how could you not stick up for your loving husband. You're going to get your turn."

"I can't wait, honey!" she laughed.

"You won't be laughing when you can't find your top, when you're in the middle of a supermarket, Adam yelled.

I'll tape two big cabbage leaves to my boobs and tell everyone I'm Eve. Her friends laughed. Adam yelled, "I'll make sure it's six isles away from the cabbage – in the frozen food section." You'll be trying to cover up your boobs with frozen corn and spinach bags.

"Some morning when you guys are taking a walk along a busy road, he'll tear off your shirt and everyone will be beeping at your boobs," laughed Nick.

"I'd be worried if I were you, Stella, said Abe.

"I know my husband. He's not revengeful when it comes to me.

"I don't know, Stella. He might change his train of thought this time and catch you off guard. I can't wait to see what he'll do."

CHAPTER THREE

While the friends chatted in the pool, with noisy music and alcohol drenched brains, they couldn't see the silent alien shadows lurking in the water canal only a few feet away. Danger was approaching, moving closer. The stalker's color made it nearly indistinguishable in the dark water of the Florida inlet. As it slid through the water with grace, the only thing noticeable from the pool was the water's calm surface.

It moved out of the water to under the deck of the pier. The huge killer rock python moved in a progression straight forward with its ribs and scales helping it push its body along the ground. Its keen mouth sensors and forked tongue led the way to the closest heat emitting flesh for its next meal. The primitive reptile mastered its slick and discreet approach.

The grisly python lifted its head out from under the end of the pier near the pool, moved across the pavement, and coiled its upper body underneath Carolyn's lounge chair.

Large beach towels were hanging off the chairs. The men and their wives were too busy having a good time, drinking and laughing in the pool, to notice the steaming for meat beast.

With fangs that could tear the thick flesh of an elephant, the hungry beast was on a journey to devour its meal of preference. A long substantial body of flesh - which fulfills its appetite.

21

Adam, still without his bathing suit, was more than a bit inebriated with his circus-mirror eyesight. He glanced at Carolyn lying on the lounge. All he saw was a curved wide nipple, sticking out of a kaleidoscope of fancy flowered bikini tops. "Hey Carolyn, fix your top, or someone might suck on your nipple," he yelled. Carolyn did not wake. "The view is fine with me," said Adam. "Oh shut up Adam!" Stella said angrily, I'll fix her top.

Adam yelled to Nick, "Take your ballerina slippers off, get the pool pole, and get my fucking bathing suit out of the lake." After a few beers, Nick's equilibrium was a bit off balance. He stood with his toes off the edge of the pier, swaying back and forth with the pool pole in his hands, as if on a tight rope. After a few tries, he managed to retrieve Adam's bathing suit from the lake.

Stella stepped out of the pool, and began to hop across the painfully hot pavement, toward Carolyn, to fix her top.

The python lifted its head from under Carolyn's chair. Stella screeched a high-pitched noise of fright, not heard, with all the commotion and loud music.

Running backwards from Carolyn, tripping and shaking, she was a crazed woman, ready to kill her friends and the python. Stella madly ripped off her bathing suit to catch attention and screamed her lungs out. *Fucking Help! You fucking oblivious drunks!*

What the fuck! Yelled Nick.

Carolyn, in a deep sleep, from the hot night, hot sun, and Merlot circulating through her veins did not wake.

Suddenly, the grisly reptile scrolled and glided over Carolyn's body and its head quickly dropped on her chest. At that moment, Carolyn's head jolted up straightforward stiff and shocked as if electrocuted, her body and eyeballs frozen solid. The deadly python lifted its body, swung far out, turning its muscular man eating tunnel in mid air, and whipped a sharp tight wrap around her neck. The beast was ready to take on and consume its weak petite prey. If her friends didn't work fast enough, she soon would be another victim, suffocated and crushed in the center of the world's infamously known lethal African Rock python curl.

After a few seconds, Carolyn began banging her fists fast against the sides of the chair; her eyes bulging and staring in a bizarre seizure of fright. She gasped and fought for any bit of breath, but the fierce python wrapped itself tight around her throat. The clock was ticking.

Everyone bolted towards Carolyn, screaming hysterically. They grabbed wine bottles and began whacking the snake as hard as possible. "We have to kill him fast"...."Get off her - you beast," screamed Stella. "She's going to die. *Huurrry up!*" They all began to sober up as nature kicked in and their bodies produced massive adrenaline.

Words and bodies flew frantically. "We have to destroy him fast!" "We have to throw him off guard and distract him…keep beating the living hell out of him. Don't stop! We only have a few minutes and that's only if she can get a few breaths. It's instinct is to squash her lungs and stop her breathing"

Maryann cried out, "No! This can't be happening-this is too bizarre…Do something Adam! She's turning pale."

Adam blew air down her throat at intervals while digging at the beast's flesh with his bare hands. On one strong dig, his fingers snapped back on one hand and he let out a roaring scream. One finger became dislocated and was hanging loose. With agonizing pain, he continued pulling and tugging hoping to shred the python's flesh.

The snake's flesh was dense and impossible to penetrate with bare hands. However, Adam couldn't think rationally. His only thought was to save the life of his friend. Another finger snapped.

Nick screamed, *Stop!* Adam didn't listen. Nick grabbed Adam and pushed him to the ground. "*Stop!*" Nick growled at Adam with anger. Your skin can tear and you can lose your fingers. Stella ran for the first aid kit in front of the clubhouse. She grabbed Adam's hand and tried to tightly wrap his fingers as fast as possible while he screamed, "*Stop you bitch, there's no time to care for me!* He had a look like he was about to explode so she moved away.

She nervously paced back and forth knowing Carolyn only had a couple of minutes left. She repeated, "You can do it girl, stay with us."

"*If anyone can heeear us…call 911*", yelled Maryann. The pool was too far from the condominiums for any one of them to be heard. No one could leave Carolyn. Everyone's help was in desperate need. A split second was a matter of life or death. The women's minds were in such intense shock; they stood and walked like longtime institutionalized mental patients suddenly dropped on the side of a highway with speeding vehicles.

The men's bodies moved with great rapidity. They banged the python repeatedly with wine bottles and anything they could find. Nick held the neck of a wine bottle and hit the bottle against the edge of the pavement. He took the sharp edged neck of the bottle and stabbed at the lower body of the python. The stab wounds did not draw any blood and had no effect on the python.

The python tried to maneuver its body under her back to make another wrap and strangle her to death. It was becoming impossible to get control of it. Nick couldn't get the cut glass to penetrate the skin deep enough to cause the snake to release or even cause a jerk so she could catch a fast breath. On a few more stabs, he did hear Carolyn gasp some air, but this was not going to save her. The python maintained massive energy and force and appeared to have enough fuel until it accomplished its goal.

Their heavy pounding hearts felt ready to detonate - but strong mental determination maintained their strength. Abe and Nick grabbed its girth and gave a mighty pull. The snake's head made a fast twist and darted at their faces causing them to fall backwards onto the ground. They heard Carolyn get a breath of air.

They arose from the fiery hot pavement, their bodies trembled, and their legs felt rubbery. Nevertheless, they recovered immediately, feeling they had the power and strength of Hercules and were ready to take on Satan with his fork of fangs. "If this fucking devil is going through this much trouble and is exerting this much energy to constrict, it must be unbelievably fucking famished." said Nick.

Stella picked up a spiral metal wine opener and jabbed at the snake's head. Its head aggressively whipped back and forth, up and down, with tremendous force. The snake's thrust hit against one of Stella's jabs with perfect timing and the wine opener became lodged into the top of its head through one of its eyes. The python became distracted but not enough to release Carolyn.

Adam, anxious and breathing heavy, stuttered, "Maybe with the wine opener stuck in its head, it will weaken and the three of us can pull its body loose."

Abe shook and mumbled, "Doesn't look like it's losing any strength at all."

Adam grabbed a thick branch and whacked the python's body while Nick and Abe repeatedly tried to pull the snake off from around Carolyn's neck until their hands bled and their veins were hanging out of their skin. However, with the python's incredible strength and the constant dodging of its strong aggressive mouth dangerously darting at them, they had no luck. On one dart, its fangs swiped against Nick's cheek and sliced it open. "I don't understand, it's acting like a rabid monster," he shouted. It must be sick.

Carolyn's lips were shouting, "*Help!*" She held her mouth open with her tongue sticking out hoping to get air. Her dark tan was turning white.

"We haven't weakened it at all. Its still constricting at short intervals like a mad beast. It's processing tight waves of wiggles up and down to squeeze her guts," said Adam. She must be close to death. God help us.

Stella, get another wine opener and try again." Nick screamed, "*Jam it harder!*"

Nick's ears were becoming deaf from the pounding beat of his overworked heart. He yelled to Bernice, "Hurry! Go get a bottle of cooking oil in the clubhouse and we'll pour it on Carolyn's neck. Its skin is dry and smooth. The oil might make its skin slippery and help us disentangle it from her neck. We're so fucking desperate....hurry the fuck up! Five minutes must have passed now." Everyone trembled and yelled, "*Hurry the fuck up!*" Bernice, with her head hung forward like a rag doll, climbed her weak body onto the second stair to the clubhouse. Hanging onto the railing, she dragged herself up a step mumbling, "*give me strength dear God.*" Jittery, the keys fell from her sweaty shaky hand. She turned to grab them and fell onto the cement pavement. She reached for the railing...what seemed like a million tries...but only three, she pulled herself back up onto the stairs. A strong wind for survival blew through her and she ran up to the door. Her hand was shaking so hard, she kept missing the keyhole.

"Hurry up, damn it!" Adam yelled.

Bernice cried and yelled in frustration, "*I can't get the key in the hole!*" One more try and the key went in.

She grabbed the oil, sped out the door, and fell down the stairs. The bottle of oil hit the cement and broke into pieces. There's another bottle, screamed Stella, I'll get it. Stella dropped the wine opener and rushed for the oil. Too much time was passing.

Bernice lay on the pavement at the bottom of the steps in a mess of oil and broken glass. Feeling like a failure – she cried out, "If she dies it will be my fault."

There was enough sweat pouring from their bodies to fill the pool. Stella dumped a whole bottle of oil on Carolyn's neck, making sure it was getting between the snake and Carolyn's skin. The snake made a slight jerk and oil splattered on everyone and in some eyes. Nick told Abe, *come on,* we'll grab the upper middle part of the snake's body and try to pull it around and jiggle it away from her neck.

The sharp fanged dick lifted its head high and its horrifying mouth opened wide and slammed shut. Its upper neck made a slithering slick movement, as if it was analyzing what was happening. "Step back!" Nick screamed.

Suddenly, Stella with a blank sturdy look, her mind not there, was at the snake's head with the sharp neck of a bottle held tightly between her hands. She swung both arms and went for a strong hit to the python's head. She missed and hit Abe on the shoulder with the sharp glass. "Get away and stay away," Adam screamed at Stella. Among all the hysteria, Stella stared as if she did not hear. Her voice whispered as she slowly stepped back, and asked, "It's dead isn't it?" The shock and horror of what was unbelievably occurring manifested into a few moments of insanity for Stella.

Abe suffered with intense pulsating pain in his shoulder and arm, from the glass cut. He could describe it as a freight train speeding up and down the inside of his arm, tearing apart his flesh, but he was overcome with a strong determination for survival and amazingly kept his strength up.

Abe and Nick continued to pull at the girth and felt a little release, but not nearly enough to untangle it loose.

The python gave a fast powerful wiggle of strangulation around her chest and loosened her neck. Suddenly, they all heard Carolyn inhale some air. "She got some air," Nick yelled with excitement. "We can't stop trying for a second."

Overwhelmed with urgency and anxiety, they felt like they were trying to unwind a colossal dick super glued to a light pole, in a split second.

"Didn't anyone think we might need a frigging cell phone?" asked Stella, as she snapped from her near breakdown state and panicked. She felt dizzy and her body moved disrupted like a hanging skeleton.

"It was your idea not to have cell phones, bitch!" Nick responded in a deep sweat as his cheek bled and he continued to tug with his spine becoming more and more strained. His back moved like waves of water from a passing boat.

"We have to shoot it, *fast!*" screamed Maryann. She remained many feet away. Her head was turned and she was heaving. She was barely able to look at the colossal creature. The python's wide fleshy throat appeared as large as a car tunnel, as she repeatedly gagged at the gruesome sight. She thought, "Is this the monster that scientists are talking about. Did an African Rock Python mate with a Burmese python?" Partially digested food fell from her mouth.

"A few bullets would do it, but the men can't leave for a second. We don't have time to run for a rifle or 38. We only have a couple of minutes," said Nick, as he relentlessly worked his damaged bloody hands, digging hard against the python's girth. His fingers oozed blood from his severely chafed skin. "It's not a good idea. The bullet could hit Carolyn. We can't become irrational out of desperation; we better watch our moves and just keep up with what we're doing."

Nick's fingers had the pain of hundreds of paper cuts as he continuously tried to penetrate and manipulate the python's thick girth from Carolyn's neck. It was the only maneuver that allowed a little air to get down her throat.

Stella was sobbing hysterically as she watched Carolyn claw feverishly at the snakes body. She dug at the scales without a pierce until her fingers drew blood. Carolyn was trying to get out of a locked casket. Horror was emitting from her popped eyeballs as she fought for her life and kicked her legs frantically for a strong enough blow to its body. She weakened and her arms collapsed. Her personal fight with a monster was ending and so was her life.

Bernice ran to the side of the woods and began to vomit. I hope she survives without serious damage, she thought.

Nick got on his knees and smothered his hands with oil and again forced his fingers in between the python and Carolyn's neck. The snake tightened up. His knuckles became stuck. "I can't get my fingers out," he yelled.

The python slithered its forked tongue and its head began darting - staking out Nick's sweaty smell. Nick ducked, as the python's head gave a strong swing over him and the wine opener shot out of its head with its eyeball caught at the end and jabbed Stella in the leg. She made a fast move to pull the hanging wine opener out of her knee and squashed the eyeball with her foot. Eyeball shreds between her toes, she screamed, I can't take anymore. God help me please! She shook her foot to try to release the dangling bits of the python's eyeball.

Abe screamed at Nick, "Get your hands out fast! It's going for your neck!" Nick gained tremendous strength from a super rush. He let out a huge growl, better than any male lion, and pulled his hands from side to side. His fingers loosened and his bloody oily hands released. At that second, he heard Carolyn catch a breath.

"I'll stab the sucker with a kitchen knife," screamed Abe. He felt his mind evolve into a mad man. He rushed to the clubhouse and grabbed a knife. "I can't stab at its upper body or head; it's too close to her body." Abe's shoulder ached, but his madness forced him to jab the knife up and down with the strength of axing wood. He felt violent with uncontrollable anger. His mind saw only the monster's flesh chopped to pieces. The salty sweat and oil blurred his vision. Currents of uncontrolled emotion made him disoriented but he wasn't going to give up. The men had determination to remain just as driven, if not more, than the python. Satan's pet was not going to win in this garden of friendship.

Abe held his knife in a tight grip and went for the jab of his life when the python made a thrashing whip and hit his crotch. The knife hit only the cement pavement. Abe's brain saw cameras flash from the pain in his scrotum. He pushed himself further and forced a deep breath into his lungs that gurgled as if it was his last. He began to collapse forward when he aimed to give the beast another jab. He missed the python, fell face down onto the ground with the knife bent against the cement forming a perfect L shape. *Fuck!* He screamed, frustrated and angry.

Everyone's behavior was exhibiting overwhelming, unmanageable fear, and emotion in excess with good reason.

The python appeared to react to the major hysteria. It lifted its head high and its mouth suddenly opened. Adam tried to speak. He babbled for words while his overheated dripping wet body swayed. "I'm going to bang this full fucking bottle of wine deep down its throat. I want the alcohol in its body."

"We only have one full large bottle, don't miss." Nick stuttered.

"*Hurry!* You only have one good hand and one good second. "This is all we have left, if we run for a gun she'll be dead," he quickly screeched at Adam.

"Adam glued his eyes to the python's mouth. A second coming wouldn't distract him. Watch my aim. Come to mama, come on, keep that fucking mouth open you sick bastard. Adam's weak body was unsteady. He aimed the bottle toward the python's head, ready to pour. He repeatedly stuttered…keep it open you sick devil. Drenched and greasy with one throbbing hand, his dehydrated body trembled, but a primitive drive kept his arms strong and his eyes focused on the snake's head. Faster than a whip, the python's mouth made a sharp swing toward the neck of the wine bottle - and *Wham!* Fueled with high-octane rage, Adam powerfully shoved and drilled the bottle so deep down the python's throat his forearm and wrist squirted blood from the inverted fangs as he pulled out. *"I shoved that bottle in so deep, he'll be more drunk than I've ever been,"* - and as if out of a horror movie, his head fell backward and he emitted a slow loud devilish laugh of relief. Victory stricken faces stood around with calm smiles looking at each other - and slow tears of happiness ran down their cheeks as the python weakened.

The python's head collapsed and fell to the pavement. Abe loosened the lifeless snake from Carolyn's neck and pulled its whole body to the ground. Carolyn made an intense barking sound while her body fought to breath. Her face was slowly getting some color as her lungs loudly wheezed for air. Her body was wallpapered with bruises and drenched with blood from those who saved her life. "I'll run to the condo and call 911," Abe said with a huge sigh of relief.

What seemed like hours, in a matter of minutes, they had overcome the vicious deadly African Rock python. To think that Florida's everglades are full of these creatures is a nightmare, remarked Adam. Everyone held their stomach.

Nick with his excruciating painful hands and Adam with only a few functional fingers picked Carolyn up off the lounge chair and walked over to the clubhouse. Stella and Bernice ran up to the front doors and held them open while the men carried Carolyn inside and gently placed her on the couch. Her coughs were nasty sounding barks. I think I'm okay, she said in a raspy voice. My neck and shoulders are aching badly, but I'm breathing, that's all that counts.

"Abe ran to call an ambulance," Stella told Carolyn.

"No, please don't. It will attract the media's attention," she whispered.

"You have to get checked out, you could have organ damage. I'll stay with you," said Stella.

Nick and Adam walked back to the snake and looked at the outline of the large wine bottle in the snake's body. "Look! - its system couldn't take the shock of the alcohol but his muscles are still contracting," Nick spoke with a look of interest. "It must be a natural spastic reaction of the body until its organs finally fail altogether. This python is an "African Rock." Do you remember when I mentioned it at the pool this morning? When I heard the news on the television - about the major infestation of foreign pythons in the everglades - I became curious and did a little research. This species could cause a very serious problem here in Florida. It would be impossible to know exactly how many are out there. The officials should have a longer hunting season just for pythons - to keep the population down. There are python squads monitoring the residential areas in the counties down near the everglades. I don't know how one of these beasts made it up the coast all the way here. It could have been a pet that was released in our area.

The police arrived and shot the python. One officer asked, "If anyone cared to slice him up and put him on the grill. It's a delicacy, he proclaimed." There was silence. No one was in a joking mood. Nick snapped at the police officer in an angry tone, "Do you realize the hell we just went through! Can't you see we're full of blood and sweat!"

The Wild Life Task Force arrived shortly after the police and removed the snake.

The tall strong voiced police officer said, "This is a deadly meat eating python. There have been many sightings of this python in the everglades area. I can't imagine how it made its way up here on the mid-coast." In a stern voice, he warned, "If there are any more sightings, report it to the Wild Life Task Force immediately."

The other two officers looked around curiously. "Where's the victim?" "Doesn't the victim need medical attention?" Abe pointed, "Over there in the clubhouse. I need help with my arm and my buddy here needs medical attention too, his hand is badly wounded." "The E.M.T.'s will take care of both of you." The two officers walked into the clubhouse to check on Carolyn. "You need medical attention. Very gently move your neck for me please," one officer asked. Carolyn slowly moved her black and blue neck to the right and to the left. "I strongly advise that you go to the hospital and get checked out. The E.M.T.'s are here and are going to help you first." Carolyn looked at the officer and whispered and coughed, "I don't want to go to the hospital. I feel lucky to be alive." She struggled with hoarseness, "My friends worked very hard to save my life."

"How will I ever repay them." she thought. Her eyes closed.

There was a cluster of news reporters in the parking lot as Carolyn was placed in the ambulance. They stared in awe, not uttering a word. They shook their heads and looked at each other with amazement. Understandably, their work must have brought them before unbelievable situations - but not anything like this. They were pushed away by police.

Stella - with her body covered with dirt, blood, and snake eyeball remnants between her toes, went with Carolyn to the hospital and spent the first night with her while she was under observation. Carolyn's body was in extreme pain and felt like it was on fire. Pain meds and oxygen allowed her to fall asleep.

After numerous tests and x-rays, a couple of mild fractures in her ribs were found that could heal on their own. Her neck was severely black and blue and covered with fingernail cuts. A couple cuts required stitches. The doctor prescribed pain and sleep medication and she was released after three days.

She felt very fortunate - but remained traumatized and suffered with severe anxiety.

CHAPTER FOUR

Noah, a retiree and Director of the Condominium Board who lives next to Spike, President of the Association, poured himself some orange juice with champagne. Give me a kiss goodbye honey, he said to his wife Cindy, who works afternoons as a computer programmer at a local company.

"Oh Noah!" Make me jealous and make yourself a mimosa before I leave for work on a beautiful afternoon like this."

He reached for her lips and gently kissed his wife goodbye. "Your day will come sweetheart, after all, you're only forty eight."

Cindy left for her three to eleven shift and Noah went and sat on his porch swing holding his drink. He enjoyed the plush beautiful forest behind his condominium. Nature was in his bones.

With their keen eyes and long elegant legs, beautiful statuesque heron birds staked out their meal in the water canal that followed his porch. The sun's rays filtered through the openings between the Cypress trees as though heaven was right there in front of him. Noah took in a deep breath of the fresh scent emitting from the newly grown greenery. He relaxed and placed his feet up on a little shabby wicker table. It can't get any better than this, he thought as he laid his head back. Although, I do wish my wife was here with me.

In the peaceful atmosphere, he began to hear leaves stirring around, a little rougher than usual. He pulled his body forward and listened carefully. His curiosity caused him to place his drink down and get up to see what was moving in the leaves behind his railing. He placed both arms on the railing and leaned forward, his eyes roaming. Noah focused hard, covering as much of the forest floor as possible. The sun's rays caused him to squint. A few squirrels played around in the brush and chased each other up a tree. It suddenly became quiet. He strained his vision moving toward the middle of some Cypress trees. He observed movement in an area of low dense brush. He climbed over the railing, placed his feet at the edge of the porch, held on to the railing with one arm, and extended his body out. He used his other hand as a sun visor over his eyes and looked again. He saw the long body of a python slowly crawling in between the ferns just a few feet behind his condominium. He jumped back over the railing. Noah had an adrenaline rush. His body was shaking. "I have to get my rifle," he quickly thought. Noah turned fast and made a dash to get his rifle in the bedroom closet. His body hit the glass slider. "Damn it Cindy! Do you have to keep the glass so clean!" he yelled aloud. His nose swelled and began to bleed and he could feel a lump coming out on his forehead. He opened the slider and ran for his rifle. He returned to the porch and scoped all around but could not see the python. "My head is throbbing," he sighed. He went to the medicine cabinet, took two aspirin, and grabbed a bag of frozen peas out of the freezer. Blood and sweat was pouring down his face. He held the bag of peas against his forehead, ran over to Spike's front door, and rang his doorbell. Spike opened the door, his eyes rolled up. "Halloween isn't for a few months." "Don't ask," said Noah. Trying to catch his breath, "I guess you didn't notice the big python behind our porch. This snake is at least twenty feet long. I ran for my rifle but when I returned he was gone." "Are you sure it was a python?"

"Yes, - come over to my place."

"See you in a few," said Spike.

Noah ran back to his condominium and called Adam.

"I just saw a giant python behind my condo."

"Are you serious?"

"Yes, I'm serious."

"I'll grab my rifle and be right over."

Spike walked into Noah's place with a machete, binoculars, and some paper folders. He leaned on Noah's railing and scoped out the forest. The old wooden railing and spindles made a crackling sound and the thin columns were squeaking. Hey Spike, you better not lay that big body of yours on the railing. It sounds like it's going to give.

I'm fine, replied Spike.

Struggling with the peas on his aching head, Noah ran to answer the doorbell. Adam and Stella arrived. "Noah, what the heck happened to your face?" asked Stella. As Noah grabbed a piece of rope and tied the bag of frozen peas to his forehead, he explained, "I ran into my glass slider after I saw the python."

"Where's Spike?" asked Stella.

"He's out on the balcony scoping the forest."

Adam helped himself to a drink at the bar and he and Noah sat in the dining room to talk. Stella kept to herself and sat on the sofa.

"Spike, get the hell in here. We have to discuss what our plan is." Adam yelled.

"I think we should keep it a secret or it will scare the life out of all the residents," said Noah.

Spike, being President of the board, gave a furious look to his director, as he walked through the slider and stood behind Noah. He said firmly, "I do not like the idea of keeping this snake sighting a secret."

Noah jumped up. I thought you were out on the balcony.

"I see where you are coming from, Spike," said Noah. "Well partially, the peas are in the way and my eyes are full of blood."

"You obviously don't see crap in that mind of yours and you can't hear!"

The residents here have to know that there is a dangerous snake roaming on the property so they can be extra careful." Spike spoke with his strong tone.

Adam took a gulp of his scotch and looked Noah right in his bag of peas. "Maybe the bang on the slider caused you to have a memory lapse and not remember the frigging living hell we went through a few weeks ago at the pool, when the savage beast wrapped around Carolyn's neck. The African Rock python is very aggressive and has a highly stretchable body. It has no problem constricting its prey to death and has the power to swallow a human."

Noah told Spike and Adam that they were right. "You bet we're right," said Adam. That few minutes of hell seemed like hours. We suffered with agonizing terror and could have lost our life to save a life. Look at the strength God gives us when it comes right down to saving the life of other human beings. I don't know if I could do it again. My back is badly strained from that incident and all the others are still healing from their wounds. I become very stressed just thinking about it.

"Okay! Okay! I agree to let the residents know about the new sighting. Better to be extra careful than sorry, even if some residents find the news horrifying and uncomfortable," said Noah.

"Better to be extra careful *than dead,*" said Spike.

I hope we never have another terrorizing experience like that again, said Noah. You and Spike should be happy you weren't there, said Adam.

I wonder if the python you saw today was the same size as the one that attacked Carolyn. Spike said with curiosity.

"I don't think so - from what has been explained to me, said Noah, the girth was smaller on the one that attacked Carolyn. I don't think she would have had a chance if it was the size of the one I saw today."

"What the hell are you saying, Noah?" Adam said nervously.

"Unfortunately, the one I saw today looked like the ugliest horrifying nightmare anyone could have - and it was right in our back yard." Noah regretfully stated.

Spike responded, "After I heard about the incident with Carolyn, I did some reading in the library on the internet. I looked at some older newspapers."

He handed a folder to Adam and Noah. "Read what I found."

"Your Most Terrifying Nightmare May Be Ahead":
"A New Deadly Foreign python is multiplying in Florida."

-- Florida's everglades have been invaded by the huge Burmese python for quite some time. Now Scientists are stating that Florida is facing its "Most Horrifying Species of Reptile." Native to Africa, the sickly, mean-tempered "African Rock Python" that grows as long as thirty feet—was recently discovered and is colonizing along with the Burmese. This meat-eating python is making its home very comfortably in Florida and could show up in any part of the state. It could crawl into or wrap itself around a component of any of the big trucks that constantly travel in and out of the everglades area.

The speed and power of the African Rock Python's strike, because of the muscular structure of its neck, allows for an extremely strong blow. A strike to the head of a human could easily occur, and would stun the human so intensely they would fall to the ground. This would give the snake its chance to coil around the body. Simply tightening its muscular coils will apply enough pressure to kill you, and there's no chance of escape. It was once believed that the shoulders of an adult human male are too broad for a snake to maneuver its jaws around, but this is not true. A fifteen to thirty foot African Rock can do this easily. --

"What a pleasant read," said Noah. "Why don't we just stick this article up on the bulletin board?" "I'm sure everyone here will have a good night's sleep after reading this!"

Spike look stunned. He scratched his head. "I've been receiving complaints from residents about their dryers not working properly, I wonder if these snakes are crawling into the outgoing air vents under the buildings." "Could be," said Noah. Noah hesitated and then asked, "What's going on with the ape-like screech or groan everyone is complaining about?"

"Actually, now that you have brought it up, I haven't heard the screech for at least a couple of days," said Stella.

"Do you really think we should care about those monkey or ape complaints at this point?" said Spike.

Noah responded, "I know it's minor compared to what we have on the property now, but I was just curious."

Noah complained, "Now there is no walking on Holly Meadow property without feeling uncomfortable. We are literally living in a frigging African Jungle." "Who would have ever thought we would be referring to Holly Meadow as a jungle because of real animals and not because of certain crazy people that live here."

Spike asked Adam and Noah, "Do you guys feel like taking a walk around the jungle, I mean grounds, and look around?" "I'll take my rifle," said Noah. "Let's go." Spike anxiously grabbed his machete. "I'm frightened," said Stella. "I'd like to help but I'm staying here." "This is the best place for you," Noah told Stella. "Yes, honey, you wouldn't want to come with us. It's too dangerous," Adam told his wife.

As the three men left, Stella helped herself to a scotch and milk. Her and Adam's favorite cocktail, especially during nerve-wracking situations. The strong alcohol hit her brain fast and she was able to relax a bit.

After about a half hour of searching around the forest, Noah noticed Spike standing with his head down, making peculiar faces at the ground full of flattened ferns. Noah ran over to Spike and they both moved further into the brush and saw something strange. They both tripped on a long obstruction. They kept walking and kicking the leaves, and after about ten more feet, they saw the large gruesome head of a dead python, and what looked like two legs of an ape sticking out of its mouth. They looked back and forth from the head to the tail end of the snake. Spike said, "This beast looks about twenty five feet long. The ape was taken in head first as typical," he said with disgust. He kicked more dirt and leaves off the body.

"Wow, I don't believe this," said Noah. "This must be the ape that everyone has been hearing. He must have escaped from the zoo."

Spike looked up and down at the long python ...."It's amazing how you can see the outline of the ape's huge body, as if he slipped into a rubber glove....Apes are extremely strong. They're five to eight times stronger than humans. I wonder if the ape had a chance to put up a fight. There are some deep claw-like wounds on the skin of the snake," Spike noticed.

Noah observed: "Look how defined the shape of the ape's head, shoulders, and elbows are. This ape's shoulders are so broad and dense, that one shoulder broke through to an extent that there's a rip in the snake's flesh, with the ape's shoulder bone showing through. It was luck that the snake's contractions and the ape's position were just right for this to happen. I mean for the snake to fortunately die as a result. What a sick sight," said Noah.

Spike hollered, "Adam where the heck are you!" "Follow my voice, we're over here." Adam walked toward Spike and Noah.

"Holy crap!" This python is huge! The girth does look much larger than the one at the pool. How much more gross can it get." Adam expressed with disgust.

"Much more, said Spike, if we don't get rid of these bastards. We have to report this to the Wildlife Task Force." He noticed the python was partially decomposed. "This is not the one you saw today, Noah."

"I wonder how many we have out here," Adam said, with a mysterious look.

"Come on guys, let's head back to the condo," said Spike.

They anxiously entered the condominium. Stella came in from the porch and asked what happened. Adam explained to her what they found.

Noah poured himself a small glass of sambuca and called the Sheriff's Wildlife Task Force. He could feel his blood pressure rise as the dispatcher asked him repeatedly what he found – his tone of voice revealed that the dispatcher thought it was a crank call. "Can't you hear?" yelled Noah. His head throbbing and his nose bigger than bozo, he took a sip of sambuca hoping it would ease the pain and relax him. "How many times am I going to have to repeat myself." He asked the dispatcher. Spike grabbed the phone from Noah. Spike told the dispatcher firmly, "We are reporting that we found a dead python with an ape in its body in the forest behind our condo. What is it that you don't understand! Are you going to do anything about it or should we call your supervisor!" "We'll send a crew over right away," the dispatcher finally said. Spike slammed the phone on the table, rolled his eyes, and shook his head with disbelief. "This is serious business."

Spike went to Noah's bar and poured a glass of coke, "I need the caffeine to keep me awake." He and Noah took their drinks and went out to sit on the porch. Stella made Adam a drink and joined them. Adam tried to calm Stella as she sat nervously. They were all drained and tired. "What is taking them so long? The sun is starting to go down, I hope they have special lighting equipment," said Stella. Noah suddenly looked at Spike with fear, "Wait a minute, this means it will be on the news and in the papers. We should have buried the frigging thing." "Not a good idea," said Spike. "We can't hide anything. It could get worse. We might need some serious help from the county." "Now we know why no one has been complaining about hearing monkey or ape screeches lately."

"I didn't want to mention this to anyone, but since Carolyn's incident, I wondered if this is what happened to the primate," said Adam. "Yes, you were right, he was gone," said Spike. Feeling bad about yelling at Noah, when he earlier had brought up the dying ape screech, Spike apologized. "My man, earlier, when you brought up the ape screech, you did have a point, but it was impossible for me to make a connection," he told Noah.

"This is horrible. The poor ape. They're only a couple of genes away from us humans you know," Stella expressed with teary eyes.

"Look at it this way," said Noah, "That huge killer sucking machine is dead because of the ape. If the ape did not kill the snake, the snake would have regurgitated the ape's body because it was too big for him to digest. The ape would have been dead and the snake would have gone on his way looking for his next prey."

"Which could have been *you*, Stella." A creepy chill ran up her spine.

"Don't say that Noah. This isn't a joking matter," said Adam. Besides, the python would be so mesmerized by my wife's beauty; she would have plenty of time to run for her life. Right honey?

"He's a *powerful predator!* You better keep your sliders shut, Stella, it might like tall slim blondes." Noah continued. "Shut the heck up Noah, I don't need her having nightmares like Carolyn."

"It's okay, Noah. I like long warm thick ones," giggled Stella as she put her arm around her husband.

Adam shook his head as if he thought his wife had lost her mind.

CHAPTER FIVE

The next few days were a media nightmare for Holly Meadow residents. The news stations and newspaper reporters from all over Florida got wind of the information. There was no cooling down at Holly Meadow. It was a steaming hot topic. There were many reporters knocking on doors and aggressively approaching anyone they could catch going in and out of their condominium.

"How sick is it that these reporters thrive on the most gruesome events in life. The more bizarre the incident is - the more they want the story," Adam said in a frustrated voice. What's even sadder is that this is the stuff that mainly attracts people to the news. Nice events are not going to keep people's attention as long as bad events. Since it's the majority of the population that's attracted to these terrorizing events – it must mean that it's innate. Our brain's system works so that we are highly drawn to focus on extra ordinary bad occurrences. My guess is that we needed this strong awareness when we were primitive.

Stella responded, "I think you're right. We are naturally forced to pay attention to devastating occurrences so we can take the information in and prepare to keep safe. It might not necessarily mean that we enjoy watching it. We need to be aware of all the terrorism in this world.

Except for plotted murder mysteries. I do sometimes find them amusing and entertaining - but feel they have no educational or instinctive concept of course. Except to keep a close eye on your husband, she laughed. Those type of movies are like a game. You challenge yourself on what's going to happen next. Unfortunately, Producers run out of unique plots and most of the time you can figure the movie out before it's over. I like a good twist with a surprise ending."

* * *

It was a beautiful bright sunny morning, with strangely, only one little tear drop shaped cloud in the sky that looked as if it was falling on Holly Meadow. Adam sat on his balcony with a cup of coffee and read the newspaper. He tilted his head a bit toward the slider opening and hollered to Stella, "Come on honey, let's get out of here, and go to Honeymoon Island Beach." Stella responded, Sure, sounds heavenly to me! They both put on their bathing suits and left for a day of relaxation.

Adam stretched out on his comfortable float and drifted lazily beside his wife, who lay beside him on the shimmering aqua warm water in the Gulf of Mexico. Her blue sea goddess eyes were closed against the hot rays of sun. He loved her. Happiness spilled over him, as he watched her tanned breasts move softly as she breathed.

You're as beautiful as our surroundings, Stella. Her eyes opened in the bright sun and she squinted a smile at him. The sun must be getting to you, Adam. However, I love hearing those words. She lifted her head and used her hand as a visor to view the area around them. There's no one around, hop on and give me a dip of your love. She threw kisses with her lips like a little fish. Hey babe, come on board, drown me in ecstasy, her lips whispered. I want to float high on these warm waves and have shooting stars while the sun still shines. The stimulating shock of her unexpected words of pleasure was so intense, Adam was about to burst through his swim shorts. He rolled off his float and she wish boned her legs and wrapped them around his pelvis. He pulled aside the crotch of her bikini and she was plump and hotter than the beating sun. Her float was down between his legs and he lowered his head and consumed her plumpness. She moaned and groaned like a baby tiger. Oh God, harder! Swallow me baby, make me bigger she whispered. She gripped his shoulders for balance and his muscular arms grabbed the sides of the float. He raised his head and slid in the love she was steaming for. Her body slid up and down the air mattress. She gave a moan as his fullness was satisfying her hot stimulated love canal. At the side of her eyes she saw some swimmers heading in their direction. It has to end babe, she whispered. Adam pushed harder and faster. He shot his stars sooner than he wanted but he was more than satisfied. He wasn't expecting such excitement on their day at the beach. She reached her hand and gently touched his face. "If we only knew what a paradise it was down here in the old days, we would have been here in a heartbeat."

They floated next to each other enjoying the scenery and gave a hello to the people who swam by.

We surely aren't letting the terror in our life affect our romance, are we Adam? You would think we would have lost interest, with the terror that surrounds our daily home life, and not knowing what's ahead at Holly Meadow, said Stella. I think we are using love making as a way to escape the horrifying thoughts and mystery of what may lay ahead at Holly Meadow, honey. Adam responded.

"Adam, you do know the best hospitals are back home up north. We've talked about this before."

He rolled his face away from her. The tone of the day suddenly changed. "Do we have to talk about hospitals, Stella. I came here to relax. I don't think we have to worry about it. I'm doing fine. I have the same blood pressure meds. We're not on another planet for chrissakes. The quality of the medicine and hospitals are just as good here. We just have to do research, like any other state."

"It's not just me worrying about your health, Adam. Take Carolyn for instance. I ran into her yesterday in the parking lot, and asked her how she was doing with the post trauma and all. Do you know what she said?" "No darling, what did Carolyn say?" "The doctors here are all pushing medication on her. She has six different tranquilizers and sleeping pills. That's all they do is write scripts and push her out of the office. It's like a deli counter with number tickets. The first thing the doctor asked was "What do you want?" Can you believe it? They don't talk to her and help her release all the suffering she experienced. I remember, back in Boston my shrink would talk to me for over an hour and let me vent all that was bothering me. Moreover, he didn't push any meds on me. He told me the more I talk about what's bothering me, the better I will feel."

He took a deep breath and closed his eyes, knowing in advance, this would turn into a dissertation on why they should have stayed in Massachusetts. "Honey, didn't you just say this is paradise?"

"She told me about her nightmares, Adam. Her *nightmares*. I can't imagine what she felt like when she had that creature coiling around her. We all suffered immensely. I don't know, Adam. I don't know if I want to stay here in Florida with creatures like that crawling around. You can't hear them, you know. Did you hear it? I didn't. Who knew?" Adam knew there was danger roaming in the area of their condominium complex and it did concern him to think of what could happen in the coming days ahead. "Stella, honey, you just said this was paradise didn't you? Once we have this problem taken care of - everything will be fine."

Something splashed in the water about ten feet away. He heard his wife suck in her breath.

"What was that?" she asked.

"Probably just a fish, Stella, relax."

"I want to go back to the beach, Adam."

"So who's stopping you!"

"Adam, I do not want to be in the water! It might be a snake."

"Adam took a deep breath and did not respond." "Adam! Did you hear me? I would appreciate it if you would please get off your float and pull my float back to the beach for me!" He opened his eyes, and squinted at her. That's when he saw her fear. Somehow, he felt it too. He rolled over, slipped into the water and began to walk his way to the beach, pulling his raft and Stella on hers behind him. He heard another soft splash again off to his right. He started walking a little faster, afraid now to look. He didn't want to see a snake coming their way. The snake attack on Carolyn caused Adam and Stella to develop episodes of paranoia, even though they knew the African Rock python is a fresh water snake.

They packed up and headed home.

Adam, "It's such a relief to be in our cool aired condo. It feels so good. I'm going into the bedroom to remove my salty bathing suit." Adam snuck up behind her and gently placed his hands on her shoulders; Stella jumped and made a shivering noise of fright. He held her waist and began softly kissing the back of her neck. Chills ran up and down her spine as the back of her hair swept his face. "Honey, if you keep it up we won't be having dinner tonight."

"You mean, honey, - if I keep it up - *you'll* be my dinner tonight," he mumbled as he continued his light soft kisses up and down her back. He kneeled down and began giving her cute velvet bum little kisses all over. "You're making me melt. Honey, you're an amazing stimulator. Your first touch gets my nice feeling nerves going, and makes them just want to keep going and going. You just have it."

Intense sounds of pleasure emitted from her gasping breath calling for more. She leaned her head further back extending her phenomenal full plump breasts with popping pink nipples heading straight to the moon. He crept his hands up her chest and felt the most desirable puffed fullness he had ever wanted, ever needed, ever dreamed of in a woman. His hands played all over the softness and the tips of his fingers swirled all over her lusciously firm nipples ready for take-off. His muscled wand pulsated hard against her skin and she could feel his love from the warm drippings. It made her weak.

They wanted each other again for the second time in less than just a few hours.

It took their mind off all the stress in their life.

She whispered, "I don't feel fresh with salt water all over my body."

"I love sea salt on my tender meat," he growled.

She turned around and gently took his hand, and with her head floating in heavenly bliss, she walked him slowly to the shower.

"Is luke warm okay?" she whispered.

"Just right, honey," he said with a gleaming smile.

"I'm so glad we got the water softener machine, it makes the water feel so sexy soft. It's *so smooth,* I always rub my body repeatedly, thinking I haven't washed off all the soap. I want to slide up and down your body and feel the softness together."

"Your soft slippery breasts feel so good up and down my body."

He grabbed her buttocks and lifted her body and she wrapped her legs around his hips. A ray of the lowering sun streamed through a little window into the shower. The water spray glistened like a rainbow of diamonds, as she poured silky body shampoo in between them. "The smooth effect will be comfortable and very stimulating," she softly said.

"How do you like the circular motion?" she gently asked with her lips and soft sudsy cheek against his.

He didn't answer, he was oblivious to everything but her soft tongue up and down his neck as she rotated her hips.

The soft wet lusciousness between her legs smothered his hardness. Her whole body disappeared. She felt nothing but her stimulated plump clitoris screaming for endless bangs.

Harder than a rock and feeling bigger than Mauna Loa, his penis was expanding with streams of flowing hot lava—he was on fire, a euphoric Hercules. She guided him into her secret grotto of divine love, thrusting and rotating his long thick succulent masculinity. The stimulation more intense with every swirl of her buttocks. Her moan was loud like a cat in the heat of the night. Feeling the height of ecstasy, she begged with tears, don't stop. He gave her the best he had, with long controlled thrusts, they were in harmony. She hung loose; he held her and took her away to heaven. Their beautiful pulsating feelings heightened. Higher and higher, further and further, the tingling orgasmic sensations extended and retracted…extending longer and more intense, she was soaked with secretion that poured. They reached a height where heaven swept through them from head to toe. "I love you," she cried out "Oh God," she felt herself reach her highest peak… He groaned his release and she exhaled little breaths, as they slowly returned to earth. God released them and their bodies were depleted of every bit of stress. Stella was so tremendously comfortable and relaxed, it felt foreign. She was a beautiful sagging and soaking wet doll, overloaded with nature's serotonin. His stars ran down her leg.

Feeling tranquility float from head to toe, they stepped out of the shower.

She grabbed a fluffy towel and dried him off. "The relaxed feeling I have is so comfortable, I could fall asleep right here standing up," said Adam. She ran the towel down his legs and kissed his religious ornament. It was sacred and hidden away just for her. A gift she could only have on special occasions - which was often.

"Let's go downstairs and I'll cook a nice dinner," she said.

Adam sat on his recliner and Stella went into the kitchen and began to cook.

* * *

The next morning on their way out for breakfast, Adam and Stella ran into Spike while he was performing his daily observations. They stopped and greeted him, with a "Good morning Sergeant." Stella liked to call Spike "Sergeant" because of his tall muscular state trooper type stature and strong tone in his voice. Stella said to Spike, "Your attributes give off an intimidating powerful image to some around here." Spike rubbed the back of his neck and looked down with a smile of embarrassment.

Those who understood Spike knew he was a very talented president. He deserved the utmost respect for his diligent work. He consistently kept up with the maintenance of the complex, and had accomplished many improvements to Holly Meadow.

"I feel confident and try to keep my thoughts in perspective, but sometimes I do get a weak spot when I receive a rude call. Some people can be so damn rude," Spike remarked.

Adam told Spike, "Of course you always have rebels that do not appreciate the good work of someone that's in control. They have their own ideas on how and which things are to be done. What community doesn't have people who like to ridicule and go against authority!"

Stella and Adam got into their car. Stella began ranting, "Especially in places where some retired long before their time. They're the ones that used to lie back in their high back leather chairs, in their offices, day after day and stare out the window thinking about the day they could walk out and never have to come back. "Oh, how wonderful it would be to have my freedom and all the days of the week for myself to do whatever I want," Stella mimicked with gestures like an actor in a play. "Well, that day came and now they're all bored out of their frigging minds and don't know what the heck to do with themselves."

"I know what you mean, honey. They purposely cause arguments and create strategies to get on people's nerves….just to occupy their time and mind. And some are so stubborn they allow themselves to get worse rather than work on improving their personalities for the better."

Stella forcefully folded her arms and looked out her side window with a disgusted face: "Live, love and laugh is just too hard for people to understand in some circles."

They returned from breakfast and bumped into Carolyn in the parking lot while she was doing her usual vigorous walk around the complex. Stella stopped her for conversation. "How are your ribs feeling?"

"My ribs are healing better than my mind. I'm still having horrific snake-related nightmares almost every night. The slithering snake slowly crawls into my bed moving his head toward my head and stares into my eyes. My head then becomes engulfed in his mouth and my eyes are staring down through his throat out his mouth at my feet." I'm trying to scream but I can't. I feel suffocated. I wake up soaking wet with my heart racing. I sit up and rest against my head board and my mind becomes anchored with images of the day I was attacked. Even in the afternoon, if I happen to dose off on the sofa, after my walk, I begin to feel like I'm choking and it wakes me up. One afternoon really freaked me out. I was dreaming that a snake slowly started to make its way up my leg. It then turned around and left. Again, it slowly started to come up my leg and made its way to my thigh. Its long tongue slowly stretched and retracted, with every stretch touching my vagina. It gave a final stretch and slithered my clitoris. Its mouth then bolted up and started sucking my whole vagina as if it was trying to swallow it. I could hear the sucking and slurping sounds in my dream. It wasn't turning me on. All I wanted to do was *kill the sucker!* I kept shaking my leg as hard as I could, repeatedly. Finally, I gave a shake and it released and I began stomping all over it. Blood and flesh were squirting everywhere. I kept stomping and stomping. That's when I began to orgasm. Killing the snake felt like ecstasy. I didn't want to stop. I woke from my dream, opened my eyes with fear, looked around, and took a deep breath of relief as if I accomplished a true desire. I had a strong sense of gratification from the kill. I think about how hard everyone worked to save my life and how they put their life in danger for me - and intense feelings of guilt set in. My emotions provoke such deep sadness; it weighs me down for the rest of the day."

"I think you better see a counselor to help you get over this," Carolyn. "It's too much stress on your body."

"The snake incident will affect me for life," Carolyn remarked somewhat angry. Stella tried to comfort her, but Carolyn said her walking helps her deal with the anxiety and frustration. "Please excuse me, she said with watery eyes; I'd like to continue my walk."

"I'm so sorry sweetheart. Call me if you need me."

"Thanks Stella, love ya!"

* * *

Late that afternoon, Stella and Adam were sitting on their living room sofa trying to relax and have a peaceful evening. Stella suggested to Adam, "There's too much tension around this complex - why don't we spread the word around to all the residents, asking if they would like to have a party in the clubhouse on Sunday." She moved closer to Adam and began massaging his shoulders. She could feel his rippled muscles under her palms. "I think it would be healthy for the residents to get together and try to have some fun," she said.

"I'll mention it to Spike. Honey, let me get the phone." She followed him into the den and he picked up the phone and began dialing. From behind his body, she placed her hands on the front of his waist. He missed a number and had to dial again. Very slowly, she moved her hands in a gentle massaging motion downward. "Sal's Pizza" answered, he had to dial again. Bit by bit, closer and closer, almost there...all over his front she swirled her fingers and played with his ever so divine softness. An elderly woman answered, he had to dial again. Her fingers slid underneath, in between, and downward, onto his muscular thighs...very slowly she moved her hands in a gentle massaging motion upward, bit by bit, closer and closer, almost there...all over his front she swirled her fingers and played with his ever so divine hardness.

This time Adam finally got the number right. Spike answered. Adam said to Spike "Oh Stella stop that bad habit of yours - always wanting to suck on my penis. Hi Mom! Stella wants to talk to you. He held the receiver toward Stella. Honey, here's your mother.

What! Oh my God! She didn't hear you did she?

I'm not sure. Here take the phone.

I can't! Oh my God! Why did you say that? I'm so embarrassed!

I'm kidding honey, it's Spike.

"Hey!" said Adam.

"Hey!" said Spike.

Stella now feeling a bit furious continued with her hands. Adam was having a hard time trying not to breath too heavy.

"Let's have a party in the clubhouse on Sunday."

"Sounds good, I could use a change of pace," Spike responded happily.

"Okay my man, talk later," Adam couldn't say that fast enough.

As he hung up, he took what seemed like his deepest breath ever.

Her talented hands spun his mind into ecstasy. "How am I doing?" she whispered ever so softly. He was breathing too heavy to respond. "I love making my husband feel good. It makes me feel good to make you feel good," she whispered.

"I feel good that you feel good to make me feel good," he managed to get out. She grabbed his testicles and squeezed them gently, but hard enough to hurt.

"Can you say that again?" she whispered. He yelled, *Ouch! That killed!* - went into the bedroom and collapsed on the bed.

"That's for scaring me!" said Stella with a big smile on her face. "Do you know how terrible I would feel if my mother heard you say such a sexual remark?"

* * *

The next day, Stella posted notices around the complex about the Sunday "Get Together" and received an overwhelming response. Neighbors brought juicy steaks and burgers for the grill and plenty of beer and wine. There was plenty of food for all, from gourmet pasta, festive salads to scrumptious sweets.

Stella and Adam felt a sense of relief coming from all their friends and neighbors. It was a pleasure to see everyone smiling and laughing.

After a few hours, Stella noticed the alcohol begin to interfere with their neuro-transmitters. A few managed to transform their personalities into big time engineers, hard-core professional lumberjacks, multi-million dollar real estate brokers or just plain clowns.

As the late afternoon approached, the men were willing to cut the pepper trees, potato vines and widen the canal. The women were willing to plant flowers and told details of what type and where they will plant them.

Then there were the conversations of "how much weight I have gained" and "how much weight I have to lose." This came after over indulging in dripping greasy meat saturated with artery clogging cholesterol. In addition, as they dug into the fivefold layers of thick chocolate cake with creamy frosting, they began to complement each other. Slurring through their muddy mouths with the fragrance of merlot, the women passed back and forth the worn out courteous remarks, "You look great for your age!" - "You look like you lost weight!" After a few glasses of wine, the vision of a woman's eyes nicely deceives her when she is with friends.

The sun began to go down and everyone started to feel tired and slowly left their house of fun.

Stella closed the glass slider and sat on her balcony to watch the stars in the night sky. Behind her in the living room, Adam watched the blaring television of his favorite baseball team.

On Monday morning as the sun was coming up, Stella could hear the car doors of those heading to work, open and close. She watched the news, and then got ready for her day of luxury and quietude at the pool. Even though she knew she always had to be on guard with the wildlife, she decided she wasn't going to let it rule her life. At the age of forty-one, she had recently been suffering from anxiety. Her doctor prescribed a mild tranquilizer to help her through her hormonal roller coaster, (and the fear of pythons), she laughed in her mind and shook her head with disbelief.

One thing that many women in the community have in common, they're all close in age.

There are those women who always get along because they're very understanding and always willing to give some support. Then there are rotating friends - depending on who likes whom at what time. The catty behavior of one or two can cause a constant recycling of friends - which in itself is entertainment and amusing to talk about. This is to be expected when you all live in the "same house."

* * *

It's nine a.m. The sun is bright, and Emerald Lake is full of nature's wild life. The birds, ducks, and squirrels are gabbing like women over morning coffee. As Stella lies in the midst of her paradise, she places herself in a meditative mood, letting go of all the hurt, pain, guilt, and sorrow of her past that remains in the subconscious mind. "It will leave if I let it go," she repeats to herself.

Spike's wife Lita was sitting across the pool with her desirable figure, glamorized by her attractive bathing suit. With the sun reflecting off her shiny blonde bob, she yelled across the pool, "Hey there woman, come and lay next to me." "I can't, I have to meditate. I'm determined for my three favorite words to be "let it go."

Lita smiled and said, "You go woman, no sense dwelling on the past and wasting time with those useless feelings." A half hour later, Lita yelled across again, "You must be brain washed by now! Come and lay next to me. I'm busy doing my nails; I won't bother you." Stella yelled back, "The polish smell will make me sick. Maybe in a while. It's too bad we won't be seeing Carolyn here at the pool for a very long time, if ever. She is really suffering with severe post-traumatic stress. Her nights are plagued with vivid nightmares."

"Maybe she should be meditating with you."

"I should try and talk her into it."

Lita closed her polish bottle and fanned her hands to dry her nails. Stella decided to sit next to her.

She told Lita, "I have a funny memory. I remember many years ago when I was single I was with a man that was so abnormally big I had nightmares of huge one eyed snakes attacking me for months. Whenever I was with him, I was in such shock my mouth would drop open. I know it's strange and a coincidence - but that's all I could think about was a huge snake. He gave me a look like he was proud. I was scared and nothing ever happened. I would say to him, get away from me with that thing! We had to break up because of it. I found out many years later, he never married and I think I know why. If you think about it, everyone always wonders why certain nice couples break up or never get married. They immediately think, "he must be gay or maybe impotent." They never think that a man could have an abnormally large penis and can't be sexually compatible with any woman."

"I have a funny memory where conditions were the opposite, said Lita. I was eighteen, and it was my first experience, so I didn't know any better. We were so in love, so I thought. One night I felt we were ready to engage further in our love. We started out and I put my hand down his pants and began caressing him. I innocently said to him "I can't find it." He never called me again. I was devastated. A few months later, after a couple of new boyfriends, I realized why he never called again." Lita and Stella giggled like young girls.

"Now that you brought this issue up, said Lita, I wonder if there are women that are by nature too tight or too wide. Imagine if a normal size man or the average size man, slid in and out of his girlfriend so loose, it wasn't possible for him to ejaculate. It could ruin the relationship. The opposite could also happen. She could be abnormally tight; it would not be possible for him to enter. These are problems that we never hear about but probably exist. If these issues were ever true, couples would always give some other excuse for the break up, because it's too embarrassing to talk about. What are they going to say?…his tree trunk is too wide so we had to break up….I love my man but his toothpick gets lost in my vagina…" I did have a high school friend who used to tell me, I'm like a small deflated balloon that refuses to inflate." I told her, "No, you're simply a virgin who needs a nice gentle man."

CHAPTER SIX

The following Sunday brought another gathering in the clubhouse. This time, with the novelty of Holly's homemade gourmet food. Holly is the specialty cook of Holly Meadow. Her cooking is delicious and adds a delightful holiday atmosphere even in the high heat of August.

As you stroll by her windows in the early evening hours, the aroma from her kitchen creates a soothing vision of mother's dinner cooking while all the neighborhood kids were out playing in their backyards or neighborhood streets - in the days when it was safe and you didn't have watch your kids like a hawk.

"You never know who is going to show up out of our three buildings," Stella commented.

"Well, look who just walked in the door. In case anyone doesn't know, this is our little lady bar maid, Lena," Stella said sarcastically.

"Cheers guys! I have my bottle of fun," said Lena with her near perfect smile and trademark sexy move of the hips.

Stella watched Lena as she flirted with the men - in her little black bikini and tropical beach wrap. Lena gave a sexy turn of her head and winked at every man that was able to focus. The crew had a good head start with their beer and wine. She lined up shot glasses and poured tequila. Most of her friends already drank themselves into thinking they were highly accomplished beings. Everyone was already feeling big and tough and felt that no one could outdo them in any aspect of life, especially Noah. "I'm the most knowledgeable of the group and a "superb engineer." "I can take care of Holly Meadow like no one else."

"Oh Noah, you're always the most superior, whether the sponge in your head is soaked with beer or not," Adam said sarcastically.

The women sat together in the clubhouse and had to stay in control when Lena was around. They did not have to act tough and take a shot when Lena pushed one. Stella whispered to her friends, "I don't understand how a petite woman like Lena can drink more tequila than the blood in her veins and survive!"

Bernice quietly commented, "How is she so manipulative with the men?"

"I'm laughing for no reason," said Lena.

"What reason could you possibly have?" Stella asked.

"I'm pouring more shots guys," Lena giggled. "This one will be our after dinner cordial."

"I think our after dinner cordial was two shots ago, *before* dinner," mumbled Noah. "What the heck - what's another." He went to the bar, picked up the little shot glass, and downed the third after dinner cordial of tequila – before dinner. That was awesome, "Lisa" I mean, "Lena." Noah slurred.

"What a good idea," said Adam, trying to be polite.

"Glad you brought that flaming bitter, gasping for breath, fermented sap. Next time, keep it home and use it to remove your nail polish. I could run an engine with that fuel," said Nick.

"You men are all coughing, choking, gagging, and spitting, I think it's time for all of us to head home, said Bernice."

"We will have to make dishes of food to take home. Holly worked hard making this special food and you all are too oblivious or inebriated to enjoy it," Stella expressed angrily.

Nick, "I think you had enough fun for the day." His wife told him.

"Fun, who had Fun?" He slurred and drooled.

"We're leaving." Bernice told Nick from across the room.

"Okay honey." Nick grabbed Stella's arm, "Let's go honey."

"Wait a minute, are you that drunk or are you kidding?" asked Stella.

"Oh sorry Maryann, I thought you were Bernice."

"*Maryann!*" said Stella.

Nick stared at Stella's face with double vision. He stood in front of Stella and moved his face toward hers, touching the tip of her nose with his. With crossed eyes, his head moved back and forth in slow motion, with the tip of his nose touching the tip of her nose several times, like a woodpecker in slow motion or a buffering movie screen. All he could decipher was blonde hair.

"You'd better lay off tequila," Stella said in frustration.

"Is she good looking? Heck! If she's good looking I'm not going anywhere. I love Spanish women," Nick slurred.

"Honey, come on let's go," he said, as the tip of his nose moved forward toward Stella again. Stella placed her hands flat against his shoulders and gave him a slight push away and he fell ass-backwards flat out on the floor.

"Yes Honey, I'll be right there, came from across the room. Honey, where are you?" Bernice looked around worried.

"He's on the floor," said Stella.

"What! Is he okay?"

"He's fine. Come get your husband, Bernice, I've had it!"

Another Holly Meadow gathering had past.

* * *

The following morning, as some left for work, those who were still in bed could hear the rise and fall of the words "upset stomach" and "headache" coming from the parking lot. Some suffered all day in their office with hangovers. Headaches that felt like their heads were cracked and nausea that forced some of them to have to leave the office early. The day-after suffering was worth it to Nick. He enjoyed a few drinks more often than his buddies - no matter how he felt the next day.

* * *

Sundays became a ritual for gatherings in the clubhouse. One late Sunday afternoon in the clubhouse, when everyone was getting ready to leave, Lena danced through the door and commented, "You old roosters don't know how to drink. I brought these bottles of tequila for nothing, you ain't men." "I sometimes wonder if you're a woman," Adam laughed. "Oh, she's surely a woman with *that* body," remarked Nick. She wobbled her way out of the clubhouse door and tripped down the steps. Adam ran out to help her. "I'm okay. I'm taking a walk down the pier." You could hear her voice scrambled in the distance, ranting, "I'm still having a good time whether you dead beats want to or not."

Spike turned to Adam and said, "Looks like she had a few before she got here. Think she's going to make it down that long pier without falling into the lake?"

"She has a lot of practice walking a straight line when she has to. She'll be okay," said Adam. Everyone left the clubhouse.

Lena sat on the planks of wood at the very end of the pier past the cheap plastic table full of dead bugs, spider webs and bird mess. The rocking of the boats tapped against the pier. The wind was getting gusty and the moon was a large transparent ball full of white fluffy strands of cotton sitting in the sky with what was left of the breathtaking fiery deep orange sun setting behind the forest across the lake. Lena reminisced about her ex-husband, and how happy they were in the beginning of their marriage. As years went by, his out of control spending made the marriage too stressful. In addition, she had fertility problems in which her husband held against her and mistreated her. She is now not fully happy and sometimes feels a deep loneliness in which she tries to cover up with drinking. However, she does a good job holding her own financially. She will take a sleeping pill occasionally to ease her mind when her sleepless nights of tossing and turning, thinking the same thoughts of her past over and over again, were obviously a hazard to her days work as a financial consultant. She told her Shrink, "These never ending thoughts make me feel crazy. I've recently noticed my sleeping pills are not working as well as they used to. (Since the python attack on Carolyn)," she said in her mind. The doctor prescribed a more potent pill and told her "I hope this will work to help you get a good night's sleep." "No alcohol and no yellow lights," he said sternly, as she walked out of his office door that morning two weeks ago. She new alcohol and pills don't mix, but she was a very daring and stupidly risky woman when it came to having a good time.

Lena stood up on the pier, sat on one of the flimsy plastic chairs at the table, and laid her head lazily back. The strong wind blew against her body. Her eyes began to close as her head hung down like a rag doll. She would get some life and bring her head up but it didn't last long before she was staring at her thighs. The tequila and hot day made her weak.

Finally, she struggled to get up and off the chair that crackled and swayed. After a few tries, her tired body sat with her limbs lying loose. Lena fell into a deep sleep on the chair. The itchy bites of big swamp mosquitoes could not wake her.

Dawn came and a strong manly voice approached her. "Good morning, Lena!" She jiggled out of her sleep. Maryann and I are taking our boat out for an early cruise to enjoy the sunrise before it gets too hot, said Abe. "The temperature has already reached eighty degrees and it's not even seven o'clock. This has been a scorcher summer. Best not to spend your nights out here, you could dehydrate," Abe spoke, as his boat crept away under the thick morning mist through the "Slow Wake" signs and into the partly clear distance. Abe and Maryann disappeared into the steamy morning air rising from the glistening water.

Lena mumbled to herself, "My head feels like its been hit by a truck, how can I make it home." She grabbed the arms of the chair and tried to pull herself up. The wobbly plastic moved backwards from the force, just missing a fall into the swampy water. She caught hold of herself, stood up, and began to walk step by step, like a baby trying to keep her gait with nothing to hold for support. The walk home seemed miles away. Her petite sagging bones swayed back and forth, as she struggled to keep her head straight. She imagined her cool living room and the relief from aspirin. Slowly and with much effort, she made it safely to her condominium.

CHAPTER SEVEN

Later on in the week, there was a Holly Meadow board meeting in the clubhouse. Spike leaned forward tapping his pen thinking maybe a few more residents might walk through the door. Adam commented with disgust, "If more than a dozen people showed up it would be a shocker for this team. There are obviously a lot of owners that don't care about the status of our budget - or the progress of our maintenance."

Spike responded, "Well, at least I know the residents that do show up are truly understanding and caring. I can't say what I think about the rest."

Spike knew that a few of the absent were spiteful, ignorant runts that hated to give credit where credit was due. In addition, there were the Holly Meadow rebels that were only interested in meetings where there was evidence of incompetence, destruction, theft, and lies, not man-eating snakes. They are leftover groupies that maintain their interest in the previous corrupt board, like a bunch of evil spirits stuck together with gorilla glue.

Man-eating pythons on the property must be too boring for some of the other residents to be present at the new board meetings, said Spike.

Everything was going well for Holly Meadow, except for the pythons, which were beyond the board's control.

"Where has the maintenance man been?" Bernice asked. Spike told his attendees, "Tom quit last week, without giving us notice. We assume he's not coming back. I tried calling him, but he didn't answer his phone. Obviously, he had no interest in telling us why he was not happy here. Secretary Luanne and I are accepting applications for a new man and we are down to a couple that we think could do the job. There's only one applicant that lives here in Palm Harbour, and he's one of the two that we picked. We'll run a background check and take it from there. I'll send a notice out when the new man is hired."

A couple of weeks went by and the new maintenance man, Jack Hardy, introduced himself around the grounds.

"Hi, I'm Jack Hardy," he said as he passed by some strange stares.

Spike mentioned in his notice, of Jack's hiring, that "He has a good solid background taking care of a variety of jobs. He can be trusted and is a hard worker. We welcome Jack to Holly Meadow." However, not everyone read Spike's letter.

Jack spent his first day wiping down the railings and touching up some paint. As the days passed, many residents got to know Jack. He became a friend to many and was always willing to help.

One of Jack's first encounters was with long time residents, Maria and Carlo, a sophisticated pair who enjoyed art. "We hardly ever join the gatherings on Sundays," Maria told Jack. "I'm much too consumed with my art classes and my husband Carlo is too busy heading tours at a local museum. Occasionally we have a splendid gathering at our place with interesting cultural food. For the most part we enjoy staying to ourselves." Maria smiled and said, "A smart idea to some."

Stella came out of her condominium to get some fresh air and stopped Carolyn in the parking lot.

"I'm doing my daily walk. Do we have to talk now, Stella?"

"Wait, can't you give me a few minutes of your time? I can't keep up with you. How have you been?" Stella asked, while she bounced around Carolyn.

"I have a new boyfriend and things are looking good. He was nice enough to stay with me through my tragedy and give me support. Another man probably would have ran the other way." You deserve a decent companion. I hope this one truly is. I know your luck hasn't been too good in recent years...hopefully this one is different...not one of those miserable lost lonely souls who latched onto you in the past." "Carolyn! I don't think you understand how much I care about how you're feeling."

"Listen Stella, I really enjoy my walk, can we talk some other time?"

"There never is another time. Most of the time you're hibernating like a bear in the winter."

"Dean is helping me deal with my phobia."

"Maybe we can all get together for dinner some night." Stella mentioned as Carolyn began to walk away.

Stella cuffed her hands around her mouth. "I'm going to give you a call whether you want one or not."

Carolyn walked fast in the distance.

* * *

The following Sunday, the clubhouse party was crowded and the music was loud. Abe, Adam, and Nick were involved in such heavy conversation, that Stella noticed they weren't acknowledging the "Hellos" of neighbors trying to be friendly. Stella went over to

CARINA NOLAN

Adam - "Honey, people are saying hello to you men and you're not noticing them. What could be so interesting to talk about?"

"Didn't notice Hun, sorry about that!"

Stella then thought to herself -"Lena's regular distribution of tequila shots always causes consistent senior moments in their train of thought. They're probably already repeating themselves. I can understand why Noah's wife Cindy never wants to join us." Stella giggled aloud. "What's so funny?" asked Adam. "Oh nothing, never mind, enjoy yourselves. Maybe I can get everyone to start eating." She walked around and told everyone there were plenty of scrumptious ribs drenched in honey-smoked sauce. She thought if they didn't drool over the display of juicy meats and salads the alcohol had overtaken their senses. On the other hand, was it, if they did drool over the display of food, they were highly intoxicated and made it repulsive.

Bernice glanced at Holly Meadow resident, Paul, who walked through the clubhouse door. Paul was Spike's predecessor on the board. "What a nerve he has to come to our gathering," Bernice angrily thought. Paul gave a pleasant look to everyone. He acted very naïve to the fact that he is despised. Bernice heard "pssst" coming from Maryann. She went and stood next to Maryann. Maryann whispered in her ear, "How can he come in here and talk to everyone with no shame? His obvious immature acts of hoarding and stealing what did not belong to him have made him the most unwanted. If anyone here throws up, it won't be from the alcohol or food." Bernice and Maryann giggled. "What are you girls whispering about?" asked Stella. Bernice whispered, "See that man over there - that just walked in, that's Paul, Spike's predecessor on the board. Paul and his wife Cathy have a disgusting reputation for a mature couple. At the time, they thought they had everyone fooled. However, some residents of Holly Meadow were too smart for them to get away with their greedy nasty illegal habits. Our newly elected board, that's now in place, and the management company that oversees the paperwork took them to court. The important issues were resolved. However, the scars in the minds of the residents will always be there. They betrayed their peers." "How do you know all this?" Stella asked. "Nick and I researched the history of the board before we moved in. We wanted to know everything we could, to make sure Holly Meadow was in a good and legal financial position," replied Bernice. "Of course everyone here was willing to tell us about Paul and point him out as soon as they met us. You know how people love to talk and let the dirty stuff out to the new residents. It's entertainment for some." "Very interesting," responded Stella.

* * *

Abe told his friends, "I feel like taking a short ride on my boat. Are any of you guys up for it?"

"Abe, are you sure you are sober enough to be out on the lake?" asked Maryann with concern. "I'm fine." "Coming with me, honey?"

"No thanks, Hun! It's too hot for me out there today. I'll stay here with the girls."

Lena headed for the bottle on the bar and poured a shot. The tequila slid down her throat so smoothly, you would think she took a shot of milk. The rest of the people finally decided it was time to grab some food. Stella told Lena, "Feel free to join our table. You could use some food with that lighter fluid."

"We won't let your stuttering and drooling bother us," said Nick. Bernice kicked Nick under the table. "Don't be so rude," she whispered.

Lena went and got herself a plate of food and returned to the table. Nick courteously pulled out her chair.

"Oh, why thank you my big boy!" she said with a flirty smile.

As she attempted to sit, Lena's body danced back and forth along with the food on her plate. Adam got up and tried to help her, but her wobbly body missed the chair and her boobs flopped out from her low cut bikini top. The fast swing of her arm to try to catch herself caused the dripping meaty ribs to fly off her plate and hit a few people. Everyone at the table helped her messy journey up from the floor.

As she managed to finally sit and tuck in her boobs, she heard cursing in the background. Angry voices yelled at length, "You can't even keep your tits in, you drunken bitch!" "Who said she had to keep them in?" "Look at my clothes, what a mess!" "Does she ever know what she's doing?" "I wouldn't hire her as my financial consultant. I'd be broke!" Lena responded, "Well excuse me for enjoying my meal with all of you, I'll be sure not to share bread with you again."

Trying to act civil, Lena wobbled around cleaning the messy drops of barbecue sauce off the floor and walls while trying to keep her boobs in place. She splattered the messy sauce all over her chest. A nasty neighbor, who was watching her closely, yelled and asked if he could lick the sauce off - while Adam yelled, "Hey Lena, have you met the new maintenance man yet." Not yet, she replied. Looks like you might need him." "Actually, he's quite good looking," remarked Stella. Maybe you should lay off the hard liquor. Men are not attracted to women that drink heavy."

"Maybe you should lay off the heavy barbecue sauce," Lena commented.

"Barbecue sauce doesn't dement your brain, but it will obviously cause a problem if your brain is already demented," said Stella.

Lena spoke loudly, "I'll be dammed if I can't enjoy myself on the weekends. Do you all know how stressful it is to sit in my office and have to listen to clients cry all day because they think I personally caused the Nasdaq to go down? They just don't understand that investing money in individual stocks is a high risk gamble. They have the nerve to complain that I'm not making them any money. I'm a damn good advisor - they don't understand the ups and downs of that stinking legal gambling casino! One client blamed me for a woman's bra company that went bankrupt. He told me I should have advised the owner of the company on how to make the padded bras properly so the company would have sold more of them. And you all wonder why I drink! "What good is the alcohol doing you?" Look at what just happened! Why can't you just sip on a couple of glasses of wine and relax? asked Bernice. Lena responded, "If you all don't mind, wine does nothing for me. I grew up with cowboys on bull farms in Texas, who taught me how to really relax." *"I'm sure they did,"* remarked Stella. "One of these days, your cowboy education might relax you into a coma."

"One handsome Texan cowboy taught me how to ride a bull when I was eighteen. He said it was the best exercise and challenge for my body, though I spent most of the time lying in mud. One day I out did five of those Texan boys and stayed on a bull for five minutes. That's a long time to have your legs open that wide and keep up your strength and balance in your arms and upper body. It was tough, but I beat'em all.

"You all can stick to your wimpy beer and wine. I'm getting out of here and going for a swim. All your hot air has made this place stuffy." Lena left the clubhouse.

After trying to clean the barbecue sauce from their clothes, everyone resumed eating and conversation. "Glad that bitch is gone," was heard from a few. "I'm sure her legs had more muscles than all those men put together," one voice said. Fortunately, some laughter and smiles returned. This was a good social outlet for some stuck in the house most of the week, because of the extreme heat, and others who worked all week.

The sun was going down and everyone was starting to leave.

Bernice made a tired sigh. "What do you think girls?" she asked.

A big yawn was Stella's answer. A yawn from Lita followed. Lita lackadaisically mumbled, "I have a long day's work ahead of me and want to hit the bed early."

"I guess that says it girls…come on let's go!"

Maryann said worriedly, "I have to wait for my husband to get back from the lake."

Adam told her, "Go ahead home, the men will wait for Abe to get back. We should all be home soon."

Stella, Bernice, Lita and Maryann left the clubhouse and began their walk home down the pier.

Abe returned from his boat ride a few minutes later. He stopped in the clubhouse to see what was going on. Nick unsteadily stood up and his chair rumbled backwards, "Where the hell were you?"

"It was just too awesome out there to leave. Where are the women?"

"They just left, they were tired," responded Spike.

"Did you happen to see Lena out there in the pool or on the pier?" asked Adam.

"No, there is no one in the pool and there is no one on the pier."

"She must have gone home," said Noah.

Nick laughed, "You should have seen the funny incident, when she fell. I pulled out the chair for her, she wobbled and fell to the floor, and her ribs went flying."

"Is she okay?" asked Abe.

"Yeah, she's fine but she got fed up with all of us teasing her and left."

"Well, by the looks of the place, seems like you all had a great time today."

"Yeah, it was a good day. Guess we'll leave the cleaning for the maintenance man and get ready to head home," said Spike.

"Yeah, sounds good. I'm beat from the hot sun and Maryann is probably wondering where I am. Good night guys."

"We're right behind you," said Nick.

CHAPTER EIGHT

Stella's day at the gym is never gratifying.

"I get bored very easily working out, she told the woman on the next treadmill. I always tell my friends that being on the treadmill is very torturous for me. It feels as though it's payback time for all my sins. I find it so boring."

"Wow! You hate it that much? If that were true, I have more than paid for my sins. I've been on this treadmill every day for years. Maybe I am a life time sinner, that's why I still have a fat ass," said the woman. They both laughed.

Stella left the gym after an hour of misery...to go home for another hour of misery, cooking dinner for Adam. She sometimes whipped up the fastest meal she could think of. "I'm sick of cooking," she thought to herself. Adam can sometimes be too fussy; it makes this cooking situation difficult, as she banged a pan on the stove.

Sure enough, that evening he complained that there should not be long stringy stems of fresh parsley in the vegetable stir-fry.

"I would like to take those long stringy stems and tie them tight around your balls."

"At least my balls would smell good, honey, and you might have a desire to kiss them."

"What woman kisses a man's balls?"

"A woman who knows what a man wants."

"Oh, so now I suck in bed. Is that what you're telling me?"

"No, honey, I would never tell you you suck in bed, because you have never sucked in bed."

"Are you saying I never sucked you in bed."

"No honey, you're good at sucking."

Stella gave Adam a peculiar stare full of confusion. With the beginning of a headache, she yelled, forget it, just forget it – leave me alone!

Adam couldn't hold in his laugh any longer. Don't worry honey, I'm just teasing you. You're a beautiful fulfilling lover.

Early that night, after Stella finished cleaning the kitchen, the phone rang. It was Bernice.

"Stella, have you bumped into Lena within the past couple of days?"

"No, is there a problem?"

"Well, Lena's sister Sarah just called me from Ohio and told me she received a phone call today from the financial firm where Lena works. They claim, "Lena has not shown up for work for two days, without calling in sick, and they were wondering if I knew why." I did not know what to tell Lena's sister, other than I would ring her doorbell and ask around, and that I'd contact her when I saw her. Sarah thanked me and hung up."

"That's strange, Bernice. I wonder where she could be. I'll help you try to find her. Let's ask around tomorrow."

"Okay, we'll talk then."

Stella sat quietly on her sofa and retraced her thoughts, to a couple of days before, when everyone was in the clubhouse and she heard Lena say she was going in the pool. No one had checked to see if she was okay before they had left the clubhouse that night, but two days have gone by and someone would have seen her if something terrible had happened. Stella called Bernice back and told her, "maybe she is sick in bed and just does not want to deal with the phone."

"As sick as she gets, she always calls work if she can't make it in," said Bernice.

"Well, let's not get too worried. We'll wait until tomorrow and see if she goes to work. Maybe she's with one of her monthly flings and they're having such a good time drinking and partying, she didn't realize it wasn't the weekend," Stella ranted on worriedly.

"She's not *that* bad. She always has some awareness when she drinks. Actually she's a very bright woman behind that ditzy personality she puts on. Don't start panicking, Stella."

Okay, I'll let you go.

Later that evening the Cypress trees began swaying back and forth and the sky filled with dark clouds. Rolling thunder ran over Holly Meadow. Everyone must have been thinking the same thing. Bernice said to Nick, "Here comes another night of tossing and turning. Maybe it will be a light storm and last only a few minutes." Nevertheless, as usual Nick was watching his favorite baseball game and *would* not hear her. Bernice stared at the ticker at the bottom of the television screen and it stated there was "tornado warnings in Panillis County."

Nick is usually very concerned about tornado warnings and hides in the closet. However, nothing could get him away from the TV when he is watching baseball. The storm didn't last long and they both had a good night's sleep.

The next morning, Bernice left her condo and walked over to Lena's car. It was ten o'clock and Lena always left for work before eight thirty. She peeked through the car windows and saw a briefcase and a pair of thong underwear on the back floor. Bernice became concerned and knocked on Lena's condominium door. No one answered.

Carolyn was not home either. Bernice called Carolyn on her cell phone and asked if she had seen Lena within the past few days. Carolyn told her she had not heard from her or seen her. Bernice slowly closed her phone. Her lips had a slight frown and her eyes looked to the side with wonder.

"Maybe I should take a walk around the grounds and ask if she has been seen within the past couple of days."

"Have you seen Lena anywhere recently, Jack?"

"I haven't had the pleasure of meeting Lena."

"Do you have any idea what she looks like?"

"I'm not sure which condo she lives in, so I wouldn't be able to definitely identify her. I see a lot of different women leaving their condos."

"Let me show you which one is hers."

"Is there a problem?"

"Yes, she hasn't shown up for work for three days and she never called in sick. This is her condo.

"No, sorry Bernice. I do see a woman leave for work from this front balcony area, sometimes, but I don't pay much attention to be able to describe her.

"I hope you find out where she is."

"Thanks Jack." Bernice continued walking. "Could she have hurt herself that day at the end of the pier and no one has seen her yet?" She took a walk to the end of the pier and saw no sign of Lena or any abnormal disturbance in the immediate area. "Where the heck could she be?" An alligator made a loud snort. She jumped and her skin chilled with goose bumps.

As much as the people at Holly Meadow liked to criticize Lena, Bernice knew no one would ever hurt Lena physically. A crawly feeling crept through her skin. She was worried.

That night Bernice and Stella walked around the whole complex and rang doorbells asking if anyone had seen Lena at all, at any time, since she left the clubhouse on Sunday. Some responded in a nice way, others were rude and said, "She's stripping at Silk Lace across the street and is shacking up with a toothless redneck."

They had no luck. "Let's call it a night," said Bernice. "But wait; shouldn't we place a report with the police? It's been over forty eight hours."

Stella said, "I feel it should be up to the family. Let's call her sister and ask her what she wants to do."

Stella held the phone close to Bernice's ear. Lena's sister, Sarah, screamed and cried totally out of control. "I can't handle this, please help me. It's so hard for me to be so far away here in Ohio. I can't leave my kids until I find a good baby sitter. Yes, please go to the police and tell them what's going on. I appreciate your help so much, thank you so much. Keep me updated. Please Stella, don't leave me hanging. Please help find my sister."

Stella and Bernice broke down in a cry and left for the police station. They filed a missing person report. Both could not sleep all night. The thought that one of their woman neighbors was missing was more than scary. The night was long for both Stella and Bernice. All crazy thoughts were going through their heads. "Maybe she left because we humiliated her when she fell to the floor, thought Stella. "No - that's not a good enough reason for a rational grown woman to disappear. But who knows if Lena is rational?"

CHAPTER NINE

The pool on the canal at Holly Meadow Bay is heavenly secluded, sheltered by palm trees, and laced with satin petals of the hibiscus flower. The century old oak trees that follow the canal, along the pier, are beautifully arthritic looking and picturesque – with their crooked thick arms decorated with long drapes of gray dry moss, reflecting a dramatic haunted look. There are exotic plants with strong long curvy tongue style leaves trimmed with needles that spray outwards, with an impression to grab. The tremendous diversity of nature at Holly Meadow creates a landscape of high interest.

Stella and Bernice lay at the pool in the midst of the intriguing atmosphere - sad, nervous, and crying. "What could have happened to her?" - dribbled out of their mouths along with drooling saliva from their mild heaves. Jack chased the tear soaked tissue on the pavement before it blew into the canal and caused the ducks to choke. He had his little secret area where he fed bread to his little pets every morning.

The whole complex is perturbed by Lena's extremely mysterious disappearance. No one had a clue, but they all were very concerned, some showing signs of panic and fear. They felt a scary but desperate need to search the forest. "Maybe she wandered into the woods and passed out," said Spike, as he stood in front of Stella and Bernice with his large shadowed stature blocking the sun. "I'm going to get a crew together with some machetes and we'll dissect this thick brush. With all our built up anger and aggression we might get lucky with our ferocious and violent whacks and slice a few pythons." *"Pythons!"* Stella and Bernice said in sync with their eyeballs looking to blast off any second. "By the way," Spike mentioned, "A detective came by this morning and wanted some information about Lena. I told him all I know, which isn't much. I didn't mention the alcohol problem, but maybe I should have. Her sister Sarah called me and said she'll be down from Ohio next week. She has a key to Lena's condominium. I hope that she will find something in there that will help us. I'm going to the store to buy the machetes and then I'll discuss a plan with the men. Talk later." Spike walked away.

"Oh my goodness Stella, do you think Lena could have been?"

"Don't say it Bernice. *Shut up! Just shut up!"*

* * *

Sarah arrived and introduced herself to all of the Holly Meadow residents she could find. Full of tears, she pled for help and let everyone know that Lena's condominium looked normal with no evidence of foul play or that she had left to go anywhere special. Nothing was out of place and there weren't any notes of interest left anywhere.

On Saturday morning, Bernice peeked out her window and saw a gathering of the men neighbors in the parking lot. They were preparing to search the deep forest area. It was going to be a very tough mission getting through that brush with the unbearable heat and the danger of pythons, alligators and God only knows how many species of pain in the ass insects. Bernice felt the search wouldn't last long before someone collapsed from heat or dehydration. With all due appreciation, the fact is, these men are not young, she thought. Swinging those machetes was a dangerous task, but a task that has to be executed - for we are all extremely concerned and curious about what happened to our neighbor and with deep pain, we now refer to her as our friend. *So!* - she had her faults, but don't we all at some point in our lives, thought Bernice, as tears fell from her eyes.

She sat on a chair and broke out in a cry, releasing her feelings alone and aloud.

She stood up and paced. She cried and mumbled, "Many people have drinking problems, drug problems, insecurities that keep them from fulfilling their dreams. Some people are shy. Some don't feel attractive or worthy. Some feel they can't be loved. Some can't love."

There are parents crying every night because their children don't talk to them and some are crying because *they lost* their children. We are all human and we all live with different problems that we battle and sometimes keep private, including me. Nick doesn't know how insecure and sensitive I am. He doesn't know how my father criticized me day after day and left me feeling insecure for the rest of my life. He thought he was teaching me or correcting me for my own benefit. My parent's recipe contained their own ingredients that they blended, thinking that as their cookies baked they would become perfectly round, outstandingly tasteful and sweet.

They finished molding their cookies when I turned eighteen and if there had been a bite taken from me it would have been bitter and under cooked. I had no direction, at a time when direction is very important for a person who just graduated high school.

My personal ideas and thoughts about life constantly clashed with what my parents had taught me. These clashes made me feel unsure, which turned into insecurity. I tried to fight my insecurities, but they were baked deep in my flesh. They became part of my personality my loving parents unintentionally conformed me to have. Some parents innocently leave a lasting pain that can stay with us until we die. Fortunately, I'm not hiding behind any alcohol or chemical addiction, like some people do.

After emptying a full box of tissue, Bernice let out a big sigh of relief. She felt better.

* * *

Spike assigned each of the ten men who volunteered a specific area to search. Each man had to have water, a watch, and return to the starting point in one hour. Their bodies were dripping with sweat before they even started. Lena's tearful sister, Sarah, hugged each one of them, thanked them, and wished them good luck. In their minds, they all hoped they would not find what they were out to look for. No one ever mentioned the name "Lena." They were driven by a sad essence, which hung in the air that surrounded them. A discreet thought that she might be out there. Only the words, "We have to search the woods" would come out. Who could believe what they were searching for anyway? Holly Meadow is a pleasant and happy community. The residents all care for each other, even for the few who have strange idiosyncrasies.

An hour went by, and slowly each man returned from the dense forest soaked with sweat as if he took a shower with his clothes on. Spike had a cut on his hand. Nick had a deep scratch on his head. Others had some scrapes. However, all were okay and it was time for them to go to their air conditioned home. They all left silently.

* * *

Monday morning arrived and Jack was busy with his regular duties, scrubbing the outdoor chairs and tables by the pool. He worked from eight until two, Monday through Friday.

After a tough day, it was approaching two o'clock and he was getting ready to leave his private workshop shed by the pool.

Stella, on her way to check the flowers she planted by the pool, noticed Jack leaving. She passed him with a joyful, "Have a good afternoon." He replied, "Thanks" and went on his way. There was no one by the pool and Stella could not stand the heat of the few moments it took to check her garden. She quickly took a glance at the plants and headed back down the pier.

On her way back, she ran into Abe and Maryann.

"Hello, Stella."

"Hi guys, taking your boat out?"

"Yeah, we're going for a short ride. By the way has anything new come up about Lena's whereabouts?" Abe stared with a curious look.

"No, nothing, I'm so confused, we all are. We just don't understand it."

"It's a tough situation to understand," said Abe. Maryann expressed, "It's mysterious. How can this happen at Holly Meadow?"

"Easily," said Stella, "Look what happened to Carolyn."

"Oh, God help us," said Maryann. "You don't actually think....." Stella interrupted and stuttered a bit..."One positive note, Spike told me the board had Holly Meadow's entire owner's and renter's backgrounds checked and they all came back clean. Therefore, we have *some* hope. Have a pleasant ride on your boat."

"Would you like to come with us?" asked Abe.

"No thanks, I'm really not in the mood."

"I understand," said Maryann.

Maryann and Abe continued to their boat looking forward to some fresh air and the speeding wind hitting their bodies. As Abe unleashed the rope from the pier, he yelled to Maryann, "Look at that thing!" Heck that sucker must be twelve feet long."

"Where?"

Abe pointed his finger. "Over there, between the two logs, see it?"

"My gosh, that alligator is huge. Come on honey, let's get going. It's too hot for me to be standing here looking at an alligator."

Abe started the engine and off they went. The air did feel a bit better than land. They wanted to rev that engine as fast as they could but they knew their limit. After an hour of having fun, they parked their boat at a pier across the lake and walked to the restaurant.

Abe noticed one of Lena's past boyfriends sitting at a table with some friends. He told Maryann, "I'm going over to ask Henry if he has seen Lena."

"Oh Abe, you know he hasn't seen her since the fight they had last winter. He woke up Christmas morning with orange hair, don't you remember?"

"Yeah, but that doesn't mean they haven't talked since, maybe they bumped into each other recently, let me check.

"Hey Henry, How's it going?"

"Hey Abe, How are you?"

"I'm doing well. I was just wondering if you've bumped into Lena in your recent travels."

"Uh, no, and I hope it stays that way. Heck, it took weeks to get my hair back to its natural color. That was no joke, dying my hair red, when I was passed out from all that tequila she fed me. That woman's sense of humor is not for me."

"I know she is capable of doing some off the wall acts, but this recent one has stunned us all. She has been missing for a couple of weeks. Nobody has a clue where she is, not even her only sister."

"Well, knowing Lena, she could be in Tahiti traveling in the company of a bunch of miserable assorted white collar scotch drinkers. Anything is possible with her," said Henry.

"Listen to me Henry. This is serious. We at Holly Meadow do not sense anything like that. Lena's only flight to Tahiti was when she drank a couple of shots of tequila," said Abe.

"She was at our gathering in the clubhouse on a Sunday, and hasn't shown up for work since. Her sister called us, because Lena's office had called her, wondering where Lena was. We all have been searching to find out, with no luck."

"Well, I'm sorry to hear the bad and quite scary news. If I do see her somewhere, I'll surely let you know."

"Thanks man."

Abe went back to join his wife at their table. As they were enjoying their healthy salads, they watched the customers that were standing by the boat docks at a wooden railing, with a shelf that held appetizers and cocktails. While they were all gabbing away, Abe noticed some were throwing bits of food in the water. "Don't those idiots know any better. You can't feed those alligators. It will confuse their brain. The dangling arms are not a safe image for them to associate with food. I'm aggravated. Let's go." "Calm down, honey. Let me finish my salad." After they finished, they got on their boat and headed home.

They pulled up to the Holly Meadow pier and Maryann noticed the big alligator was in their slip. She screamed to Abe not to go near their slip. He said, "He will move as we start to pull in."

"What! Are you crazy? Those things can jump and climb fences."

"Turn the boat now or I'll scream bloody murder."

"Oh come on, Maryann, he'll go away, they always do. They don't like us. I'll swim to the slip to scare him away then you can drive the boat in, okay?"

"*Bull Crap! Don't you dare!* They're opportunists. A hungry gator will eat just about anything, carrion, pets, *humans!*"

"As far as we know, they have never been fed around Holly Meadow," said Abe.

"What if he traveled from another part of the lake, where they *do* feed them, as you just witnessed."

"Okay, you win; I'll take the boat down the pier to one of the empty slips by the pool."

Abe parked the boat and they walked down the pier looking forward to relaxing in their cool-aired condominium.

They ran into Spike in front of their building and mentioned, "there's a huge dinosaur out there that needs to be shot and sent to the alligator factory. He'll make some women a few new handbags and some shoes," said Abe.

"Yeah, like fifty pairs, size 12 double wide, great for women with big bunions," said Maryann.

"Okay, I'll call the Sheriff's Wild Animal Office first thing in the morning," said Spike. They should be giving out hunting permits soon. It seems like we have a higher population of those dinosaurs this year."

"Yes, and a much larger body size population," said Maryann.

The following week, residents could hear gunshots on the lake in the middle of the night. It was one a.m. and Maryann and Abe had trouble sleeping with the noise of the shots.

"I don't care about the loud gun shots keeping me awake." "I feel good to know that hunters are on the lake. The more gun shots heard the better everyone we'll feel. It'll make us feel the town is giving out hunting licenses and is making a serious effort to eliminate the numerous large alligators roaming in Emerald Lake," said Abe. "The experienced older hunters from the deep south are good at getting the big ones. As a matter of fact, the next time I see gator on the restaurant menu I just might try some. I'll tell everyone it's delicious and start a demand for it. That might help keep the gator population down."

"Abe, I'm sure the animal activists will keep a watch on what's going on with the alligator population. They were almost extinct only thirty years ago here in Florida and they worked to bring them back." Maryann replied.

"I don't understand you. You were the one screaming and terrified about the giant one in the boat slip and now you're sticking up for them."

"I don't want to swim with them or have a giant one leap on my boat, but they are God's creatures." Ready to end the conversation, she turned and closed her eyes.

CHAPTER TEN

It was a hot Saturday afternoon and Spike, Nick, and Noah were enjoying the blinding bright sun while lying by the pool. Their bodies laid lifeless as the warm sensation against their skin relaxed every part of their body. The soothing free time was recently rare and therefore, highly appreciated by each of them.

After about an hour, Noah squinted his eyes open and rolled them over toward the water canal and noticed a large alligator head peeking out of the water. "Hey, take a look at the big gator in the canal, he whispered." The three men jumped up and watched the reptile's head while it slowly tread the stagnant water.

Nick said, "In the past, while lounging by the pool alone, I'd find myself with my only companion, an alligator, sun bathing on the grass just a few feet away. I couldn't lay there with my eyes closed. The alligator has a three thousand pound bite per square inch. Of course, the small ones are less threatening. However, if it is more than three feet long, I always have to watch their movements and where they're heading. I know it's a natural human instinct for survival. And these days, around Holly Meadow, if you don't have a natural instinct for survival, it's best not to leave your home. Every day feels thundery here. As if lightning could hit you at any moment and each day that feeling grows stronger."

"It really sucks," said Noah. "You could be taking a nice after dinner stroll along our beautiful path of trees and *Bang!* out of no where, you're struck on the head by a python. "I would rather be hit by lightning than have a python curled around me, if you want to know the truth."

"I'm not sure about that Noah. At least you can try and fight the dam python off, with lightning, most of the time you have no chance." Spike commented.

Noah said, "Imagine what the residential areas near Miami and the everglades are like. You can't leave your kids out in the back yard of your own home or they could be snapped in a second. That's why there are python squads monitoring those areas. It's a very serious problem and it's going to get worse. There are thousands of pythons populating the everglades every day."

Spike placed his hands on the wooden railing that trailed along the pier. Noah's words forced him to look across the canal into the forest and get a flashback of when he was looking for the python behind his condominium. The creepy feeling placed him in a trance for a moment. His head shook slightly and the recollection let loose.

"If you take a good look at these alligators with their armored lizard-like bodies, muscular dinosaur like tails, and powerful long jaws - it's extremely obvious they're envoys from the dinosaur era. I think that's what makes them so interesting to observe." Spike explained.

There had never been a dangerous incident with an alligator at Holly Meadow. However, after the knowledge of a few pythons being on their property, and the attack on Carolyn, the residents became extremely fearful. As each day went by, it was hard not to think about the dangers of the huge alligators and monster pythons that were roaming on their land. "Dino," now his branded name at Holly Meadow, was the largest alligator they had ever seen in Emerald Lake. This new knowledge added tremendous stress to the members of the board. Especially, since the residents depended on them to take care of everything and anything.

The weeks flew by and it was almost two months since Lena's disappearance. The women decided to form a support group. Saturday afternoons they shared stories about how much fun it was watching Lena play bartender and push tequila shots on the guys. Everything about Lena that used to be referred to with negative criticism now turned positive. She was missed terribly. The story of her disappearance would occasionally flash on the local news and the stress was just too much for the women at Holly Meadow to bear. They sat together in the clubhouse and cried. There were storms of emotions expressed between them. Lena's sister, Sarah, was staying in Lena's condominium praying for her sister day in and day out. "Every time I hear a sound, I look at the front door hoping to see her walk in. At night, the slightest noise wakes me up and I run to the door. I want to stay - but my family is calling me every day from Ohio and telling me they miss me and they are begging me to come home."

"A friend or relative isn't realized how much they mean to us until they're gone," said Stella. "Even the ones that get on our nerves or the friends we sometimes get aggravated with and complain to other people about what we don't like about them. Every one of us has a different character in our personality and as long as it's within reason and not criminal we should be more patient with the people in our lives. Most people don't have patience for anyone that's not just like them. They expect everyone to think and act like them. That's not a fair way to think. It's very selfish. We all have little idiosyncrasies that are within normal means. If you want to have lots of friends or people that respect you, it's all about kindness and patience. Sarah's eyes became watery. She told Stella, "You couldn't have said it any better.

* * *

Sarah informed the group she had to go back to Ohio in a few days to care for her children.

That night after the group meeting, Bernice grabbed a thick beach towel and bug spray and took a walk alone along the pier. She laid her towel down at the end of the pier, rested on her back and stared at the spilled bucket of diamonds in the black sky. The burnt out bulbs on the light poles allowed the stars to appear crisper. Like a little girl, she pointed her finger at one that stood out, glistening brighter than the rest. She thought, "I bet that one is fifty thousand carats, mommy." She let out a deep breath of sadness. "How I wish those days of being an innocent little girl were back."

Suddenly, a narrow laser light beam passed over her body. She became very nervous. She yelled as loud as she could, "Hey out there, watch it, I'm human." Her voice echoed across the lake. There was no moonlight. The distance looked pitch black, like a black hole, as if nothing existed. But the alligator hunters were obviously out there - with their high tech laser beam rifles. Bernice could not see any boats and she didn't hear anyone respond. She knew high power green laser reflects intensely off the eyes of animals, allowing the hunters to quickly detect alligators over two hundred yards away. The expertise of the hunter was rewarding. Whoever killed the biggest or most alligators was proud. He was fast and had good aim. It's a strong male ego thing with hunters. Bernice tried to relax, but the long beams of laser light kept passing over her. After about thirty minutes, she heard a rifle go off in the distance. The atmosphere became too unnerving; she got up and headed back down the pier to her condominium. Another shot went off and her body jerked. As she continued a few feet further down the pier, an alligator let out a loud snort. Her body made an awkward jump, almost causing her to lose her balance and fall into the mysterious murky water. Shaking, she managed to get one leg to step backwards, toward the middle of the pier, and then the other. That was close, she sighed with relief.

Dashing, dying to get home, she made a fast turn onto the barbecue deck in the middle of the pier, and a giggly "Hi Bernice" came out of the darkness. A teenage couple ran ahead of her. Bernice began a fast walk to the pool area. The evening lights were on timers and had shut off. All she had was the little light from the stars. Bernice was heading to exit the gate when she stepped on a frog that croaked so loud she jumped, tripped, and pranced on one leg and fell backwards into the pool. Bernice lifted her head out of the water, a green laser beam passed her eyes with a loud - Bang! - from a rifle. She felt rapid wind from a bullet speed by her ear. Her mind spun as if in the center of a tornado. Her dizziness and the darkness confused her way to the pool stairs. She felt the side cement wall, pulled herself up, and rolled her body onto the pavement over a large colony of red ants. She turned and coughed trying to catch her breath from the sudden and violent shock of the bullet, squashing the red ants all over her body. Bernice struggled and brought her body to stand. The red ants were crawling up her arms and all over. Her knees were wobbly, as if they had screws that became loose. Her skin was pinching all over like crazy. She began sweeping her hands fast all over her body, stamping her weak legs up and down trying to get the ants off. She scratched every part of her body and begged, please help me dear God, I can't stand it. She held the nearby pole of the outside shower and washed the ants off in the cold water. Shivering and itchy from head to toe, the bites left a creepy crawling feeling that she kept trying to sweep away. Bernice felt she was losing her mind. She frantically hurried to exit the wooden gate and found the gate door stuck closed. She banged her body hard against it - but it did not budge. She stepped a few feet back and charged her soaked body full force, with all the strength she had left, and hit the gate open. Her body swung with the door and she fell off the side of the pier. She was hanging off the bottom of the gate by her long hair snarled in the splintered wood.

Partially submerged in the black water of the canal, shaking with fear, she grabbed hold of the planks and lifted her body back up onto the pier and onto her knees; she stretched her arms and pulled at her hair. Her hair broke off in pieces as she tugged and finally released her head from the gate door. Anxiously, she wobbled fast down the pier to her home.

She could barely catch her breath as she tugged at the handle on her screen door. "*Nick!*" she screeched and banged. He came to the door and held it open as she walked in, keeled over, holding her stomach, and went and lay on the sofa. Nick ran out to the front balcony and scoped around fast then hurried back in.

"What the heck happened to you? "Give me a minute. I have to catch my breath."

"Try to calm down, honey. Tell me what the heck happened? Should I call an ambulance?"

"A bullet just missed my head."

"Bullet! Who?"

"I started out lying on the pier, then left because there were alligator hunters out on the lake. On the way back, I fell into the pool and a hunter's beam caught my eyes by accident. He obviously couldn't see clearly enough through his scope that his target was human, because my head was low in the pool. I heard a shot and a bullet sped by my head."

Nick began screaming..."Why do you do such stupid things like that? Never go down there when it's dark during hunting season. You were almost killed! I don't want you out there at night."

She was scratching all over, "Hurry honey, get some vinegar for my ant bites, the itch is making me insane!"

Mad, he stomped his foot on the floor. "You're already insane, dam it! I need to take you to the hospital, your head is bleeding."

"No, it's just some hair that got caught. I'm okay" She wept.

CHAPTER ELEVEN

The Holly Meadow crew put off their usual gathering on Sunday for the time being. Too much time was passing and they knew the more time that passed the less of a chance it would be that Lena would come home.

It was time for the residents to stay in, stay cool, and relax with a good movie or baseball game. Of course, Adam, would never miss a baseball game this weekend, his Florida Stingrays were playing the Boston Sharks, pure ecstasy for Adam. Stella prefers to enjoy mystery movies in the guest room. The game extended into an eleventh inning. Suddenly a special news broadcast took over the television, announcing the long awaited good news, that Osama Bin Laden was killed and wiped off the face of the earth by U.S. Navy Seals. Adam had served as a navy seal and was extremely proud of their accomplishment. "Now if we could only get them to wipe out a few psychotic snakes here at Holly Meadow," he thought.

It was after midnight, Adam said, "Good night honey," as he walked up the stairs to the bedroom. Stella didn't respond. "She must be sound asleep."

Monday morning arrived, and Adam awoke without Stella beside him. She must have fallen asleep watching television in the guest room, he thought. After showering and shaving, with his cell phone blasting the sports news, as it did every morning, Adam went into the guest room to tell Stella he made coffee, but she was not there. He wondered, "Could she have gone out already? But she usually tells me she's going out." He looked out the window and saw her SUV parked in her usual spot. He scratched his head with a curious look. "She does always check the flowers in the morning and likes to check the progress of her plants by the pool." With a pleasant smile, he thought, "My wife wishes there could be many brightly colored flowering plants everywhere in sight around Holly Meadow. Simple things make my wife happy. She will know where I am when she gets back." Adam left for work.

It was approaching ten a.m. when Adam was sitting in his office and decided to call home. Stella did not answer. He dialed her cell phone and she did not answer. He continued his workday with Stella in the back of his mind. After a few minutes, he laid his head back and shut his eyes. He felt her silky hair touch his face and a light scent of her perfume blew by him. He moved forward in his chair and drummed his fingers on his desk. He was worried. "We have had days where we simply just didn't connect," he thought.

When Adam returned home from work, he began to head for the stairs to his condominium and saw Spike standing out front. He took a deep swallow and asked Spike, "did you happen to see Stella today? No, Spike answered. Adam hesitantly continued up. He stopped after every few steps and looked around the parking lot. When he reached his front door, he scrambled quickly for the right key. As he opened the door, he heard the loud noise of a vacuum.

"I thought I would get this done before you got home." Stella complained, "There's cat fur and your curly gorilla chest hairs everywhere in this place. I'm just doing a fast job for now."

"Okay honey," Adam responded. He turned away and let a tremendous amount of relief expel from his chest.

Of course, even though the men refused to show it, everyone was on edge at Holly Meadow and with good reason.

CHAPTER TWELVE

Sophia, a long time resident of Holly Meadow, frequently went out early in the mornings and worked diligently in the small pond under her balcony. She took lots of pride in her efforts to improve the looks of the sometimes overgrown filthy spot of water that stood below her balcony, and that of many others. After many months of raking, pulling and planting, the pond looked beautiful. Because of Sophia's generous hours of cleaning, you could enjoy the view.

Every now and then Sophia would have a conversation with her neighbors, Maria and Carlo. During their walks - they stopped by the pond and watched her work.

One early morning, after talking to Sophia, Maria and Carlo left the parking lot and headed down the pier. Suddenly, Carlo stopped and stared ahead with curious eyes. "There's something very long floating in the middle of the canal by the pool. Can you see it?" he asked his wife.

Maria said, "Let's get closer." A very determined and strong woman, she struggled with her cane. Her knee had been sore, but she managed to bring herself all the way to the pool where she and Carlo observed a dead alligator.

"It's a big one. Maybe Dino?" said Carlo. The huge one that everyone has been talking about.

"Why would the hunter leave him in the lake?" Maria wondered. Deep in thought, her eyes casually fell on Carlo's crotch. "That size is a show piece." "Yes, Honey you finally realized, it took you long enough," responded Carlo with a big smile. She lifted her cane and hit her husband on the calf of his leg, "Don't be a wise guy. No hunter would leave a huge alligator behind. He would want to hang it on his boat and brag about his kill. Maybe he didn't realize he actually killed it. Sometimes they get them right between the eyes and don't even realize they shot their target. That's one problem when you have to hunt at night. We better go and tell Spike, I can smell the odor. The rotten flesh will stink up the whole area."

Maria and Carlo walked back to the parking lot and told Sophia.

Sophia, "You would not believe the huge dead alligator that's floating in the canal."

"Where? How far up?" Sophia ran down the pier, observed the gruesome dead alligator, and could not believe its size. She ran back to the parking lot.

"You better watch yourself in that pond, Carlo told her. I sometimes see one in there."

Sophia said, "Don't worry, I'll run and tell Spike."

She knocked on Spike's door. Spike, "You're not going to believe the size of the dead alligator Maria and Carlo found floating in our canal. Come fast, you have to see this!"

"Holy Mackerel!" That's a huge sucker," exclaimed Spike.

That afternoon, the "See Ya Later Alligator" company came with their truck and took the dead alligator to the county laboratory. The technicians noticed some scrape marks on the alligator's body, but scrape marks are not uncommon on these reptiles. Alligators often fight and wound themselves, or get scraped by wood or boats.

The lab technicians and scientists almost always dissect the body of dead animals, to make sure there's not something out of the ordinary going on with nature's eco-system. There were no bullet holes in this reptile, so an autopsy was performed.

Even with a large razor sharp surgical knife, the lab techs had a hard time getting through the tough thick skin of this reptile. The head surgeon of the lab, Larry, took the long knife and held it between both fists above the stomach and pushed it in. "A chain saw would have made this autopsy much easier," one tech said. Larry had a hard time pulling the long sharp autopsy knife out of the body. There was an obstruction caught on the knife. He took a wrench, tightened it around the handle of the knife, and pulled back and forth until finally it broke through the flesh.

"Quite a fancy rhinestone dog collar. By the looks of this collar it must have been one of those rich spoiled poodles," Larry commented.

The lab workers surrounded the table and took samples of blood and flesh. They opened the stomach and intestines as wide as possible and found a few different objects. A golf ball, a couple of fishing hooks, a beer can, a few bird beaks, a couple of condoms and many small bones. Not anything human looking. Thank goodness.

The results of the alligator's blood test came back normal. Except a swab specimen from the alligator's skin did show an infectious bacteria called MRSA. Larry explained to his trainees - as strange as it may sound, alligator blood does indeed contain antibiotic components called peptides, and it is hoped that one day these components can be synthesized for treatment of many human diseases and bacterial infections. There is already some preliminary evidence that certain antibiotic peptides found in alligator blood can kill drug-resistant bacteria such as MRSA. That may be why MRSA was not found in his blood. However, obviously the bacterium is in the lake. It is not uncommon for this bacterium to be found in many bodies of fresh water in Florida. And it can make humans with weak immune systems very sick.

As bad as everyone wanted this beast dead, it was unlawful to kill an alligator by any means unless it was self-defense or if you had a permit to hunt for it by gun.

Larry concluded that it was almost useless to try and figure out what caused the death of this alligator. He estimated the alligator to be close to fifty years old, the normal average life span of an alligator. Its torn up wounded old skin was not good enough to send to the factory for women's accessories. "We'll keep the specimens from this gator in the freezer for the time being," Larry told his staff.

The next day the Sheriff came to the laboratory to check on the circumstances that led to the death of the old reptile. Larry explained the details to the Sheriff and he left with some lab reports and the dog collar for record keeping.

The Sheriff stopped by Holly Meadow to inform Spike of the findings and gave him a copy of the report, along with the dog collar, in case someone around the lake was looking for their dog. "I understand an alligator this size should not be kept alive in this area, but any elimination of animals or reptiles has to be executed legally unless it's self-defense," the Sheriff told Spike.

Spike remarked, "Are you insinuating our community killed him?"

"No, it's a reminder of the law." It's standard procedure to recite it."

The Sheriff continued, "A couple of years ago on a hot mid-afternoon in July, along a bank on Emerald Lake, I observed a small unsuspecting deer that had bent down for a drink. It did not see the very large black beast in the water and with a mighty vertical leap from the water, it grabbed the innocent little deer by the head and dragged it in, rolling and rolling it over and over again, drowning it. I'll never forget that gruesome sight." At that point, Spike realized it was obvious that the Sheriff did not personally care whether the alligator was killed legally or illegally.

Of course, no one in Holly Meadow cared whether the alligator was legally or illegally killed. They were just happy that "Dinosaur" was gone. Alternately, was it not *actually Dinosaur* that was gone. Could it be another reptile his size? Some thought.

CHAPTER THIRTEEN

It was a Saturday afternoon and the women's support group met in the clubhouse. Stella stood up and spoke - "The days are slipping away. It has been three months now since Lena's disappearance. I know we are all mentally worn out and tired from tearing to shreds any possible theory of what could have occurred that Sunday when she left the clubhouse. Maybe she did go home and had gone out again. Maybe she had a date with a man we never heard about. That would be the reason her car was never moved. However, we will never know. There were no sightings of her leaving her condo or walking through the parking lot that day or night. We're left with absolutely nothing to go on. But we will remain strong and stick together with lots of hope."

"Maybe if we all got together like we used to every Saturday afternoon, it would help distract us from our sorrows and fears about Lena," said Stella. All the women agreed.

Stella also decided it was time to make a few phone calls that night and ask some friends and neighbors how they felt about having a party in the clubhouse the next Sunday. They all thought it was a good idea.

The usual crew showed up around one o'clock. Each brought a scrumptious dish and placed it on the long table against the wall. It had only been a short time since their last gathering, but the feeling of what seemed like old times was refreshing and some felt a sense of comfort.

Noah offered to barbecue some steaks and burgers, but the reaction was neutral. "I think we have enough food. You don't have to sweat over the hot charcoal. Help yourself to a cold beer and relax," said Bernice.

Everyone seemed to be more caring and humble. They all left their snobby, tough, big shot personalities behind.

There were no characters or actors. The atmosphere was more subdued. Their real selves were there. Even after consuming beer and wine, their personalities did not change.

When Lena was mentioned it was with love and beauty. It proved the severe impact a missing peer can have in a close community.

A couple of hours had passed and the sky was turning dark and gloomy. They heard a radio news cast of a possible hurricane heading toward their area. Suddenly, huge lightning bolts lit up the lake like fireworks and everyone jumped from their chairs. The first bang was deafening and shook the building as if the B-3 Stealth Bomber had struck nearby. It sounds trembling like a tornado, Stella commented. They discussed whether they should stay in the clubhouse or head home. They all were having a good time, but decided to leave quickly before the downpour. They picked up their belongings and walked the pier home as their bodies fought a high wind and drizzle. The women hesitated to say goodbye to each other. "We'll all talk tomorrow," said Stella. "Yes, I'll call you girls tomorrow," said Maryann. They were not fond of the word goodbye. It scared them. Their hearts were full of pain and anger and their minds soaked with confusion. They hugged each other and left.

* * *

During Florida's rainy season, the nights have harsh violent rainfalls with thunder and lightning bolts that sound like atomic bombs. Lights flicker and the energy viciously shakes the buildings. The loud rumbling and banging is like that of a battlefield. Episodes of bright light flash through the windows like giant cameras going off every minute.

A crash, bang and bowling ball rumble, sped through the building like a freight train. Stella grabbed Adam and cuddled under the sheets....."Sounds powerful out there honey," she said.

"He doesn't impress me honey, I can make my own powerful bangs"...Adam mumbled half asleep.

Four loud massive bolts flickered in front of their bedroom window.

Adam swung the sheet off and bolted upright in bed. His eyeballs popped out like ping pong balls and glowed in the dark with a straight frozen stare, as if he heard a poltergeist.

"What was that?"

"What was what?" Stella asked.

"Goodnight honey," Stella whispered.

CHAPTER FOURTEEN

Every couple of days Jack would go around all the front balconies with the leaf blower. One particular week no one heard the blower or saw him cleaning the railings. Most thought nothing of it. Maybe he was side tracked with something more important.

One day, that same week, Maryann and Bernice were on their way to the local mall for a fun day of shopping. Bernice drove her SUV toward the front exit, and as she was going over the bridge, Maryann noticed something strange on the grass by the pond on the right side of the bridge.

"Stop, back up, there is something foreign-looking lying near the pond," Maryann said.

Bernice backed up and looked out the passenger window. "It's very long. Let's go park and take a better look," said Bernice.

"Maybe I should call Abe before we get out of the car," said Maryann.

"Yes, call him."

Abe didn't leave for his morning golf game and was able to take a walk over. He came up to his wife's window and asked, "What's the problem Maryann?" "Look at that freaky looking thing near the pond," she told him.

"Heck where?" asked Abe.

"Over at the end - in the corner, in that muddy area. See it?"

Abe walked over to the other side of the pond and took a closer look. "Damn!" He gave it a hard kick repeatedly.

"What is it?" Maryann yelled from the vehicle. "It's a decomposed python. I'll go talk to Spike and we'll call the Sheriff's Office and get someone out here. You girls go ahead and have a good day." "Well, we'll try." Abe walked over to Spike's place to explain to him what he found. Spike called the Sheriff's Wild Life Task Force and then walked over to the pond with Abe. "Now we have two dead reptiles," said Spike.

"It's over here," said Abe.

"I've never seen one this big in a zoo. Look at his gross mouth stuck wide open. I can see down his throat," said Spike.

"Do you see anything special down there?"

"Maybe, let me take a closer look." Spike looked down the python's throat as if he was observing something in particular. In a very serious tone he said, "I see a skeleton of five toes with very long toe nails. They do say our nails keep growing after we die."

"*What!*" Abe took a step back. His stomach began to churn.

"I'm kidding!"

"You freaked me out. You're going to give me an ulcer."

"I usually get complaints as soon as a small alligator is seen up here. A snake might be more difficult to notice in the mud. Maybe someone hit him with their car and threw him here," said Spike.

"I don't think so, Spike. Wouldn't they freak out if they hit a huge frigging python and inform people of the incident?"

The Task Force Team came and three men lifted the python, placed it on the parking lot, and hosed it off. They threw it in the back of the truck and off they went to the lab for the routine exam that had to be performed.

There were no bullet wounds found in the python. One odd thing that perturbed the laboratory techs, was that they found the same exact rhinestone dog collar attached to a piece of flesh in this pythons body as was found in the dead alligator, that the lab previously dissected.

The head tech, Larry commented, "This one didn't belong to a poodle. However, I don't think it would be seen on a German shepherd either. Maybe it was one of those large poodles."

Larry gathered his technicians in a room for a meeting. He explained to his workers, "The circumstances could have been that the two reptiles were in the same place when they each fed themselves a dog that belonged to the same person. The two dogs must have been in one of the backyards that border the lake. Not that the chance of two dogs having the same exact style collar on opposite sides of the lake is far-fetched, no pun intended.

Larry continued, "The metal holding the rhinestones has not oxidized yet. It's probably platinum or rhodium plated. It is still shiny, almost like new. They must have been expensive collars because the acid from the reptile's bodies did not turn the color of the metal. However, it would have with time. That could mean there is a family out there that's not happy right now and still mourning their loss.

"The pieces of dog bone were broken down by the python's powerful acidic system. We found only tiny bones that looked like toothpicks and splinters stuck in the lining of the flesh." Larry also stated, "These two reptiles being found dead on Holly Meadow property is a mystery to me. It is a possibility that chemicals from dog and cat collars can interfere with certain animal's biological systems and cause them to die. But since these collars did not yet have signs of deterioration, the small amount of chemicals released from the material was not enough to kill a reptile of this size. I am ruling out that the prey was the cause of death."

CHAPTER FIFTEEN

The Sheriff stopped by the lab to pick up the second report and took the torn but sparkling large collar.

He dropped off the second report and collar at Spikes. This time the Sheriff showed more concern about the second death and told Spike, "It is pretty serious that there were two reptiles found dead here at Holly Meadow. It could be just a coincidence of course, but I might be ordered to conduct an investigation of the residents. It's routine." "Okay, Sir, talk soon." Spike shut the door.

Spike had been dwelling on how such a large alligator could be killed and tossed on its back. A human wouldn't be able to tackle any alligator that size in any way and turn it on its back while it was alive. Unless, maybe, they used raw flesh and had a technique that would manipulate the body to a point that would cause it to flip over - or it could have had a fight with a python and the python's twists and turns could have tipped it over.

Now, as much as he was happy the python was found dead, he wondered what exactly could have killed *this* reptile. Spike felt a spin had taken place in his situation. He was working hard to figure out how to eradicate the deadly reptiles and make his community safe, but now the Sheriff's department made him feel he had to watch out for the safety of the deadly reptiles. Spike was a bit confused and with good reason. "Why doesn't the Sheriff think anything strange about the fact that there are dangerous African Rock Pythons on our property?" he thought. "Does the Sheriff actually think it's normal to have this giant foreign species roaming around a quaint community?" Spike felt he had a twisted responsibility and that the Sheriff had a partially twisted mentality. He *was* an older fellow. Maybe all the years of being in the animal welfare department and the constant rescuing of animals changed his way of thinking. "No, it can't be," Spike thought. Maybe the Sheriff never saw what the python looked like and thinks it's like a garden snake.

Spike knew it was crazy to think he had to worry about the deadly reptiles being killed, unless they were savagely murdered by a psychotic person. However, this wasn't the case or *was it?*

Of course, with Lena still missing, the perspective of what was important to most residents differed from that of the Sheriff's Animal Welfare department.

They figured it was just a coincidence and there could be a million reasons why the snake and alligator died. Old age for number one, poison from dissolved badminton birdies, kids rubber or plastic toys, fishing line bobbers, or maybe a heart attack. No one in the lab takes time to check the heart of a snake or alligator, because it's not worth their time. And if someone did have a tactful way of killing them - *at this point* - most residents would be all for it, whether it was legal or not, at least until the python problem was resolved.

With their sad thoughts of what might have happened to Lena, Stella and Bernice did not like the sound of any type of hanky panky going on around Holly Meadow, even if it was the beastly creatures. As much as they wanted the snakes gone, any type of mysterious death that surrounded them, gave them an eerie feeling. However, so far there was no proof the reptiles were killed by humans.

Spike thought about the rat exterminators that had been to Holly Meadow just a couple of months back. Therefore, he wrote a letter to the residents stating, "One possibility for the recent two reptiles being found dead could be that they ate a rat that had ingested poison." However, this theory did not make sense to the residents because of the clean blood tests from the lab. Wouldn't the rat poison show up in the reptile's blood?

The laboratory doesn't test for one hundred different chemicals, Spike explained.

CHAPTER SIXTEEN

Emerald Lake is crowded with hundreds of alligators. No guest has ever missed an exciting sight of this ancient reptile.

Residents who lived at Holly Meadow for a couple of decades never heard of a dead alligator being found. Talk about the strange incident with the dead alligator and python went on for days among the men. They became mesmerized and thrived on sharing their theories on what could have happened or who could have caused it to happen. However, Lena's whereabouts was always the main priority with the women. They knew the story about the disappearance of a forty-year-old woman with nothing to indicate any acts of foul play, would soon start to get stale in the papers and on the news.

As Lena's story faded out of the limelight, all they could do is wait. There was not anything to do but wait. Lena's sister, Sarah, was back in Ohio taking care of her family. Lena had no children. She had been married for a short time, but no one knew to whom. It was a story she had told, maybe a handful of times, during her few years living at Holly Meadow.

* * *

Spike on his way out to do some errands stopped his truck by a few friends and neighbors chatting in the parking lot near the water canal. He asked if they had seen Jack around. "He wasn't around yesterday doing his regular duties," said Noah. "I know," said Spike. Has anyone seen him today?" "No, not yet," they responded. "Maybe he's sick. I'll check my messages when I get back. Spike drove off. Spike was still out and the neighbors noticed Jack coming up the pier toward the parking lot. "Hey Jack, we were just talking about you. We haven't seen you around," said Noah. Jack responded, "Hi guys. Sorry I didn't show up for work yesterday. I had a stomach virus, but I'm back to feeling myself today. I'll catch up with my work. Maybe I'll stay an hour later today." "Oh no, just do what you can," the crew told him.

About an hour later, Spike was driving back in through the front entrance and saw Jack by the front ponds. He yelled, "Hey man, where were you yesterday?" "I was just telling the guys I had a virus." "Next time give me a call." Spike drove away down to his parking space. As he parked, he wondered what Jack was doing up at the ponds with a rake. His duties today didn't have anything to do with the ponds. Maybe he was just doing miscellaneous jobs in between his regular stuff.

Jack raked and filled up numerous plastic bags with rotten weeds and trash from the front ponds. He divided the bags between all dumpsters in the buildings, so one dumpster would not be completely full. This took up most of his workday, so he decided to stay over his time, and blew out the dirt and leaves on the front balconies and doorways to catch up. Spike was not happy with the way Jack used his time, but he didn't mention the issue to him. It was hard to find a decent maintenance man and he did not want to lose this one over a couple of messed up days. He let it go for now.

* * *

Recently, in the afternoon, Stella made it a point to lay by the pool and relax after the strongest rays of sun.

It was three o'clock and the heat index felt like a hundred and ten. The pool water was extremely warm, so she only felt a little relief when her wet body hit the air as she left the pool. She wanted to have a dark tan before she and Adam left for Massachusetts in a couple of weeks. Adam hadn't seen his sons for a year and he was looking forward to taking them to a baseball game.

Stella was at the pool alone. She turned on relaxing music and tried to concentrate on her meditation technique. She was trying hard to bring herself into a relaxing trance, but in the background, she could hear a loud strong mating snort from a male alligator, which disturbed her concentration. She sat up on her chair and listened carefully. Another strong snort caused her to jump up off her chair. If I were a female alligator, I surely wouldn't want to mate with *that monster*. Imagine what his moan is like. I wish someone was here with me. I'm too curious. I have to go look at this alligator. He sounds gargantuan.

I usually hear a few small snorts, but this one is exceptionally masculine. This sucker is loaded with testosterone.

She took a walk down the pier to look around. The dense brush that covered some of the water area by the pier, sometimes made it very difficult to see an alligator. He has to be close by. It was too loud for him to be far away. Those hunters obviously have a few big ones left to kill. She was looking out at the calm lake and noticed a few playful river otters. Suddenly, she heard a snort that sounded much too close for comfort. She folded her arms in front of her chest and began to walk down the pier back to her comfortable area by the pool. Suddenly, a massive snakehead bolted out from the side brush and encased her ankle with its mouth. Her heart jumped erratically. Its colossal jaws gave her leg a jolt, bringing her body down.

She could feel the pressure gaining and began to scream. She bent forward and gave it her best blow to the head. It let go of her ankle, and as she rushed to stand, it whipped and banged its body around her leg so fast she had no chance. Its body continued wrapping around her leg causing her to lose her balance and fall off the opposite side of the pier, face down, into the old wooden moldy moss ridden Holly Boat. The fright and strange grotesque emissions caused her to gag and fight for air. Her dizzy mind thought if the snake didn't kill her, the stench might. The putrid odor - worse than rotten post mortem flesh - was so unbearable, her severe gagging choke like cough caused a torturous pain in her chest, as if splintered ribs were shredding the inside walls.

Her gut wrenching heaves became so strong all her eyes could see were her intestines hanging out of her mouth coiling in circles like a snake.

Her body lay among the fungus and bacteria with two focused eyes and a long slithering tongue on a mission to consume its next meal. Disoriented, she screamed frantically for her life, but she was too far down the pier to be heard. She tried to lift her body up and crawl with her hands along the outer edge of the boat, but its weight on her leg dragged her down. The shock of seeing its lengthy body erect like a dinosaur's penis, still traveling up from the other side of the pier, made her fear her dead ex was getting his revenge for all those nights she said no. Bugs were munching on her skin. Pain was shooting in her ribs. Her head was spinning and her thoughts were racing. "I can do this. I'll do this," she cried with green muddy water rolling down her face. She tried with all the strength she had left to lift her body again, but with the slippery algae and moss covering the inside of the boat she kept sliding down.

"God help me, I have no chance." She imagined her obituary in the Palm Harbour News. "The poor woman, what a way to go," the readers were saying.

She turned her aching neck and her vision kept focusing in and out like a camera. She looked at the pier and her mind evolved into a state of paranoia. The snake had no end.

As the python slowly combed the slabs of wood making its way into the boat, she was hallucinating hundreds of feet of python reeling in around her body. She tried endlessly to scream, but all that came out was a weak cry. She was slowly losing all her energy as the monster tightened up on her leg. Her only hope was that because she was lying down it might not be able to give her another wrap. However, she knew the truth was, the strength of this beast could easily slide under her slight body and make a full wrap as if she were merely a toothpick.

Stella's glance at its colossal jaws open wide enough to grasp her whole neck and squash her throat caused a feeling of mushy tonsil and thyroid flesh in her mouth. Her cheeks blew up from her morbid fright driven thought. She heaved to release the flesh and then passed out.

The sun began to move down behind the horizon. Stella awoke in a stupor, her vision fuzzy. It took a few seconds to realize that she was alive and the snake was gone. She raised her arms, held onto the side of the boat, and brought herself up to a sitting position. She crawled with her arms along the edge of the boat and slowly wiggled her hips and legs down to the end of the boat near the pier.

She caught a reflection of her horrific face and hair in the water and stared with delusional admiration. Trying to keep her sanity she thought, "It's amazing what a few hours of sleep, strangled by a snake in a swamp, can do for a woman."

Still feeling the weight of the missing snake and numbness on one leg, she slowly pulled her weak body up, out of the boat, and onto the pier. Drenched with muddy moss and algae, she struggled to stand. It was difficult to keep her body balanced. She slipped on the slime and fell off the pier and into the lake. She was shaking so severely, her screams made no sound. With some life-saving adrenaline left flowing through her veins, she managed to get one leg back up on the pier. Stella grabbed the end of the wood planks as hard as she could and pulled herself up. Lying limp on the pier, a lifeless haunting doll, her lungs were starving for oxygen. Terrorized through every bone and piece of flesh, her strained muscles fought to breath. A large contraction of air sucked into her lungs and released. She was catching her breath. Her soul was strong. Her spirit strived to regain its desire to live. It was not time to leave her beloved husband.

After a few minutes, she took in a few deep breaths, sat up, pushed her whole body to a standing position, and wobbled down the pier dragging one leg through the parking lot. No one was around to help her. "They're only nosing out their windows when you don't need them," she sighed. "Isn't that always the way."

She got to the elevator and when the elevator door opened, she had to kneel down and crawl in as the door was shutting on her body. Stella was so weak she could barely crawl to press the button to her floor. The doors opened on her floor but she did not have the strength to get herself up and out. She lay in the elevator in agony – crying with no tears - a weak squeaky tone came from her dry throat, *somebody please help me.* Her life force was ebbing away. After a few minutes in the closed elevator, the temperature rose and she was becoming more dehydrated and began hallucinating. Traffic was too slow in the building to wait for anyone to use the elevator. Stella may have been an average girly type woman – but she had a strong love deep inside and valued herself highly. Suddenly, her survival mode became so strong she struggled to push herself up and make it out of the elevator and onto the front balcony. I don't want to die, she sighed. Stella dragged one leg as she walked to her condominium. When she reached the front door, her body felt like led as she banged against the doorbell with her back and slid down the wood slabs.

Adam came to the door. "Honey, what happened?" "When I got home from work, I saw your car and figured you were down at the pool or out with the girls. I fell asleep on the recliner until just a few minutes ago when I noticed you never came home. I'm calling an ambulance." "No, no…she barely could whisper - water fast. Ice, she pointed to her ankle." Adam ran to get water and ice and then carried her to the sofa and quickly placed soft pillows behind her neck and head.

"What the hell happened to you? You're all beat up and you stink. I think I should take you to the hospital." "Vinegar for my bites," with an extremely dry mouth and throat, she gasped, barely able to get words out. Her head hung loosely forward. "Lots of water with straw." She sucked and drank fast. "More, more, hurry!"

"You must have fallen into the lake."

"Worse."

The water she drank was helping her tremendously. She whispered, "I fell into the Holly Boat. That's only part of it. Get me a valium. Let me sleep. It was bad. I feel like I'm going to have a nervous breakdown. I'll tell you later."

Stella fell into a deep sleep. Adam spent most of the night with a warm washcloth trying to get the green stuff off her body. He noticed terrible black and blue bruises all over her and was tempted to call an ambulance. What the heck happened to my wife? He kept checking her breathing. He asked himself repeatedly as he paced, "Should I call an ambulance?" Late in the night, Stella woke and said she was going to soak in the tub. She cried, "My ribs are aching. I was strangled by a python."

"*What!* What do you mean you were strangled by a python?"

"I told you that's what happened. He must have been thirty feet long. It's a miracle I'm alive. I don't understand how I didn't die.

It must be the holy water my mother sent me. I put it on my forehead this morning.

"Are you serious? Stella, this is not something to joke about. Thank God it's not a venomous snake. I think you should get some x-rays. You could have broken ribs or sustained organ damage. Come on, never mind the bath for now, I'm taking you to the hospital whether you like it or not."

Adam took his wife to the hospital and fortunately, the tests and x-rays came back showing no very serious problems except for a hairline fracture on a right rib, a sprained ankle, numerous black and blue marks and some minor wounds. The doctor stated, "Fortunately, his fangs and teeth did not penetrate your skin deep on your ankle. You're a very lucky woman. This snake must have somehow been distracted or he would have swallowed your head. They have no concept of size when they're hungry." The doctor gave her a tetanus shot and a strong antibiotic. The police were notified and an officer came to the emergency room and forced her to give a verbal report. Tired and angry, knowing it would be in all the newspapers, she reluctantly told her story out of courtesy.

She would have preferred her privacy but new this wasn't a good time not to please the local police department.

When they arrived home, Stella took her much longed for warm bath. The clean soapy water felt like heaven. She laid her head back and Adam gently washed her hair while his eyes watered with sadness for his wife.

"How can I enjoy my home anymore, Adam? From this day forward, I have to live with more fear than ever. It's not safe to be around Holly Meadow. We have to move," she cried.

"Listen, we are going to find this monster and kill him."

"What if there are more out there?"

"We will kill them all."

Adam tried to hide the tears falling down his cheeks.

"This was our dream - to come to Florida and not have to put up with those cold snowy winters. Trying to maintain a strong voice, he told his wife, those evil creatures will not overtake us. Lay your head back, honey, so I can rinse your hair under the faucet."

Adam composed himself and ran his fingers softly through Stella's hair with clean warm running water. Adam lifted his wife out of the tub and wrapped a fluffy thick towel around her precious body. He hugged her gently and held her in his arms with love and thankfulness that she was okay.

"Stella, your deep love is what keeps me going every day, it keeps my heart beating, my blood flowing." Adam recited a few lines from a love letter he wrote to her the night before they wed. She remembered and tears fell from her eyes. "Losing you is the only thing I fear, said Adam. We will not give up without a fight. Together we can conquer it all. Please don't get discouraged. I beg you sweetheart."

She moved away from Adam. "It's easy for you to say. You haven't been attacked yet."

"What do you mean, yet?"

"I'm sorry; I didn't mean to say that. I hope you never will." Stella then looked into the mirror and wiped her face dry. She was searching for some sign of sanity in those eyes staring back at her. "Was this real?" she asked herself. "Of course not, it was impossible." She reached out her hand and slowly touched the mirror. "Maybe it was a hallucination brought on by grief and despair," she thought.

"What's wrong, Stella, are you okay?"

She buried her face in his fluffy bathrobe like a little girl. Then burst out a cry. She grabbed his collar open and smothered her tears and kissed his chest for love and support. "Oh, Adam, I wish this was all a dream and I was asleep somewhere."

* * *

The lights were low, the air conditioning was comfortable, and a few sips of wine allowed them to relax on the living room sofa."

"Honey, let me explain. I left the pool to check out where a very loud snort was coming from. You know, we all do that out of curiosity."

Adam angrily responded. "What do those alligator hunters do out there all night? We hear enough loud gunshots to disturb our sleep. Most of them must be misses. Maybe there are all amateurs out there this year. Stella, I know it's human nature to be curious and everyone likes to see something out of the ordinary, but it's dangerous out in that wild swampy lake. Especially these days. You should know better. I'm sure you learned a lesson. Get it through your head, you almost died!"

She took her last sip of wine and set the empty glass on the coffee table. Feeling a little high she became teary eyed. She lay comfortably against her husband's shoulder and he placed his loving arm around her. Water falls rolled down her cheeks. "I don't want to go out on the pier anymore, Adam. It was a horrifying event to say the least and I still cannot believe I survived."

Suddenly, she made a slight giggle and mumbled, …."Maybe when I passed out there was no challenge left for him and that's why he left. On the other hand, maybe he thought I was dead and didn't find my smell appetizing. It was the gruesome odor of the boat that turned him off." Seeing his wife's irrational state, Adam tried to comfort her. He held her close and gave her a hungry kiss to try to relieve her pain. "Honey, relax. Everything is going to be okay."

However, Stella continued, dizzily laughing and crying at the same time, "He thought he would develop acid indigestion from all the mold."…"*This is all so sick!*" "*I can't get this bizarre life we're living, out of my mind. Hear how crazy I'm talking. I'm looking for excuses why a python didn't devour me. This is insane! It's saturating my brain cells. I've been saying crazy things to protect myself. I'm creating a story in my mind! I want to believe this is a novel I'm writing to protect myself. It's my mind's natural reaction to keep me from having a nervous breakdown. The mind can do that!*

She got up from the sofa and limped back and forth…. Lena is still missing. An alligator and python were found dead and *two of us* were attacked by snakes!" "We will have to cancel our trip to Massachusetts for now, honey." She sobbed with disappointment. We won't have a life outside of Holly Meadow until this nightmare is over.

"It's time we get some sleep. Let me carry you up to bed." Adam lifted his wife gently, took her upstairs, and laid her carefully onto the bed. He tucked her in and kissed her cheek. He understood her irrational state.

"Try to get a good night's sleep," he whispered as he lay next to her.

* * *

Spike wrote a letter to every resident explaining Stella's unfortunate incident. Stella told Spike, "It was much worse than an "incident." "I would say it was a life threatening attack." "I apologize, you are right. It was a horrifying attack. Guess I did not want to scare them too much, but if I describe it as a life threatening attack, it will be for everyone's benefit and force them to be even more careful. We all have a major responsibility now to watch out for each other and ourselves. The county should step in and help us. It's like having a serial killer hiding in our neighborhood. I wish I could shred those savage man eating tunnels. Maybe Abe and I can come up with some type of idea to make a snake grinder trap. It would take some time to create because we would only want it to attract snakes. If it caught other innocent animals it would be a major disaster," said Spike.

Spike called Abe that night.

"I was wondering if you want to discuss some type of innovative machine that we could test out for trapping the snakes." If you have time tonight, we can get started." "It doesn't sound realistic to me, Spike, but I'll come over to talk about it."

"Okay, why don't you come down around seven and we can come up with some ideas."

They sat and talked that night for hours. Their thoughts and ideas went back and forth like ping-pong balls. It was tough to be creative when dealing with such an alien creature that was totally out of their control. "How about a high powered turbine vacuum in a heavy weather proof container that would suck the snake in and slice it up like a deli machine as it entered the box." With a high eyebrow, Abe expressed his opinion with an insecure tone.

Spike said, we could get the pheromone scent of a female python and have the trap spray the area at intervals. The python scent might also keep other animals away. Female snakes emit odors that attract males. It's sort of like when a woman uses perfume to catch the attention of a passing guy. Male snakes will pick up these pheromones when they stick out their tongue. That is how they find the female snakes.

"Hey, just like us men," said Abe.

"Alright, that's enough Abe. It's not the same concept. Sometimes more than one male finds the female and a battle takes place between the males."

"I have seen that take place with humans," said Abe.

Abe told Spike, "When I was on the computer reading about snakes, I couldn't stop, it got so interesting." "I know this has nothing to do with our python problem, but just for conversation, I know about male rat snakes, king snakes, and rattlesnakes that have ritualized fights to see who is stronger and gets to mate with the female. Each male raises its head into the air to see who can get his head the highest. Then they try to push the other one down to the ground and pin it. A little, like world wrestling. Once one male shows that he is stronger, the other male will leave. Again, like us men when we are all drunk and horny during last call in a nightclub."

Spike mentioned, "I know in other species, like garter snakes, a bunch of males will swarm the female. Female garter snakes are usually larger than the males, and the smaller males chase after her and wrap around her. Often they form a large mass of snakes all wrapped up together, called mating balls."

Abe laughed. "You mean orgies! Hey, they all become entangled in their garters and then they die of dehydration and starvation – what a way to go – strangled in a bunch of garters."

Abe, quiet! Spike continued, "Male garter snakes are tricky. Sometimes the males will emit pheromones that smell like a female to confuse other males and lure them away from the actual female."

Abe commented, "Nature is remarkable. Do you realize how ingenious that is? It's like when men are fooled by beautiful cross dressers. They are wasting time talking to a man and it allows their friends to have more of a pick of the real thing.

"Then when the heterosexual guy figures out he's kissing a gay man, the gay has a good chance of getting the crap kicked out of him. Sexuality is not something to fool around with when it comes to humans. Spike commented."

Abe continued, our universe is so massive – there could be a planet out there, where alien beings transform from male to female, or vice versa, by just using a mental program. When they need to mate, they turn into whatever gender they need to - depending on the situation in the area. There could be an anti-rejection program that would allow an even amount of females and males that are attracted to each other - so that when they are in a nightclub, no one would feel sad or lonely. Or feel alienated, laughed Abe. They could all be programmed to have an appropriate mate for the evening. No complaining or unhappiness.

There could be a geek alien, with a name like Meteor Stein that was sitting in its cosmic dorm one night and figured out how to hack into their minds and screw up the gender transformation program.

Alright Abe, that's enough about the alien stuff. Are you sure you didn't have a few drinks before you got here?

Spike retraced his train of thought and continued, "That way the male snake can sneak in and mate with the female snake. After mating, the males will release another pheromone that can temporarily make other males unable to mate." Abe was astounded and said, "So instead of fighting with force like the other snakes, they use chemical warfare. Wouldn't our wives love to have control over us men with a pheromone?"

"Heck, that's scary. Imagine if a human scientist invented a spray that made men instantly impotent. If that got on the streets, it would be a nightmare beyond imagination. There would be terror beyond any ever heard. The murder rate would be extremely high."

Stop going off track, Abe!

Spike said, "Since we are not fully familiar with the African Rock, we should study its behavior thoroughly before trying to build a trap."

"Now that I really think of it, building a trap for a fifteen to thirty foot snake doesn't sound feasible to me," said Abe. "I don't think we can do it, Spike, but I'll study as much as I can about any possibilities that could help us and we'll put our ideas together and take it from there. The African Rock is new to this country so I don't think many people know much about them, except for the task force down in the everglades. In addition, I'm sure the task force is much too busy to be thinking about a killer machine other than a rifle. However, a super strong vacuum hose to suck up the eggs might be a good tool for them to use. We can come up with all kinds of ideas, but I honestly don't think we will invent a machine that will work to the expectations we'd need to get the job done." "I suppose an ax is the best remedy," said Spike, as he paced back and forth with his hands pressed to the sides of his head as if preventing to keep his brain from exploding.

By the way, Can I take you off this subject for a minute? – Sure Abe, what else is new? Spike commented.

The other day, my wife asked me if I would please go to Walmart and buy her a selfy pole. I said to myself, is she serious? Walmart would never sell selfy poles. I stopped at an adult store and bought a very nice one. I wrapped it up beautiful - and when I brought it home to surprise her, she hit me over the head with it, and called me an idiot. Spike, do you have any idea why she was mad?

Maybe you forgot the batteries, Spike responded.

CHAPTER SEVENTEEN

Abe stayed home the next night, to study more about the African Rock python and pythons in general. In the meantime, he caught a news broadcast on a Tampa Bay station that the African Rock is overpowering all pythons and migrating further out of the everglades. They put out a warning for all parents in Spade County not to leave their children alone in their backyards or anywhere in the neighborhood. A child could be attacked very easily by surprise and would never survive. They talked about extending the python hunting season.

He called Spike. "I did some more reading about the African Rock python and to my surprise, I found another recent interesting article in a Florida newspaper. This article says the African Rock pythons are so innately aggressive that they begin their attacking movements as they're leaving their eggs. Those little bastards are born ready to strangle." It also explained how the python can digest its prey's skeleton completely, no matter how large, with very few exceptions that may be too overwhelming, like a large hippopotamus or a giraffe.

Spike, I'm very impressed that the python has such a powerful biological ability. Moreover, it instinctively knows what part of its prey is the head so it can give it a blow and knock the prey out. *Even more striking*, no pun intended, it identifies a human head, as tall as we are, erects and knocks us out faster than a bolt of lightning.

"You might be frigging impressed, but I'm frigging stressed to the max," responded Spike. "My hair is turning gray and my stomach feels like there's a bowling ball laying on the bottom of it."

Spike began to sweat. He became so intensely nervous about the fact that Abe did indeed find this information, he thought about taking a shot of whiskey. Now, being extremely concerned and anxious, he knew he had to post permanent official warning signs on the property. He already had signs that said "Beware of Alligators." Now he had to add "Beware of Snakes" on the property. Should I post beware of twenty to thirty foot frigging man-eating pythons? What the heck is next? He mumbled to himself.

The next week, Spike gave Jack six "Beware of Snakes" signs and told him to spread them out evenly and nail them to a tree. Spike received numerous calls from residents who wanted to know how serious the situation was at this time. He told them to be very aware of their surroundings until the problem is totally eradicated. In addition, if he had to, he would call the county or state to come in and help.

* * *

The Sunday gatherings were back on a steady basis now, almost as if things were back to normal, which was not the case. However, a few drinks and some social talk once a week relieved some of the nervousness that was "roaming" around the community.

Conversations were more down to earth than in the past. It was fear that changed their tone. Fear for the future of their community. The real estate market was down and it was not worth it to try to sell their property. They would all have to take a tremendous loss. Moreover, with the gossip that was out about the life-threatening occurrences and odd happenings at Holly Meadow – selling would be almost impossible.

Stella mentioned to Bernice and Lita, "We have to create a task force that only concentrates on Lena's disappearance. It has been over four months now and the people here are losing sight of the fact that we have a human being missing. It will never be too late to try to find her. We can set up office here in the club house three days a week to take or make phone calls - and set up flyers for distribution in the surrounding towns," she suggested. Bernice and Lita agreed.

Spike and Abe discussed their trap plan with Adam and Nick. Nick told Spike, "This crazy machine that you plan on building, would need state and city approval which would take a long time to acquire."

"You're right. I hadn't thought of that." "I was thinking I could just set the trap in our back forest area like a mouse trap. Nick cracked up...the word "mouse" hit him funny. You're comparing a frigging snake trap to a mouse trap? Now I know this idea is totally crazy!

Spike continued, however, it wouldn't be that easy. It would be a highly outstanding invention, which would take lots of time and thought. Many years of work.

Spike realized. "Wow, what an idea! You might think this machine is crazy and funny, Nick. However, did you know imagination is what's makes this world progress and succeed. Without imagination, we wouldn't exist. Some people don't have any imagination. Without imagination, you can't create anything. Therefore, even if we don't succeed with our so-called crazy idea, at least we had the imagination to create it in our mind. This idea displays a lot of intelligence. It's not stupid and no one should ridicule us. "Do you know one of the first missiles created was with a cat inside? With the idea that it would be so scared of water, its paranoia would give it energy to run and move the missile through the air." "It's all about trial and error," Spiked preached to his buddies.

* * *

The next day, Maryann and Lita decided to take their minds off everything and play tennis. Maryann took a swing that brought the ball flying over the fence and into the pond next to the court. Lita grabbed a few balls and they started playing for fun, hitting the balls any which way to get the most exercise.

"We look like a couple of drunks dancing during an earth tremor," Lita said, while barely catching her breath. With surprise, Maryann swept all the balls over the fence and into the pond.

"You're playing tennis not baseball! You are wasting balls. Go get those balls out of the pond," said Lita.

"Like heck I will! Do you actually think I would go in that muddy puddle?" Maryann sat on the bench drenched with sweat.

"It's not part of Jack's job to retrieve tennis balls that were intentionally thrown into the pond," said Lita. In addition, we can't pollute the pond.

"We had a good workout. I'll try and rake out a few, one afternoon this week. I'll buy more balls and bring them the next time," said Maryann.

"I suppose it was worth the fun and calories we burned," said Lita.

* * *

That night Lita fell asleep on Spike's lap as he was watching one of his action movies.

"What's up with the tiredness babe?"

"Maryann wore me out today on the tennis court. She turned it into a playground with some twisted moves. Hope you don't mind that there are a few balls in the front pond."

"You girls have fun messing up our place don't you? Why don't you go to bed? You'll be more comfortable honey.".

"Okay babe. Goodnight," said Lita.

Maryann also fell asleep early on the couch that night.

She called Stella the next day and told her about the fun time she and Lita had out on the court.

"You should come out and play with us one day. It's a fun workout and it takes your mind off of all your problems."

"I'm so out of shape, but I'll take you up on it one of these days. I'm still sore from my horror film. The director was excellent," Stella joked.

"I can't imagine how you made it through that nightmare. You must be a strong woman," said Maryann. "The last thing I remember, I was staring at his open jaws. That's when I must have passed out and I don't know what happened after that. As crazy as it sounds, I sometimes wonder why he left without my head in his throat. With all my tanning emollients he probably thought my body would cause major acid reflux."

They both laughed.

"Aren't we lucky to be able to laugh at such a bizarre, real life occurrence," said Maryann.

"Actually, it's the valium. I have severe post-traumatic stress. I'm trying to hide it from Adam so he doesn't worry. Now I know what Carolyn is going through and why we hardly ever see her. It's a wonder I'm not in an institution for trauma rehabilitation."

"You poor thing. Let me know when you want to go for a nice quiet lunch," said Maryann.

"I will," said Stella.

That evening, Adam wanted to stay up and finish the ball game that had been postponed. It was after eleven and Stella told Adam she was heading upstairs to bed.

"Okay, I'll be up soon, he said."

Stella threw her clothes on the chair and put on a slippery soft satin nightgown. She hopped into her fresh sheets and slid her body down comfy and cozy. Wrapped in a hint of lavender scent she fell fast asleep.

In just a few minutes, her mind turned into a twisted dreamland of terror. Stella was on a cliff looking down into a pool of pythons and a force kept trying to push her off the cliff. Her body jerked back and forth in her bed. The jolts got stronger and she was getting closer to the edge of the cliff. One more jerk and she slipped off the cliff and her body was spinning in mid-air. Before she hit bottom her mind woke out of sleep and her eyes opened wide. She sat up in the bed with her heart racing and sweat saturated her nightgown. She didn't want Adam to know about the dream. "My poor husband has enough to worry about," she thought. She put on a fresh nightgown and ran the hairdryer quickly over the sheets.

She popped a sedative. Maybe I should take two? She popped another and went back to bed. I hope I don't become addicted to these pills. I can see how people do get use to taking them; they allow me to feel relaxed. Everyone would probably like to feel relaxed by nature, all the time. However, they can't, so they pop a tranquilizer and then another and another. Before they realize it, their brain is used to working with the chemical and then it's very difficult to come off them. She began to feel the calmness set in.

I hope I don't become a prescription addict, she thought. Her eyes began to close and she fell asleep.

CHAPTER EIGHTEEN

Spike called the Town of Springwater and asked for some help with the African Rock Pythons. The office made an appointment for Spike to come and talk to the town officials. Spike collected all the police reports and hospital reports from Carolyn and Stella and a statement from Noah to make himself well prepared for the meeting. Spike posted a notice of the meeting on the community bulletin board and said the outcome will be discussed at the next board meeting.

A few days later Spike went to the town hall, sat in front of the town committee, and explained the situation at Holly Meadow. Right from the beginning of the meeting, Spike was very disappointed in the officials' attitude.

The committee stated, "The circumstances of the environment at Holly Meadow are part of the risky consequences that surrounds wild life preservation."

Spike emphasized that the African Rock python was very dangerous to humans and foreign to the state of Florida. Their response was; that it should be understood by all residents, that there are hundreds of non-native species of animals and reptiles in Florida. The officials stated, "It was up to the residents to be aware of their surroundings at all times and they would send a special task force to analyze the situation at Holly Meadow." Spike left very disappointed with the meeting and felt the committee was incompetent regarding his issues. "What a bunch of useless, uneducated political cronies," he thought.

The residents were too anxious to wait for town officials to go through all the channels they would have to go through before anything could possibly be done. They called Spike, one after the other, stating they were "sick of being threatened and frightened by their environment." "It is more than bizarre to not be able to step out of your house without feeling terror could be lurking in their shadows. We want the press on this now," the residents strongly complained.

Spike thought, how unfortunate is it that we are the only complex in this area inhabited by a python that was recently discovered down in the everglades. It is quite a mystery, to say the least. Spike held the phone calls slightly away from his ear. He tried to calm each resident, telling them he would find a solution as fast as humanly possible, to make Holly Meadow a relaxing and comfortable place to live.

That night, Spike sat with Abe, Adam, Nick, and Noah in his condominium to form a think tank on their issues. Their thoughts were all on the same track. They all read the newspaper every night and they watched the local news on a regular basis. As far as they could see, Holly Meadow was the only area in Panillis County, where the African Rock python was being found.

"What do you guys think? - about the fact that there have been no sightings in any other area of our county?" Spike asked his close buddies.

"How could that possibly be?" asked Adam.

"Even though Holly Meadow has the perfect environment for the python to thrive, it is still very strange that the species is not being found or seen anywhere else in our county," said Noah.

"So! What are you thinking guys?
I know we are all thinking the same thing," said Spike. "I can feel it."

"You say it first Spike," said Adam.

"Say what?"

"You know. Go ahead say it."

Nick told Spike, "Since you are so sure we are thinking the same thing, and you brought it up first, you are now obligated to say it, whether you want to or not."

"What we are all thinking is that - let me grab a soda first, then I'll say it," said Spike.

Spike got up from the sofa, went over to his bar, poured himself a soda, went back, and sat in between Adam and Noah. He took a few sips and said, "I'll say it in a couple of minutes."

"I know what Adam and I are thinking right now. I can feel it," said Noah. "That our president is a frigging wimp. You grabbed that soda, like it was a shot of whiskey to calm you down!"

Adam mentioned, "Jack Hardy was the only new person on the property since the bizarre incidents began to happen."

"Where did Jack live before Palm Harbour?" Noah asked Spike. "Let's look over his background check and resume."

"I'll get the files," Spike said.

He placed all the papers on the table as they each took a turn looking at them. Adam noticed that his previous place of residence was "Chokoloski." "Do you know where Chokoloski is?" asked Adam. "It is a small island down near the everglades. Just because Jack has a clean past doesn't mean he did not bring snakes with him." "Oh, come on Adam, do you really think a fifty year old man like Jack could all of sudden have a demented desire to terrorize a community with snakes?" said Noah.

"Why not?" Maybe he had a sudden urge to Chokoloski the hell out of people," said Adam. In his own mind, he could be the Choker Joker of Holly Meadow."

"Alright guys, that's enough of your stupid funny stuff, said Spike. This is too serious to choke about. I mean joke about, damn it! Damn, I thought I was under stress many years back when I was sitting in my hometown corner donut shop and a disheveled filthy slight man walked in with a gun in his trembling hand. He walked up to the register and told the worker, "Give me every single donut in this place or I'll kill everyone here." I couldn't help but break into a laugh, while I was sitting at a small table with a cup of coffee and donut. While the nervous worker was filling bags with donuts, the thief came up to me and put the tip of the gun up my nostril. He said, "You think this is funny fella? If you don't shut that ugly face of yours I'll fly a few fleshy donut holes out of your chest." His jiggling hand caused the gun to crack the bridge in my nose. I was in agonizing pain and surely wasn't going to laugh anymore. He kept yelling at the worker – "Don't give me any raw ones. I can't cook them on the sidewalk, it's too cold out there. Hurry up! All of them! If I find one donut anywhere before I leave, I'll shoot you."

He barely could keep his hand up. The gun was too heavy for his weak arm.

I had blood pouring out of my nostril.

"He then stuttered, "If you don't have any Boston Crème I'll shoot all of you." One woman sitting by the window began to cry. "You can have mine," she said.

"You want me to make a few donut holes out of you lady," he yelled. He was becoming very anxious to get out of there. He grabbed all the bags he could and ran out the door.

I asked the doctor, while he was fixing my nose, if he could straighten out the hook I have. He said he would get his little electric saw and give me the straightest nose anyone could have. That's why my nose is nice and straight.

"Gee, Spike, we were all always wondering why your nose was so straight." "Nobody could figure it out," remarked Adam.

All right, don't be a wise ass.

Well, you geniuses, how do we approach this situation without directly attacking Jack?" Spike asked.

Jack displayed a very humble personality and was easy to approach. Nevertheless, Spike still felt very uncomfortable asking Jack unusual questions like; "Did you ever own a python?" Alternatively, "Did you ever see any of those recently discovered African Rock pythons down in Chokoloski?" However, maybe Jack would think that they were just curious for some knowledge about the snakes, since he had lived close to the everglades.

After a few days of thinking about his strategy, Spike just simply went out looking for Jack and asked him an array of questions that he thought might be valuable in solving the snake problem. Jack answered Spike with all he knew and it was not much. Jack claimed he spent most of his spare time fishing in Chokoloski and at the time he was living there, there was no talk of any newly found python.

Spike was disappointed that he didn't learn anything new or pick up anything strange from his conversation with Jack. He called his friends back to his condominium for another meeting.

"Don't you understand that Jack could be a snake himself, and as you know, snakes are very sneaky." Adam told Spike.

"Listen, I don't care what he told you, we still have to keep an eye on him more closely, but we should be as discreet as possible," said Noah.

The heat was on Jack. He could not move without the board men checking on what he was doing most of the time.

They all knew where he lived in Palm Harbour, but they were not at a point where they felt they should invade the privacy of his home nor did they have the right to.

A few days with heated breath down his back - Jack finally asked Spike if there was a problem with his work.

"*Not at all!* We are just a bunch of bored old men. You are doing a fine job. Keep up the good work."

"Looks like we are getting on Jack's nerves," Spike told his friends. We had better cool it, because if he is innocent and finds out we think he may be the culprit, we might lose a good maintenance man. And you know how hard it is to find a good worker." They all agreed.

"We need some other strategy," Adam said.

"Listen Adam; don't be so fast to judge this man. We have no proof of anything," Spike responded.

"Now let's go get that smelly old Holly Boat out of the water and decide what we want to do with it," said Spike. Noah commented, "I think it would make a good planter. We can place it on the grass, fill it with plants and flowers, and paint Holly Meadow on the sides. It has a legend, not a long one, but it has one. Remember many years ago when the boat was new, couples would sneak out in the night and have romance in it. It was so much fun in those days." "I'll think about," said Spike. "I don't think Stella would agree to keep it after what she went through," said Adam.

They all walked to the pier and tied a couple of ropes to the Holly Boat and began to drag it along the side of the pier when Adam suddenly screamed, "Holy Crap," and threw his guts up at the sight of a gruesome corpse with a head bobbing up and down. "Is this a nightmare?" said Adam. Wake me the hell up! Spike began to hyperventilate and called 911. As he began to talk, he threw up on his phone and it went dead. All four men couldn't stop heaving at the smell and sight of the gruesome rotten corpse. Spike babbled out, "Noah, frigging dial 911." Breathing heavy with his mouth drooling on the cell, Noah spoke into the phone, "Help us. We found a corpse." The communication dropped, but fortunately the GPS system kicked in through the cell phone and sirens were heard.

Noah ran down the pier. "Over here, Over here!" he yelled to the E.M.T.'s and police. All five friends were ordered to move away. They waited and watched in the parking lot.

The coroner showed up. The body was wrapped and taken away. The pool and pier area was taped off, making it off limits.

Crowds of residents were screaming and crying, "It's Lena, I know it is. God please help us!"

After hours of devastating sadness, while sitting in the parking lot, there were no tears left, and it was time to go home and wait out the long days for the identification and autopsy results.

Neither Spike, Abe, Adam, Nick, nor Noah could recognize the body. It was too decomposed. Even though it was almost five months since Lena had been missing and closure would be a relief, everyone prayed hard that it was not their beloved friend. There was delusional talk that maybe it was a float-in from far away, or an alligator that was so decomposed you couldn't recognize that it was not human. The residents were not thinking straight, for a coroner would not take a dead alligator. All these hopeful thoughts raced through everyone's mind that night. Nevertheless, sadly, most believed what was probably the truth.

Bernice called Lena's sister, Sarah, to inform her of the finding. Sarah could hardly speak and hung up the phone.

Because Sarah lived in Ohio, she gave all legal power rights to the Holly Meadow Board.

The guys were extremely exhausted and could not sleep. They were drained from the stress and shock of finding a dead body. They sat together like worn out rags lying on Spike's sofa all night, and could barely talk. As the sun began to come up, they finally fell into a deep sleep and all snored as if they had not slept in days.

It was around one o'clock in the afternoon when Noah got up and left. Adam slept another hour and then Stella came looking for him.

This morbid finding added a tremendous amount of pressure to the board and increased fear in the residents. It was evident that Spike, Abe, Adam, Nick, and Noah were a solid team and the true caretakers of Holly Meadow. They had lots of pride in their home and even after this difficult incident, their strength and ambition continued. They never gave up, even under the most challenging circumstances.

Five days had passed since the coroner had removed the body from the lake. Spike called the coroner's office to ask how much longer it would be for the official reports. He was told it should only be one more day. The coroner's office had to take material samples from Lena's home, to check the DNA, and that prolonged the process.

Two more days had gone by and Spike's phone rang. He hesitantly picked it up and said hello. "Hi Spike, this is the Panillis County Coroner's Office calling to tell you we are finished with the autopsy report. Spike was scared but anxious. "Is it Lena?" He asked hesitantly.

"The dead body you found in Emerald Lake is not your resident Lena Kotta." Spike gave a sigh of relief.

"At this time we have no identification of the body - other than it is a male and that the decomposition analysis shows that it was in the water for at least eight weeks, the official stated. The rate of decomposition depends on many factors such as temperature, stagnant water, insects, animals, bacterial conditions and so on. We would not be able to give you an exact time period the corpse was immersed in the lake."

Spike was in shock and lost his breath.

"Sir, are you there?" asked the official.

"Yes, sorry about that, guess I just never thought it would be a *Man*. Why did you take DNA from our resident Lena's condo if you knew it was a man?" asked Spike.

"The missing woman is on file with the Sheriff's office as a possible victim of foul play, so we had to try and verify if there was a connection. The man's body was too deteriorated and decomposed to evaluate a health condition or evidence of foul play. We will have to wait until we receive another possible missing person's report that would match this man and take it from there. If there is anything more you need to know or if you have any more information that could help us give us a call anytime." They hung up.

Spike called the police department and asked if the crime tape could be removed from the property. They refused his request. It was too early in the investigation. Spike went to his computer and e-mailed the good news that "It was not Lena" to all the residents. Nevertheless, even still, it is a very sad and tragic event that a man is dead and we should respect that fact, he wrote.

Spike's phone started ringing, *"What do you mean a man?"* The residents were all just as shocked as Spike - to learn that it was a man. Some were rude and yelled at Spike, Adam, and Noah for not being able to recognize at the finding that it was a male.

"Couldn't you three assholes save us all this heartache and see that it was a man in the water. Don't you know balls when you see them or tits when you don't?"

Spike ignored the stupid question.

"It's probably one of those drunken fisherman they find every couple of years," a few expressed.

As the news got around, most residents felt a sense of relief, to a certain extent. Lena's sister, Sarah, in Ohio was surely relieved, but of course still nervous and upset. "Where on God's earth could my sister be?" she thought.

The board men didn't do much during the wait for the autopsy results. Now that they knew they found an unidentifiable body, they were able to go on with their projects.

The county detectives began to visit Holly Meadow on a regular basis. They knocked on every door in the complex, asking questions to anyone they could find who set foot on Holly Meadow grounds in the past few months. At first they had an aggressive approach, but as time went on, they had no leads to go on and discontinued their visits.

CHAPTER NINETEEN

It was a bright sunny morning and the banging of a hammer was heard, along with lawn mowers. Adam left for work around eight. Stella hopped out of bed shortly after in the nude. She stood in front of her bathroom mirror and as usual massaged tanning oil all over her body and gorgeous breasts. Stella's mother had been instrumental in encouraging her to feel good about her body. She repeatedly admired her pretty pink nipples like she never saw them before. "It's not important, but when I notice other color nipples on my friends, I prefer my color," she thought. "I don't think guys care what color they are, they just want to suck on them - the horny bastards."

Stella stared into the mirror directly at her eyes and made a promise to herself. "Each day I will work hard to overcome my trauma from the snake attack. I do realize it will take time to rid my mind of the fear and anxiety it has caused, but I promise I will not depend on medication for long. Life is about being strong and happy and enjoying all the beautiful natural gifts that our creator has giving us."

The sun's rays shone through the bathroom window and reflected a gleaming silky shine off her dyed golden blonde hair as she slipped into her provocative bathing suit. Stella wrapped a towel around her waist and headed for the pool.

On her way to the pool, she bumped into Jack who was whistling away while replacing a damaged plank on the pier at the entrance to the pool. Stella said, "excuse me," made her way around him and stopped. "Boy, they have you doing everything around here, don't they? Looks like you are a "Jack of all trades," no pun intended of course," she remarked with a big smile.

"I just do what I'm told."

"By the way Jack, we all haven't had a chance to really get to know you. Why not join us at one of our Sunday afternoon gatherings? I'm sure everyone would enjoy having you there. We don't have them every Sunday, but the next time we do, I'll let you know." Jack glanced up at Stella, "Maybe I *should* have a beer with the guys. I might take you up on that, Stella."

"Your wife is welcome too, of course."

"Oh, I don't have a wife."

"Bring your girlfriend."

"I don't have a girlfriend."

"Now what's a handsome man like you doing without a personal companion?"

"After my divorce five years ago, I lost interest in relationships."

"I understand, *I think!*" Stella with a look of wonder folded her arms and toyed with her hair. "Maybe you just need a sunny prospect to come your way."

"I just got screwed so bad, I'd rather not deal with any of the problems that could come along in a relationship, so I decided to stay alone."

"You must get lonely. Maybe one of these days you'll change your mind."

"I doubt it. She took me for practically every penny I had, including the house we built with my father's inheritance."

"I'm sorry I brought back bad memories, Jack. I'll go now and lay by the pool. But if you ever feel a need to talk let me know."

Stella resumed her walk down the pier to the pool.

"Hmmm! I wonder how Jack's ex-wife was able to accomplish such an unfair deal in their divorce," she thought.

She could feel the sun's hot rays stimulating her tanning oil. Many things were going through Stella's mind. The python problem, the dead body, Lena missing.

* * *

That night Stella had a gourmet candlelight dinner waiting for Adam. When he entered the door, she greeted him with a warm kiss. He glanced over at the candle light shimmering in the darkness and said, "Looks like we're in for a very special evening." "Yes sweetheart." She gently swept the back of her hand across his cheek and whispered in his ear, go take your suit off and let's have a glass of wine. Adam went upstairs to the bedroom hung up his suit and returned downstairs in just his underwear. Stella handed him a glass of Merlot and acted like she didn't notice.

"Hope you're hungry darling. Let's sit at the table."

After a few sips of wine, they both couldn't hold in their laughs any longer.

"You are too funny Adam!" Stella stood up from the dining chair, lifted her dress up over her head, whipped it around a few times and threw it on the floor.

"Now we have matching attire."

They both laughed.

"How was your day at work?"

"The same as usual. I had one amusing conversation with a customer. A woman called to ask why her printer was not working. Of course, it was not a banking issue, but I helped her to realize she just had to plug it in. She said she was going to write to the president of the bank and tell him how amazingly helpful I was."

"What did *you* do today honey?"

"Well, after you left I realized I did not have any errands to do and I was caught up with the house work, so I decided I would take myself over to lay by the pool."

"I'm proud of you honey. I've been a little worried about your psychological well-being."

"On the way to the pool, I bumped into Jack while he was fixing a plank on the pier and held a light conversation with him. I figured I would make him feel more at home and explained to him that he was more than welcome to join us in the clubhouse on a Sunday."

"That was considerate of you, honey."

"Adam, he did tell me an interesting story - about how his ex-wife took him for everything they owned, including the house they had built with his father's inheritance. I thought it was strange, because I know they had no children."

"That does sound strange. She must have had a great lawyer. How long ago was that, did you ask him?" "He said five years ago. He's not over it, Adam. I could still feel the anger in his voice when he told me." "Well, honey that just makes our relationship seem all the more special. Some people are just dealt a bad deck in life. Cheers!" "Here's to us."

After they finished dinner, Adam helped his wife clean off the table. She noticed how he wiped every crumb off and mentioned, "Honey, you don't have to be so fussy." He then lifted her body into his arms and laid her on the table. He lifted one of her beautiful long legs and kissed her ankle gently and slowly all the way up to her silky soft thigh. Her deep breath turned him on. He took her other leg, held it up, massaged her pretty foot, and made stimulating little massages all the way to her panty. Her breath became heavier. It turned him on more. He took both her ankles and placed them on his shoulders and ran his hands gently all around, up and down the inside of her smooth thighs. Her hands lay loose above her head and her eyes dreamy. He slipped her hips close to him and his motion of love took them to a universe filled with shooting stars. She lay like a cosmic rag doll as if a glorious spiritual asteroid shot through her head out her toes and dragged every bit of stress in her body out with it.

He lifted her body off the table and into his arms, carried her up the stairs, and laid her in bed placing a soft blanket over her. As she fell asleep, he kissed her cheek, and whispered, "Thanks for the nice dinner, honey," and went downstairs to read the paper.

CHAPTER TWENTY

Carolyn called Stella early the next morning and asked if she could come over for a cup of tea. Stella was surprised to hear Carolyn's voice on the other end of the phone.

"Is everything okay?" Stella asked.

"Yes, I just feel a need to talk to you."

"Okay, see you in a bit Carolyn."

Stella threw on some comfortable clothes and boiled some water. She wondered why, all of sudden, Carolyn was ready to talk to her. A few minutes later Carolyn knocked on her door.

Please sit, Carolyn, I'm so glad you came to talk." Carolyn began to cry. She told Stella, "I'm so sorry about your snake attack, I know what you went through and it's so awful."

"It's okay Carolyn, fortunately we are strong women. We got through it and we will continue to fight it. As time passes, we will gain more strength."

"I haven't told Adam about my crazy dreams. Last night I dreamed I walked into the bathroom and stared at my ghostly looking face in the mirror. My hair was all snakes like that of the Greek Monster Medusa. I sprayed mousse on my head and styled each snake, sliding it through my hands, twirling and twisting it all around. The longer I could get them to stick out the better I felt I looked. It was so real I woke up and ran to the mirror."

"Stella, it doesn't sound much different than most of the hairstyles teens dream of having these days." Stella looked down and up into Carolyn's eyes with a big laugh. She barely could get out, "thanks I needed that" as she wiped the tears from her laugh. Carolyn told Stella, "At times I dream that I am just sitting on a chair and I feel great sadness. It's strange; the sadness slowly tightens around my chest and heart. It feels like the crushing coils of the snake, and as it continues to constrict it squeezes tears from my eyes. The more it tightens up - the harder I cry. I start sobbing so hard it feels real. I wake up out of breath, like I finished my cry."

"I assume our friends must think we both have some type of post traumatic problems," said Carolyn. "Actually, it appears that most residents have anxiety about just living here and I can understand why. Who in their right mind wants to live in an environment like this one."

"Stella, There is something I want to tell you." "What is it Carolyn?"

"I know I have not been social with my friends and it is a little rude that I don't even pop in to say hello at the gatherings you all have been having on Sundays, but I'm just not ready."

"We understand, said Stella. Don't worry about it, honey. You had one of the most bizarre tragedies that anyone could have."

"Carolyn, The only reason I might appear to be handling my tragedy a little better than you is because of the medication I take every day to calm my nerves and help me with anxiety. And after I told my doctor about the dream I had the other night, when I woke up with palpitations and my nightgown drenched with sweat, he changed my prescription. He said it should work better for this type of problem. At first, I felt guilty taking it, but I have a very valid reason to take it. I just don't want to become addicted to it."

"Carolyn, I seriously think you should see my shrink and let it all out, you'll feel much better. Some psychiatrists just like to prescribe medications and some will listen to you."

Let's have something to eat. I have some fresh cut fruit in the fridge and some delicious Danish."

Stella got up, dressed the table, and served Carolyn. Carolyn was feeling so sad it made Stella begin to cry.

"I'm so sorry," Carolyn wept. "I shouldn't have come over."

"No, don't feel that way, this is good for us. Crying is a healthy release. I'm glad you said what you wanted to say, said Stella. Let's try to relax and eat some fruit."

"That's not what I wanted to say, said Carolyn. I mean, I did want to tell you how I felt, but there is something else I need to tell you." Carolyn gently wiped the juice on her lips from the sweet pineapple. Stella lifted a brow and sipped her drink calmly. Now curiosity set in and Stella waited patiently for Carolyn's next words. "First, thank you for this breakfast, I really needed it."

"Your welcome dear. It's so good to see you and have you here.

Stella lifted her fork with a small ripe red strawberry and swallowed it nervously without a chew. The pain in her esophagus was hard to hide. She sat in silence until the strawberry made its way to her stomach where it lay like a brick. "I'm too curious, Carolyn, what do you need to tell me?"

Carolyn drew in a deep breath and exhaled, "On the Sunday Lena disappeared I noticed Jack's truck in the parking lot, when I arrived home from Dean's place in the early evening. It was parked in an odd spot, away from the buildings, near the hose for the car wash. I know he doesn't work on Sundays, so I thought he was in the clubhouse with all of you guys. I wondered why he didn't park in his usual spot near mine, since it was available."

"A few days ago when I said hello to Jack in the parking lot, he was sweating and swearing over a nail. I joked with him and said, "Go grab a cold beer in the clubhouse, you work too hard." He responded, "Funny you said that, Stella mentioned I should join you guys on a Sunday in the clubhouse. I might take her up on it."

I told Jack, "I haven't joined my friends lately in the clubhouse, but I thought you were already playing with them, because I noticed your truck in the parking lot one Sunday afternoon."

He turned bright red and stuttered, "It wasn't *my* truck, Carolyn."

"Maybe it wasn't your truck, I said, but Stella's idea does sound good, I'm sure you will enjoy it."

"I left and continued up to my condo."

"Stella, I know for a fact that it was his truck, because he always parks in the same guest spot next to my space and I recognized his plate number."

Stella responded, "Maybe he was dropping off some supplies or had to do a small job for one of the residents and didn't remember."

"Then why did he act like I caught him off guard? He didn't hesitate to think and he denied it was his truck right away. I swear it was his truck. It hasn't left my mind since."

"You have an interesting question, Carolyn. I think the both of us need to clarify this or we will drive ourselves insane."

"I really don't want to get too involved in this, Carolyn said nervously."

"I'll try to find an answer," said Stella.

"I think I better go home and try to relax," Carolyn whispered in a depressed tone."

"Okay, honey, if it will make you feel better. But I'm really glad we finally could be alone and talk."

"And maybe I will go see your doctor."

"Let me give you his card."

After Carolyn left, Stella curled up on her sofa and dwelled on what Carolyn had told her. Stella knew that anytime Jack was on the property, other than his regular working hours, he was to report it to Spike. She decided to call Spike.

"Spike? - It's Stella. I was just wondering if Jack had any side jobs on the property that were on a Sunday since he's been here."

"Let me check my book. I see that on the Sunday Lena disappeared, I have written down, change showerhead for Lena. And on one more Sunday, he changed the hose on Mrs. Gilbert's washing machine. I don't see anything else written down on a Sunday. He probably changed Lena's showerhead before she came to the clubhouse that day."

"Okay Spike, thanks."

"Hey, is there anything you want to tell me, asked Spike."

"Not right now. Don't worry, it's nothing."

Stella remembered the day when Lena told her she "had not met the new maintenance man because of her working hours." "That didn't mean she could not have had him change her showerhead. She could have made the plans through a neighbor and left her the key."

Stella thought, maybe she, and Carolyn are getting carried away. After all, Jack does have a clean criminal record. *However*, Stella said aloud, as she got up from the sofa and walked back and forth. "Just because he has a clean record doesn't mean he had an amicable divorce with his ex-wife."

"They could have verbally fought to the high hills with vicious and nasty criticism and comments thrown back at each other. Maybe Jack has lots of anger built up inside. There are always two sides to every story, she thought. But what would any of his personal problems from a past marriage have to do with Lena?

A woman he has never met. Maybe I should find his ex-wife and try to have a talk with her. She will either be the snotty type and tell me it's none of my business or she will be the type that enjoys bashing her ex-husband. It won't hurt to try," thought Stella.

Stella called Carolyn and told her she was going to try to find Jack's ex-wife and have a talk with her.

"It's the only way we can find out about Jack's true personality," she told Carolyn.

"His ex-wife is not going to have much good to say about Jack - and you'll never know if she's telling the truth," said Carolyn.

"I think sometimes women break down with other women and a lot of the truth does come out, said Stella. I might be able to get bits and pieces of information that will clear our mind and we won't have to wonder anymore." "Well, it's your case detective; I could never bring myself to do it. If you feel you are strong enough to track her down and go through with it - lots of luck to you woman."

"Please don't mention what I'm doing, to anyone, Carolyn."

"I won't, Stella."

"Thanks, I'll keep you updated."

Stella called the Chokoloski directory assistance and asked for any resident number with the name Hardy. The operator told her she could not find any Hardy in Chokoloski.

Adam walked in the door that evening and Stella was more quiet than usual. "Is anything wrong, honey," he asked as he placed his briefcase on the table and took off his suit jacket. "No, honey, I'm just feeling a little tired today for some reason. Maybe I didn't get a good night's sleep." "Yes, come to think of it, you did a lot of tossing and turning last night. I hope you're not having any bad dreams." "If I am, I don't remember them. But it's possible."

"Why don't I go get some take-out and you can hit the bed early tonight," said Adam. "I'll appreciate it, honey, thanks."

* * *

The next morning after Adam left for work, Stella anxiously got up out of bed and looked at a map of the cities and towns near Chokoloski. Stella read; "Its population is extremely small and that it's a fishing community." She could see why Jack's ex might not be living there. She read that Chokoloski is part of Capri Island and thought Capri Island would probably be more his ex-wife's style of living. Stella dialed directory assistance in Capri Island.

"Do you have any residents with the name Hardy?" she asked.

"Yes Madam, we have a few but I can only give you three numbers in one phone call."

"Give me any three, please."

The recording came on and Stella jotted down the numbers. She called the first one and a woman answered. "Hello!" Stella anxiously said, "Please excuse me for bothering you but I was wondering if you knew of a Mrs. Hardy that was once married to a Jack Hardy who lived in Chokoloski.

"No Maam, I'm sorry I do not know of any Jack Hardy that was ever in my family."

Stella dialed the next number and there was no answer. Stella dialed the next number and this time a man answered.

"Mr. Hardy?"

"Yes, said the man."

"Please excuse me for taking up your time Sir, but I'm looking for a long lost friend who was married to a Jack Hardy approximately five years ago. Would you happen to know a Jack Hardy?"

"Well, my brother's name is Jack but he doesn't live down here anymore. He moved further up north for better job opportunities. I'm not sure it's the same Jack you are looking for Madam."

"Can you give me the name of his ex-wife so I can find out if it's my old time friend?" asked Stella.

"I think I should leave that up to Jack. I'll give you Jack's number and you can ask him."

"That would be of great help, Sir."

Stella jotted the number down and thanked the man for his time. She ran to her desk and shuffled through the papers, looking for the introduction letter from Spike that had Jack's number on it. She couldn't find it. Stella called Carolyn and asked her if she had the letter lying around somewhere. Carolyn had the number on her list on the fridge and gave it to Stella. She heard her say, "Oh my goodness, this number matches." "Matches what?" asked Carolyn. I just spoke to Jack's brother but he wouldn't give me any information except Jack's phone number.

"What good is his number going to do you?"

"Absolutely nothing! I told him I was looking for a long lost friend that was married to a Jack Hardy - but he wouldn't give me her name. He said his brother should give it to me. Of course, I would never ask Jack for his ex-wife's number, he would think of it as weird or suspicious. I was so close Carolyn. I'll keep trying, talk later."

CHAPTER TWENTY ONE

Spike received a phone call from a crying woman who said she had just called the Sheriffs office to ask if anyone had found two poodles. The woman could barely talk she was crying so hard. She said the office told her, "you have my dog's collars."

"I'm so sorry Madam; I don't know what to say."

"I guess it's my fault for leaving them in the backyard near the lake. I should have known better. My poor little babies, I loved them so much."

"You can pick up the collars any time. If I go out, I'll leave them in an envelope behind my screen door. Again, I'm very sorry for your loss. I know how hard it must be." Call waiting kicked in, it was Adam. Spike excused himself from the woman and told Adam about the sad phone call.

"Maybe if you tell her one of our neighbors is missing it will make her feel better."

"Don't be so sarcastic."

"Feel like coming to my place for a cold beer? asked Spike. Lita is out doing errands."

"Sounds good."

Adam and Spike sat at a table on the back porch. They talked and laughed about all the craziness that was happening in their complex. Suddenly, the doorbell rang. Spike opened the door and it was the woman who came for her dog collars. "Hello, I'm Michelle Stein. How did you end up with my babies collars?" she wept. "We found a couple of dead reptiles on our property. The lab had to dissect them to try and find the cause of death and unfortunately they brought us your dog collars." Adam came to the door.

"We are sorry Maam, he said."

"I'm Michelle Stein."

"Glad to meet you, Ms. Stein. I wish we didn't have to meet under these circumstances. We are still trying to figure out how the alligator and the python could have died," said Adam.

"*Python!*" Ms. Stein said with surprise.

"Yes Madam, we here at Holly Meadow are having a problem with pythons." Spike gave Adam a slight kick on his ankle.

"Of course we care about your dogs - but finding two dead reptiles on our property is very mysterious."

"It is," stuttered Ms. Stein. Her dentures rattled. "I have lived on this lake for twenty years and I never heard of such a thing. I always wondered what happened to the alligators that died of old age. They are never found. The Sheriffs must shoot them before they reach old age. Well, I'll be on my way. I'll set up a memorial now that I have the collars. Thank you so much for keeping them." Spike shut the door. He was furious.

"Why did you mention the word "python?"

"Oh come on Spike, they can't just be only in Holly Meadow."

"Well, so far it seems that way," Spike said angrily. "We haven't heard any talk of them being anywhere else."

Spike grabbed a soda and Adam grabbed another beer and they went back and sat on the porch. Noah yelled from his porch,

"Will you guys be quiet over there or I'll have to call the police." "Noah, come on over and have a beer." Adam and Noah sat on Spike's porch enjoying a few cold beers until Lita came home and reminded Spike they had a late dinner date with her brother and his wife.

Noah invited Adam over to his place. "Cindy doesn't get home until after eleven," he told Adam. "I can't Noah, Stella is home waiting for me to have dinner."

They all went their separate ways for the evening.

Noah sometimes felt exceptionally lonely in the evenings when Cindy was working - and his friends weren't around. This night he decided to go out to a local bar.

There were no seats at the bar so he sat in a booth and ordered a beer. He took a good swig of his cold beer and could not help but over hear the conversation in the booth behind him. Noah listened closely to the two guys arguing back and forth.

"I told you to bring raw steak and swing it in front of the boat."

"I brought raw chicken, what's the difference?"

"It's not bloody enough for them to pick up the smell, damn it!"

"That's bull, they have a very keen sense of smell." "I had to hide the boat near a little island with some brush. I had my flashlight but the only other light I had was the pole lights at the end of the pier and the full moon. I didn't want to use my flashlight too much, because I thought it might attract attention. I hung the chicken out in front of the boat and focused my flashlight over toward the dark mysterious grass area. I couldn't believe what I saw. The wide opened mouth of a huge python heading toward a gator in the grass. The gator didn't move. All of a sudden the python grabbed the gator and placed his whole frigging mouth around the gator's head. Talk about a living nightmare. My heart was pounding out of my chest. I wasn't expecting a twenty foot python to be around Holly Meadow. I placed some more meat on the rope and *Bang!* - out of nowhere a frigging alligator jumps up and misses the chicken meat and lands on his back. Another huge python aggressively attacked the second gator while on its back. I couldn't believe my eyes. The python wrapped its whole body around the second alligator. I took a fast look toward the grass. The first python was making huge muscular contractions and the head of the alligator was now moving slowly *out of his mouth*. My boat was too small to hang around this horror scene. I didn't think I was going to make it out of the area alive. I tried one more piece of meat to attract more alligators but there were none around. I was nervous and shaking."

"The deal was five alligators. You screwed up."

"If you think I was going to hang around the lake looking for more alligators, you're nuts. You really piss me off. You didn't tell me there were frigging monster pythons in that area. I waited to see if the python that regurgitated the alligator's head would leave. The alligator never moved. If it was alive to begin with, I think it quickly succumbed to the lack of oxygen in the python's body. I was hoping it had suffocated, because my only hope was to drag the dead alligator to shore and get it in my truck. My head was so screwed up. I was terrified of the python in the grass. I don't give a damn about the money. I could have been seen by someone or killed. You should have done it yourself. Let's get out of here."

Noah heard the men leave. He felt too nervous to turn his head to see who they were. He waited a few minutes, took his last swig of beer and went home to his condo.

When he arrived home he tried to relax on his sofa. In his mind he repeatedly went over the conversation he overheard between the two men in the bar. He wondered, "Could there possibly be a relation between the men and the mysterious occurrences at Holly Meadow. Should he mention this to Spike?" He regretted that he didn't turn his head around to see who they were. "What were those men trying to achieve?" he asked himself.

CHAPTER TWENTY TWO

The next couple of days, Stella stayed home trying to track down a Mrs. Hardy. "I think I'll try Capri Island again," she thought. She dialed directory assistance. "Do you have a Mrs. Hardy or a Jack Hardy?" "Yes, I have a Jack and Lena Hardy, would you like the number?" Stella dropped the phone.

"Excuse me, are you there," echoed from the floor.

Stella picked up the receiver. "Did you say Jack and Lena Hardy?"

"Yes Maam, would you like the number?"

"Ah, yes please."

"This must be a coincidence," Stella thought. "I have to take a pill for anxiety before this phone call." She ran upstairs to the bathroom cabinet and took a pill.

Stella then came to her senses. If this number is in Capri Island, than it must be a different Jack and Lena. However, I would like to find out if there is any relation, she whispered to herself. She drew her courage and began dialing. A man's voice answered.

"Excuse me, Mr. Hardy?"

"No, Mr. Hardy is not available. He is away on business."

"Is Mrs. Hardy home?"

"Well, sort of, but she is not able to come to the phone. Can I take a message?"

"No thanks, I'll call her later."

Stella hung up. "How bizarre was that! What did he mean, sort of? I have to call Carolyn."

"Carolyn, I just had the strangest conversation with a man at a number that's supposed to belong to a Jack and Lena Hardy in Capri Island. I dialed the number and a man answered and said, Mr. Hardy was away on business. Then I asked if Mrs. Hardy was home and you would not believe his response. He said, "she is sort of home but could not come to the phone." "Is that weird or what? What kind of person responds with "she's sort of home." She is either home or she is not." "A woman could be a dead corpse in a closet and one could refer to her as being sort of home. It's weird, Carolyn, what do you think of it?"

"I don't know, Stella. *It is* very strange."

"If it is Mr. and Mrs. Hardy's house, what would a man be doing in it, while Mr. Hardy was away on business?" asked Stella.

"Maybe it's the butler? When he picked up the phone did he say "you rang." Carolyn broke out in a laugh.

"Stella, I think we are getting carried away. There could be a million reasons why a different man answered the phone. It could have been a friend or relative, and Lena Hardy could have just been busy washing clothes. You better cool it for a while."

"Maybe your right, Carolyn."

* * *

It was a weekday morning and while Adam fixed his tie in the bedroom mirror, he quietly admired the reflection of his beautiful wife as she slept on the bed unaware of her luscious position. Adam's heart palpitated as he thought of a light gentle lick of her beautiful soft lips. Nevertheless, he had to get to work to finish a project, so a kiss on the cheek and a quick "Have a nice day honey, I made coffee," had to do.

Stella heard the front door close and could not sleep any longer, so she threw on a sundress and grabbed a fresh cup of coffee and some cookies and took a walk down to the end of the pier and sat on a chair at the umbrella table. I can feel this is a strong caffeinated brew. He knows I'm very caffeine sensitive, she mumbled to herself. Adam must have needed a good jolt to get him going this morning, she thought. I hope it doesn't make me too jittery.

If Stella had made the coffee, she would only add in a half of a teaspoon of caffeine, which was just enough to give her a little morning lift.

A slight breeze hit her face. Oh, what an awful smell, I wonder where it's coming from. As her eyes roamed over the glistening water she glanced at the docked boats. When she saw Abe's boat, she noticed an empty bottle of tequila under a seat. Abe and Maryann would never drink that stuff on the boat she thought, as her eyes focused back to the glistening lake.

Stella finished her coffee, got up from the chair and stretched. She bent forward to look at the baby ducks on the side of the pier and baby talked to them, "I think I'll go up and take a nice long shower, sweeties." The mother duck swam from under the pier and Stella noticed a piece of black material around her neck. "Oh, you poor thing, what do you have around your neck, let me help you." Stella broke a long thin branch from a nearby tree and used it to try to slip the material off the duck's neck. However, of course the duck was confused and made it difficult. "Looks like I'll have to break the rules and give you a little piece of cookie." As the duck pecked down for the cookie pieces she got hold of the material around its neck with the branch and pulled it off.

"Oh my goodness, a little black bikini bottom. Too funny. I wish I had taken a picture of it around the ducks neck, cute story," she thought. Stella headed back down the pier to her condo.

Stella entered her condo; she threw the black bikini bottom on the laundry room floor.

Heading upstairs for her shower, she heard the beep of the answering machine. She went into the den and pressed the answering machine message button. "Hello, this is Mrs. Hardy. I don't recognize the name, but I saw you on my caller I.D. and was wondering if it was something important that you were calling about?" The woman sounded very elderly so Stella lost interest.

* * *

The sky began to darken and energy from the thunder traveled with such intense force, Stella could feel the usual rumble through the building. She stared out the window at the blackened sky and heavy rainfall. The phone rang and it was Carolyn.

"Hey woman, you know we're not supposed to talk on the phone, when there's lightning."

"Wasn't that the old cord phone?" Carolyn asked.

"Oh, I don't know, what's up?"

"I was wondering if you found anything."

"An elderly lady who said she was Mrs. Hardy left a message on my answering machine, so I lost interest."

"So does that mean you are going to stop the phone calls to Hardy residents?"

"I think for now. I'll let you know if anything else comes up."

After about an hour, the rain stopped and the sun broke through the clouds, bright as can be. Stella thought, "What a beautiful afternoon. I think I'll take a walk around the complex."

Stella's brain was subconsciously working in detective mode - all the time now.

As she was walking, she noticed a small ladder behind Noah's porch. Maybe Noah is cutting some branches. She took a walk over to get a closer look. The legs of the ladder were embedded deep down in the soil and the ladder rested against the bottom of Noah's railing. This is his way out the back door, she thought.

Holly Meadow residents had no back exits in their condos, other than the sliders that led to their high balconies.

Stella noticed Adam's car driving down the parking lot. He stopped his car, rolled down his window and said "Hi Honey!" "I finished my project before my deadline so my supervisor told me to take off for the afternoon. Do you want to go out for an early dinner?" Okay, let me just run up stairs and freshen up a bit. Stella ran up to her condo, washed quickly and brushed her hair. She hurried out and jumped in the car. "I miss you so much during the day, I wish you could retire early," she told Adam. "I feel the same way sweetheart. Now let's discuss where we want to eat. How about Italian food?" "I'll enjoy that," said Stella.

"Spike called me today; he wants the board members to have a meeting tonight at his place."

"He sometimes can be too spontaneous, don't you think? What if we had plans?" asked Stella.

"We would go ahead with our plans," Adam responded.

"With all the problems Holly Meadow is having, every meeting is important, whether it's official or unofficial." Stella remarked.

"We do have major issues that have to be discussed constantly now," said Adam.

"What did *you do* today honey?"

"I had a cute little encounter with a duck. I managed to retrieve a little black bikini bottom that was stuck on her neck."

"A black bikini bottom!" Adam confirmed with surprise. "You mean a bathing suit?"

"Yes," answered Stella.

"Don't you remember the last time we saw Lena she had a black bikini top on?" said Adam.

"Barely," said Stella.

"Well, she must have had the bottom on too - under the beach wrap she was wearing," Adam said anxiously. "How do you remember all this," Adam? "All what, Honey." Adam's face was as red as an over ripe tomato. Men remember those things. Yes, I can see that. Stella folded her arms and turned her head toward her car window. I bet you don't remember what I had on.

Usually when a person is missing, everyone is informed and knows what the person was wearing. Haven't you kept that in your mind?"

"Guess not. You really think it could be Lena's bathing suit bottom? What would it be doing in the lake?"

"That's what I would like to know. I'll bring it up tonight at Spike's. Where's the bottom?"

"I threw it in the laundry room. I'll rinse it out and dry it."

"No! Don't rinse it out. Leave it the way it is!"

CHAPTER TWENTY THREE

That night Abe, Adam, Nick, Noah, and Luanne went over to Spike's place and sat in the dining room. Adam felt anxious. Spike said, "We are going to have to buy extra insurance to cover any more possible snake attacks on the property. Luanne said, "I'll call the insurance company tomorrow and let you know the numbers when I get them."

Adam took a deep breath and couldn't wait any longer. He said, "I have to show you all something. You are not going to believe what my wife found in the lake today." He held up the black bikini bottom. "Oh my God," said Luanne. "Does it have a size?" They all laughed.

"I don't think it has to, you all know what it looks like."

Abe said, "That's the bathing suit Lena had on the day she went missing."

Noah's eyes gave a surprised look and he began sweating profusely. "Are you all sure it was a black bikini that she had on?" he stuttered.

Spike stood up and began pacing back and forth. Anticipation and anxiety burned his stomach. Spike spoke with force. "I'm damn sure....*maybe she's in the lake!*"....Spike kept pacing.

"Wouldn't the body have floated and been seen by now?" Noah commented.

"Not if she was anchored down," said Abe. *Anchored down!* What are you guys talking about, you're scaring me," Luanne cried out.

Spike told them, "If we can definitely verify that this is Lena's bathing suit, we can get a diving team out here to search the lake.

"There's probably no DNA left on it, it's been too long," said Noah.

"I'll talk to the Sheriff's Office and send it to the town lab along with another piece of her worn clothing from her condo, said Spike. This could be a good lead. Tell Stella, thanks for being so observant. We'll wrap it up for tonight and I'll email or call you after I find out the results."

While Adam was at the meeting, Stella decided to call the elderly woman who left a message on her machine. "Hello, I'm Stella, Maam. I'm the one that was on your caller I.D." "Oh yes, dear, I know sometimes people are shy and don't want to leave me a message so I always call and ask how much money they want. If they say five dollars, I tell them that's too little, I will send ten thousand. I tell them I'll put it in the mail as soon as I can and hang up. Of course I don't send anyone any money. I'm not a stupid old lady. Once it was my doctor's office and the young girl didn't leave a message that my appointment was changed. Needless to say, I made a trip to the doctor's for nothing. Another time, there was heavy breathing on my message machine and it sounded like the poor man was having a heart attack before he could even say his first word. I called 911 and told them a man was having trouble breathing and all I could do was give them his phone number. I didn't recognize the number so I didn't know who he was. The dispatcher said they would do a trace and thanked me."

"Uh, Mrs. Hardy, the reason I called you is because I'm trying to track down an old high school friend. A Mrs. Hardy that was married to a Jack Hardy."

"Let me get my hearing aid dear."

"My oldest son is Jack Hardy and he is divorced. He currently lives up in Palm Harbour. Is that the Mrs. Hardy you're looking for Miss?"

"Why yes, do you have a number so I may talk to her?"

"It's been a long time but I still have the address book. Wait one moment dear. Dear are you there?"

"Yes, Mrs. Hardy."

"This is the last number I have for Tina. We kept in touch for a little while." It took twenty minutes for Mrs. Hardy to communicate the number to Stella, but she finally had it written down.

"Thank you so much for your help. I really appreciate it." Stella hung up.

Stella could not dial the number fast enough.

"Hi, my name is Stella and I was wondering if we could talk a little about your ex-husband."

"My *ex-husband!* Why would you need to talk about him?"

"Listen, can we meet for lunch one day next week – please?" Stella begged.

"Well, okay, I work Monday through Thursday, would Friday be good for you?"

"Sure, I live in Palm Harbour so I have a very long way to drive, but it will be worth it to me."

Stella hung up and called Carolyn.

"Carolyn, I spoke with Jack's ex-wife, well I think it's his ex-wife. His mother said her son Jack lives in Palm Harbour...it has to be her."

"Stella, calm down."

"I'm driving to a restaurant on Capri Island next Friday to meet with her."

"Are you crazy?" said Carolyn. That's too far for you to drive.

"Well, maybe I'll fly."

"I can't believe you're going through all of this."

"I have to, Carolyn, for Lena's sake."

"Why can't you just talk on the phone?"

"I'd rather talk with her in person, then I'll really get a feel about their relationship and what Jack is like.

"Okay, detective, talk to you later."

Adam entered his condo as Stella hung up the phone. "Who were you talking to?"

"It was Carolyn just calling to say hello. How was the meeting?"

"Everyone was impressed that you found that bikini bottom. If there is a DNA match, Spike is going to try and get a dive team for the lake."

"Just the idea frightens me, Adam. It will frighten everyone."

"We have to do all we can to help solve this case, Stella. I'm going to bed....are you coming with me?"

"Yes, honey, I'm exhausted."

Stella laid her head on Adam's chest. Adam yawned, "Honey, did we ever think that in beautiful sunny Florida we would be living among deadly pythons and alligators, a possible murderer, a dead body and a missing body. I mean a few feet of snow can be a pain in the ass but this is ridiculous." Stella broke out in a laugh with tears pouring from her eyes. "I don't mean to react like this, but you said it so bluntly." She grabbed the box of tissue on the nightstand and saturated all that was left. Stella sat up and keeled over. She couldn't stop her hysterical laughter. "Oh God, I can't catch my breath." She finally calmed down and placed her head back on Adam's chest. She took a deep breath and sighed with relief.

"By the way, Adam, do you think we should get a chain ladder for the balcony?"

"Yes, it would be a good idea in case of a fire. What made you think of that?"

"I was walking by Noah's porch today and noticed he has a ladder standing against his balcony and he is on the first floor. I never noticed it before, but it has been there a long time, because it looked slightly weather worn and the legs were embedded deep down in the soil." "Funny, I never noticed it either," said Adam.

"Oh well, it's just a ladder. It's painted green like the forest... that's why it's hard to see. Good night Adam, Honey."

Morning came and Adam left for work. Stella had her coffee and then left to get the mail. She bumped into Noah in the parking lot and greeted him with a "Good Morning!" I'm going down the pier to help Jack replace a couple of slabs that are loose, he said. I hope I don't find the top to that bathing suit, Noah choked out with a frog in his throat. I hope not either, said Stella.

Stella went on to the mailbox to get her mail and Lena's mail. Lena's sister Sarah gave her the key to hold all the mail for her. Sarah told Stella, if anything looked strange or seemed important to call her. Stella neatly stored all of Lena's mail in a paper bag. She was on her second bag now.

First, Stella grabbed her own mail then she opened Lena's mailbox. She noticed a letter far back in the mailbox that she must have previously missed. "Oh how could I have not seen this? It looks like a special occasion card. It obviously has to be from someone who doesn't know she is missing," she thought. She looked at the postmark and noticed it was dated six months ago. She brought it up to her condo and looked it over. Stella opened the card and it read, "Miss you sweetheart….I think of you every minute of the day…you're in my bed my love. Can't wait 'till you step up into my arms again and join me in my Ark."

Just one of her crazy lovers, Stella thought. She saw there was no return address, but took note that it was stamped Palm Harbour. Stella placed the card in the paper bag along with all the other mail. Asking God for forgiveness, knowing the "type of woman" Lena was, she wasn't surprised at such a note.

The next morning while Adam was shaving, the phone rang. Stella ran to the den and grabbed the phone. "Hi Stella, it's Tina Hardy. I have a meeting in Springwater next week. I think it will make it easier for you if we meet then."

"Oh that would be great. I'll call you when I get to the Sands Hotel."

"Okay, talk to you then."

"Who was that, Honey?" Adam yelled from the bathroom.

"Oh, just a telemarketer. I'm going back to bed."

CHAPTER TWENTY FOUR

Spike was sitting in his office and the phone rang. When he picked up the phone he recognized the voice of the former maintenance man's wife, Carrie Albertson. Hi, Carrie. How are you? Spike asked with a suspicious tone.

"Tom hasn't answered his phone in over three months. Can I leave him a message?"

"Carrie, I know you and Tom are separated, but he hasn't been here for many months. One day he just didn't show up and I haven't heard from him since. I hired a new maintenance man."

"Did you try calling him?" asked Carrie.

"Yes, I tried calling him but he didn't answer his phone."

"This was supposed to be a trial separation and he disappears into the clear blue sky." Carrie sounded very frustrated. "That bastard must be shacking up with some rich slut."

"Listen Carrie, I know you're angry but it really isn't any of my business. Just thank God you don't have any children involved. I don't think I'll ever hear from him, but if I do, I'll be sure to let you know."

"I'm sorry, I don't mean to take it out on you. Thanks, Spike."

"Whew, I hope I don't hear from her again." He hung up with relief.

That night, Spike was sleeping, when Lita was awaken by gurgling noises coming from Spike. He began yelling in his sleep -"No, No, it can't be him." Lita tapped Spike on the shoulder.

"Honey, wake up!"

He opened his eyes. "What's wrong?"

"You must be having a nightmare."

"I'm okay."

"What were you dreaming about?"

"I just remember looking at a man in the water and yelling."

"Do you remember who the man was? Because, I heard you say, "No, no, it can't be him."

"No, not right now. Maybe it will come to me tomorrow. Let's try and go back to sleep." Lita turned around, stared at the moon shining through the window, and fell asleep.

The next morning Spike and Lita were having coffee in their kitchen. Honey, do you remember anything more about your dream last night? It's not like you to talk in your sleep.

It was just a freaky nightmare. I think I was looking at a corpse in the lake and I remember Noah being there. Noah said something like, it's him, I know it's him, can't you recognize him? That's all I can recall right now. I really don't think it means anything.

"By the way, you wouldn't believe who called me yesterday?"

"Who?"

"Tom Albertson's wife."

"What! Why did she call you?"

"Believe it or not she was looking for Tom.""Looking for Tom!"

"Can you believe Carrie thought Tom was still working here!"

"How could she not know where her husband is?" asked Lita.

"They're separated. I think she thought he was being spiteful and wasn't answering his phone, so she wanted me to relay a message to him. She was shocked when I told her he hadn't been here for a few months. She thinks he's shacking up with some rich woman somewhere. Knowing Tom, he probably is. Remember when Abe and I caught him with that young woman in the dumpster shack. Boy, were they embarrassed. How classy can you get? For weeks, every time he saw me he walked with his head down."

"Yes, that was the most excitement we had going on in Holly Meadow in those days," laughed Lita.

"Today, I'm going to bring a piece of Lena's clothing from her condo and the bikini bottom to the police station so they can send it to the lab," said Spike. "Okay, you can hop in the shower first. I'll call Maryann and ask her if she wants to play tennis. Maybe I'll even get Stella on the court."

Maryann told Lita she could play around three o'clock. Lita then called Stella. "Stella, how about joining us on the tennis court today?" "I can't make it, Lita, I have a lunch date with an old friend." "I'm sick of trying to get you on the court. When you decide you want to play, let me know," said Lita. "Oh, okay. I'll make it someday, said Stella. I do miss playing with you guys. Right now I just happen to be caught up in a few things I have to get done." After they hung up Stella ran to the shower. Today she was going to meet Tina Hardy for lunch in Springwater. Stella was nervous but excited at the same time. She scrambled through her closet looking for the best suit she could find. "I have to make a good impression or this woman might not give me what I want," she thought.

It was a forty-minute drive to the restaurant to meet Tina. Stella was on her way. She entered the restaurant parking lot, parked her car, and took the keys out of the ignition while her nerves began to rattle. Her fingers drumming on the steering wheel, she thought, "How am I going to do this?"

She took a sip of bottled water, fluffed her hair, got out of the car and entered the front door of the restaurant.

"May I help you, Madam," the host asked.

"Yes Sir, I'm looking for a Ms. Hardy."

"Yes, Ms. Hardy is here. Follow me."

Stella followed behind the host with a slight wobble in her new stilettos.

"Hi Tina, I'm Stella. It's very nice to meet you."

"You too," said Tina.

"Now where or how should we start? asked Tina. How about with a glass of Chardonnay?"

"I would love to have a glass of wine but it will just go right to my head and I won't make any sense when I talk," responded Stella.

"That's fine, you must not have anything in your stomach so we will order fast," said Tina.

"So what is it that you are so interested in knowing about Jack?

"Please don't get the wrong idea, Tina, but we have a missing woman at my condominium complex. It's been over five months now, and I'm probing all possible channels that could have led or misled my dear friend to some sort of endangerment."

"Are you saying that Jack is a suspect?"

"Not at all. Jack was the only new person that came onto our property at Holly Meadow when our friend went missing. Jack is our maintenance man. Oh, I see he's moved up in life," Tina commented with a smirk.

"I don't think Jack and our friend who is missing had ever even met. But if I can find out what type of person Jack is, I can feel more comfortable about him being with us at Holly Meadow."

"Well, for one thing, I can tell you that Jack is not a murderer. He's a lazy crap ass husband, but I can assure you he's not capable of murder. Our marriage did not end because I had any fear of him. I just got sick of being the breadwinner, explained Tina. He was a supervisor for the traffic department and was laid off. After that, he only wanted to fish, as a sport, not to make money. Do you know what it's like to have a husband whose only interest is fishing?"

"Jack told me that you got his father's home that he inherited," said Stella.

"Oh please, we took out a mortgage on that home and at the time I couldn't afford to pay all our bills by myself. I simply got fed up with the situation and filed for a divorce. *He couldn't* afford to keep the home. Oooh, try this lobster salad," said Tina.

"So, in general, Jack is not abusive and doesn't have an abnormal temperament in any way, just maybe a little lazy about getting a good paying job? Is that how you would describe him?" asked Stella.

"Yes, that's about it. Sorry I didn't solve your case," said Tina.

"Well, it was very nice meeting you, Tina said as she picked up the tab."

"Oh no, let *me* get that!" said Stella.

"The pleasure is mine, Tina said with a smile. If you do find something that might surprise me, please give me a call," Tina told Stella, as they walked out to the parking lot.

"Damn it!" said Stella, as she opened her car door. "I feel like a fool." Suddenly, she heard a voice from across the parking lot.

"Not for anything, but after the divorce I heard rumors he was having an affair with his bookkeeper, Ally, while he was working in the traffic department," yelled Tina.

"Okay, Tina...Thanks for meeting me."

When Stella arrived home, she called Carolyn.

"Looks like things are clean with Jack, or Tina is a good actress."

"What was she like?"

"Actually, she was very nice. She didn't display any anger when she talked about Jack, just a little frustration about his laziness. I can hear Adam walking in the door. I'll talk to you soon."

"Hi, honey, how was your day?" asked Stella.

"It was pretty smooth. I had a late lunch, so you don't have to cook anything. Just give me a kiss."

Adam hugged Stella and grabbed her ass. "Why do you have a suit on, babe?"

"I felt like looking professional today. But it's coming off fast. I'll beat you up the stairs."

The two of them ran like children and Adam grabbed Stella's skirt in the middle of the steps.

"Are you trying to slow me down or keep me here?"

"You just gave me a good idea," said Adam.

"Oh Yeah!"

Stella tried to make a fast run up the stairs but Adam grabbed her slip and then her shoe. They both sat half lying on the stairs and laughed. He took off his jacket and threw it up the stairs and it came down and landed on her head. He began unbuttoning her blouse while she took off his belt. "I love you so much," she said.

"Yeah, how much?"

She unzipped his pants and snuck her hand in. His well-endowed manhood made her body weak and anxious. I want it bad, very bad, her mind called, as she ran her hand up and down his pulsating wand. Her body lay loose on the stairs as she craved his thrusting force. He began breathing so heavily she felt she wasn't going to be satisfied. She tried to make another run up the stairs to the bedroom. She didn't make it. Adam caught her panties and pulled them down her legs. He slithered his saliva all over her plump long hard stimulated spot and sucked her soft velvet lips – he softly pecked and sucked a bit to tease. She was wanting badly. Her legs opened wider and wider - she held them with her hands under her knees and pushed against his mouth. He wrapped his lips around all of her and sucked a bit pulling away over and over again. She gave a push and he sped his tongue fast, faster and faster, harder and harder. An intense moan began to emit like he never heard before. Her deep sound of ultimate pleasure reached a peak and a long screech of release followed while tears ran down the sides of her eyes."You conquered me on a set of stairs." He responded, "that's been one of my desires for a long time. This is what keeps us feeling young. Honey, all our problems totally disappeared for a while. It's the best therapy any one can have. It only lasts a little while but our minds escape from the world." Adam, I love escaping from this world – if only we could escape forever. I was brought up being taught that heaven was a place of everlasting ecstasy and love. Imagine if heaven was a galaxy of orgasms." "Well, it's a good thing we don't know for sure," Adam responded.

CHAPTER TWENTY FIVE

The next day Abe, Adam, Nick, and Noah received a call from Spike.

"I need you to come to my place tonight - we have to have a meeting."

"Two meetings in three days," each complained.

"I have something to discuss."

"No kidding," said Abe. "I didn't think there was ever nothing to discuss these days. What's going on?"

"I'll see you at seven." Spike hung up.

They went to Spike's and they sat at his dining room table as usual, each with a look of despair and curiosity - with a yawn in between.

"Where's our secretary Luanne? Nick asked.

"I didn't think she would be able to handle tonight's conversation - so I didn't call her. This is a very serious subject. I don't want any jokes or sarcasm tonight."

"Okay, said Abe. How long are you going to keep us hanging?"

"As long as I want," said Spike.

"Keep it cool guys, he's very serious tonight," remarked Adam.

Spike sat at the head of the table. "I think I know the identification of the male corpse that we discovered." *"What!"* They all said in sync.

"I think it was our former maintenance man, Tom Albertson."

The men stared back and forth at each other in shock.

"What the heck brought you to this conclusion?" asked Nick.

"Never mind," said Spike. We are going to have to inform the detectives and have his wife get some of his DNA and bring it to the lab. She called me the other day and said she hasn't heard from Tom in over three months."

"They're separated," said Adam.

"Carrie told me it was a trial separation and I remember overhearing him talk to her on his cell phone once in a while."

"How do you think he drowned?" asked Abe.

"Well, let's all take a guess!"

"I have no idea. He was a smart man and he knew how to swim," said Adam. "He could have had a heart attack. He smoked."

"Don't you remember the cough he had?" said Nick.

"You mean to tell me not one of you Einstein's can figure out how he may have died?" Spike got up from his chair and began his famous pace, back and forth - his hands on his waist and his face beet red.

"Not one of you schmuck heads is going to leave tonight until you can figure it out."

Their eyes were glued on Spike.

He looks ready to kill, whispered Nick.

Kill! Did you say kill? Spike spoke aloud.

"You all figured it out!"

"Figured what out?" asked Adam.

Spike gave Adam a fast glance with a wise crack in his lips, as if Adam was playing dumb.

"*Now*, who's going to be the first one to say it?" Spike asked the guys. They all sat frozen with their eyeballs asking each other "who's the next one to talk?"

Nick stood up and spread his hands upward. "Spike, calm down. I've been thinking about it for a couple of weeks now."

Abe stuttered, "It can't be."

Nick said, "I'm thinking the same thing Spike is thinking. Tom Albertson was killed by a python. We should have talked about this possibility much earlier."

"The corpse was decomposed beyond recognition. Why didn't anyone smell the odor sooner? asked Abe.

"It was encased in dense brush - with the wood boat on top of it. There had been a strange smell around the pier area - but we all know because of the swampy elements and the fishermen's bait - there is always some sort of strange smell around there," said Adam.

Abe stood up. "Wait a minute. Right now we're assuming. We have no facts. Let's wait until we get more lab results from the town, before we start spreading it around that Tom was killed by a python." "I agree, said Spike. I'll call Tom's wife in the morning."

The next morning Spike reluctantly picked up the phone and dialed Carrie's number.

"Carrie, it's Spike."

"Hi, Spike. Did you find *"my wonderful husband"*?

"Possibly. This is going to be very hard for you, Carrie. I apologize for having to be so blunt about what I'm about to ask you - but I need a DNA specimen from Tom to be brought to the county's forensic department." "A DNA specimen? Did he commit a crime?"

"No, it's not anything like that."

"What I'm about to say may not be true. But we have to prove it one way or another. We found a male body in the lake a few weeks ago."

"A body? You mean -"

"Calm down. I could be totally wrong. Would you be willing to allow a DNA search in your house, so it can be sent to the town lab for verification?"

"Yes, Spike. I'll cooperate and do whatever is needed," Carrie responded in a fearful tone of voice.

"I'm sorry we have to do this, said Spike. Please don't mention this to anyone until I get back to you." He hung up the phone.

Spike called the Sheriff's Office and they sent their forensic team to Mrs. Albertson's home. The town lab was taking many days to perform the DNA work.

Spike waited patiently while his insides felt jumpy. He did everything he could to keep anyone else in the complex from knowing about the lab work. "Why startle and depress everyone and then find out the DNA doesn't match," he thought.

Ten days had passed. Spike called the lab. "What's taking so long?" he asked a technician. "Sir, this case is being treated as a possible homicide." Spike thought to himself, "He was killed alright, but not by a human."

"We had to acquire permission and signed releases from the town court. We'll get back to you as soon as we inform Mrs. Albertson of the finding."

"What about the bikini bottom?" asked Spike.

"Actually we have finalized that report, but we had to send it to the police station first. It's an official procedure, under the circumstances, of a missing woman." Spike hung up and then called Adam right away. "Adam, we need more than a DNA match. We need specimens of a python on the body - to prove the body was attacked and partially consumed. The python regurgitated the body. Tom was a very big man.

Spike said, "Even though Tom was large, the speed and power of the python's strike could have brought him down, especially if Tom was struck on the head. If the snake was twenty to thirty feet long, he could have coiled around Tom with no problem. The tightening of its muscular coils would have applied enough pressure even to kill a man his size. Swallowing a man Tom's size could be a difficult process for a python, but it can be done. The python could have maneuvered its jaws around him and swallowed him, but then Tom's body was probably too large to digest and it regurgitated him."

Adam said, "You could be right," Spike. But I don't think the python made it further than his head and then that's when it began to have a problem. God rest his soul, but Tom was an unusually huge man and always had trouble maneuvering his body because of his weight and broad shoulders. Remember when we were considering laying him off because he wasn't fit enough – no pun intended – to do a lot of the jobs required around here."

Spike responded, "Either way, there will definitely be python specimens on or in what is left of his corpse. We have to acquire another court order for the python lab work. I'll leave work early. Let's go talk to the detectives and tell them what we need to know."

In the meantime, Stella had been home feeling relieved that Jack had nothing to do with Lena's death. "Where do I go now, she thought. I feel so helpless."

* * *

Stella was on her way to the pool when she spied Noah through the corner of her eyes. "What's he breaking apart in such a nasty manner?" she thought. "Hey, Noah! Are you letting out some frustration or what?"

"I just thought I'd get rid of this old ladder and buy a new one," he responded. "Just throw it in the dumpster. It's a small one. You don't have to go crazy trying to tear the wood apart," she told him. Stella continued on and walked through the gate to the pool and laid on a lounge chair facing the sun. As she began to relax and fall asleep, she suddenly got a whiff of what smelled like smoke. "Where could that be coming from?" she thought. She got up from the chair and looked around and didn't see anything suspicious. "I'd better look into this further." She walked down the pier and half way down she noticed a burning barrel behind Noah's porch. She watched him as he placed the pieces of wooden ladder into the fire in the barrel. "What the hell is he doing?" She called Spike on her cell phone.

"Spike, what the heck is Noah doing burning wood in that barrel?"

"It's not wood, Stella. He's getting rid of the piles of leaves behind our building."

"Spike, I saw him tear up that ladder behind his porch in a angry way. I'm down on the pier and he's throwing the pieces of wood in the barrel of fire."

"I guess he's just getting rid of the old ladder, Stella!"

"But he was working so hard trying to break it into pieces. Why didn't he just throw the wooden ladder into the dumpster?"

"You sound suspicious about something, Stella."

I am. It's ninety frigging degrees. Who the heck burns stuff when it's this hot! Stella was whispering as if she could be heard by Noah, but it was impossible, she was too far away. She went on....."

The ladder was in good condition. I walked over and looked at it one day, because I had never noticed it before and I thought it was a very good idea for a fire escape, since the first floor porches in our building are unusually high. It gave Adam and I the idea of buying a rope ladder for our second floor."

"Why are you so suspicious? It's only a little ladder."

"I'll talk to you later, it's too much to explain now."

"So you're going to leave me hanging! The only thing I don't have left hanging is my body and it's beginning to sound like a good idea." Spike hung up before he heard Stella's last words. "Don't worry. I will talk to you soon."

Stella returned to the pool and laid on her lounge chair. Her eyes began to close and she started to fall asleep.

Suddenly her eyes popped wide open. She moved her legs and sat up on the side of the chair. Paranoia was setting in. She had a recollection about the card she found stuck in the back of Lena's mailbox. At the time, she had wondered what Lena's lover had meant when he wrote the words, "When you step up into my arms again." Those words remained in her subconscious from that very day. But today was different. The quote entered the conscious level and a frightening feeling came over her. Goose bumps shot out up and down her arms and a creepy shiver shot up her spine. Her eyeballs moved with wonder.

Feeling nauseous and uncomfortable she walked fast back to her condo. She called Adam at work and told him she was not feeling well and asked him if he could come home a little early.

I'm going upstairs to lie down while I wait for Adam, she thought out loud.

At approximately four o'clock, Adam entered the door. "Honey, where are you?" He didn't hear a response. She must be sleeping, he thought. He went upstairs and Stella was lying on the bed.

"Honey, are you awake?"

"Who is it? She lifted her head and asked with squinty eyes."

"It's me honey, what's wrong?"

"Honey, what's wrong? Sit up."

"I'm so nauseous."

"What's bothering you?"

"Adam… … … Noah… … killed Lena."

"What the fuck are you saying?"

"He did it, Adam. I know he did. I found a love letter in Lena's mailbox and it says, "I can't wait until you step up into my arms and it had x's & o's. You know the x's mean kisses. Winston Churchill created them in 1763 in a letter he wrote to someone he loved. He was tired and his writing was getting messy so he wrote I love you and wrote a few x's after those words."

"How the heck would you know that Noah was tired while writing his supposed letter."

"I mean Winston Churchill you idiot!"

"So what! You found a letter, big deal!" said Adam.

Stella continued, "Today, I saw Noah tearing apart his little ladder in which he purposely had against his porch as an escape in case of a fire. Then I saw him burning the pieces in a barrel. Why didn't he just throw it in the dumpster? He was pretending to burn leaves. It was ninety degrees today, Adam. No one burns leaves when it's ninety degrees." "It was insufferable out there, a steaming sauna."

"Why not? They were piling up quite a bit back there and the leaves are a fire hazard in this weather."

"Don't you get it? The love letter was from Noah. He meant, "Step up the ladder into my arms." He and Lena must have been having an affair."

"You're assuming, Stella."

"No, I'm sorry honey. I can feel it. He had the perfect set up. Cindy works three to eleven. Lena would sneak up the back porch so none of us would see her. Where do you think the body is, Adam?"

"Oh, come on Stella, Noah has been with us at all the meetings. He's been just as caring and emotional about Lena's disappearance as any of us."

"Good act he plays, huh!"

"I don't know, Stella, I think your thoughts are traveling a little too far. What we can do is get a specimen of Noah's DNA and send it to the lab for them to look for his DNA on the black bikini bottom. I hope you're not going to make a fool of yourself. Do you realize the seriousness of your accusation? I'm going to call Spike."

"Spike, would you mind coming up to our place?"

"Yeah, sure. I'll be up in a few."

Stella broke into tears. "I know that son of a bitch did it…I know he did." "Let me get your pills." "I'll get them, I have to put on something decent." Stella went into the bathroom and then back to lie on the bed.

Approximately fifteen minutes went by and Adam heard a knock on the door.

"Hey Adam! What's wrong? You look like you're preoccupied with something."

Adam poured two shots of scotch. He handed one to Spike and they sat on the sofa. "Here's to the Hell of Holly Meadow," he said as he lifted his glass and took a big gulp. "You know I don't drink," said Spike. Spike dumped his scotch into Adam's glass.

"Ready for this?"

"Ready for what?" asked Spike.

"Stella!"

"Yah Adam?"

"Stella!"

"Yahhh!" Spike said drawn out with anxious ears. "What the fuck Adam…Stella what?"

"Give me a sip of that scotch. This must be shocking news if your having this much trouble telling me." Adam handed Spike his glass. Spike took a sip and a warm rush flew through his body.

How long do I have to wait for that *big* sip to kick in? asked Adam.

My brain is saturated with scotch. I'm intensely inebriated and in a total oblivion. Nothing could bother me at this point. Now what the fuck are you so afraid to tell me?

Stella thinks Noah killed Lena." Adam mumbled it out so quickly, it came out sounding Chinese.

"Spike downed the whole glass of scotch and choked out an ice cube. Did I hear you correctly? Why in God's name does she think that?" he asked.

"She found a love letter in Lena's mailbox and she thinks it's from Noah."

"Are you kidding? Noah is a good man. He always helps us."

"The card that Stella found must have contained something very convincing, because I can't talk her out of it."

"Lena has been missing for over five months," said Spike. "Wouldn't we have picked up some strange behavior from Noah by now?"

"Let me look in the paper bag where she stores Lena's mail," said Adam.

"We'll never find it. There's too much mail and junk in this bag." Adam took every piece out until he found the card.

"Here it is!"

It says, "Can't wait until you step up into my arms and join me in my Ark." "Noah's Ark! Get it Spike?"

"I don't believe this," said Spike. "It just doesn't seem to fit his personality. The note could just be from a guy who has a boat that she was having an affair with. I don't sense anything weird about Noah's personality. Noah *a murderer! I just can't conceive it.*"

"Stella did call me from the pier today and thought it was peculiar that Noah was burning his wooden ladder," Spike told Adam.

"She thinks he was burning *evidence,*" said Adam.

"This is going too far without positive evidence, said Spike. "We first have to explain the situation or scenario to the police. Then we have to somehow obtain Noah's DNA and see if the lab can find his DNA on the bikini bottom."

"Let's first find out if the bikini bottom is indeed Lena's, Adam said with frustration." "With the bikini bottom being in the lake for a long length of time, there may not be any DNA left on it. We are surely paying the salaries at the town lab this year," Spike commented. "Our condo association financial report will be the first in history to have an allocation for DNA research. How bizarre is that!"

"I can't go to work tomorrow. I'm calling in sick," Adam told Spike.

"We have to form another think tank about this serious issue. I'm going back to my condo. I'll talk to you in a couple of hours. You better check on Stella." Spike left.

CHAPTER TWENTY SIX

As Spike entered his condo, he heard his answering machine beep. It was the crime unit. Spike's nerves began wracking. He dialed the crime unit number.

"Hello, it's the Holly Meadow President calling about the results of the lab work."

"Yes Sir, we have the results of both DNA tests. We have informed Mrs. Albertson, and since we have no known relative of Ms. Lena Kotta, and the Holly Meadow Board is her Power of Attorney, we have permission to inform you that the bathing suit has Ms. Kotta's DNA and the corpse found in the lake is Mr. Thomas Albertson." "Okay Sir," Spike said with sadness. The officer then stated, "Just because a bathing suit bottom found in a lake has the missing woman's DNA does not mean a crime was committed. The same goes for the man. For now, we will continue to treat these cases as possible crimes. And it's routine that we will be sending detectives out to Holly Meadow to ask a few questions pertaining to Mr. Tom Albertson and Ms. Lena Kotta." Spike reluctantly told the officer, "Unfortunately we will have to have some further DNA tests done, Sir. We have put some pieces together and have a possible lead pertaining to the missing woman. We also need to know if there are any python specimens on Mr. Thomas Albertson. We recently have had a couple of very serious python attacks here at Holly Meadow. We have police reports to prove it."

"We are questioning a possible python attack on Mr. Albertson," said Spike.

"Have you told the lab about the new tests?" asked the officer. "I'm not sure if snake specimens would be covered under forensic," he stated.

"No Sir, I haven't told the lab. I'll go to the lab and fill out a report and if the specimens are not covered under forensic, my association will pay for the tests."

"When I receive the results I'll call you," said the officer.

"Thank you very much Sir."

Spike then called Carrie Albertson. "I'm very sorry, Carrie."

"Do you have any idea how he died?" Carrie asked, in a weak tone. "Not yet. We need further tests done on the body and the lab will need your permission. There have been a couple of python attacks here at Holly Meadow, so we need to have the lab test for python specimens on the body. A detective will be coming to your home to ask some questions and get your permission for the tests. Please, Carrie, I know how very hard this is for you, but we need you to cooperate with the Sheriff's Department." "I will," she responded in a raspy voice. "Feel comfortable to call me anytime." Carrie cried out, "Oh God, this is terrible!" as she hung up.

Spike sat on his sofa and tried to figure out how he could obtain a piece of Noah's DNA to give to the Sheriff's Office. He decided to call Noah and ask him to come over and have a beer, but there was no answer. He then looked out his front door and observed the parking lot to see if Noah's car was there. It wasn't. He would have to wait.

"Maybe I can go around to his corner porch and see if I can find something of Noah's that would be easily accessible," Spike thought.

Spike left his condo and walked around the side of the building and looked along Noah's wrap around corner porch. He noticed a dirty t-shirt hanging over the railing in the back. He carefully went to the back of the porch and pulled the t-shirt off the railing. As he made his way back around to the front of the building, Noah was pulling into his parking space. Spike thought, "I'm going to keep walking as if I don't notice him." Spike continued walking and as he placed his foot on the first step of the front stairs he heard, "Hey Spike, what are you doing man?" "I'm just checking out the grounds. How are you doing?" "I'm doing okay. I just went and got myself some food for tonight. How would you like to join me for dinner? Cindy will be working as usual."

"Let me get back to you in about an hour." Spike continued up to his condo and called Adam.

"Adam, I grabbed a dirty t-shirt off of Noah's porch."

"Perfect!" said Adam.

"Noah caught me as I was heading back to my condo. He was cool and asked me to have dinner with him. How can I sit across from him and eat? He will be talking, and all that will be going through my mind is; "Where's the body?"

"Have dinner with him and play it cool," said Adam. "Now that you're tuned into the possibility that he did it, you will be more observant when he talks and you'll pick up on anything unusual in the conversation." "Good thinking," Spike responded.

"I'll call the lab and the detective and tell them I'm bringing in the t-shirt."

Spike then called Noah and told him he would join him for dinner.

It was six p.m. and Spike knocked on Noah's door. "Hey Spike. Come on in. Let me get you a beer."

"No thanks."

"Sit down and make yourself comfortable. I have some ribs cooking in the oven."

"So have you received any information from the crime lab about the DNA?" asked Noah.

"Yes, unfortunately I did. The black bikini bottom is Lena's and the body is Tom's."

"I'm shocked! What could have happened to cause Tom's death?"

"I called the lab and told the technicians I need more research on the body."

"For what?" asked Noah.

"I think he might have been killed by a python. What else could it have been?" said Spike. He was just too big for the python to digest. The python that might have attacked Tom might have saved Stella. Tom's body was under the boat at the time Stella was attacked. The python might have picked up the odor of the carrion and became distracted. I've been doing some reading about the African Rock python in between the budget work. In the wild, snakes, like most other carnivores, will usually take any opportunity to get an easy meal, and will not pass up a freshly killed prey animal if they happen to come upon it. Snakes are known to eat a fair amount of carrion, which has been dead for some time, and the stomach contents of wild snakes often contain prey that had been in an advanced state of decomposition when it was eaten. Thus, although the python may prefer to eat live prey, which it kills itself, of course, through constriction; this is not at all necessary for the health of the python. In fact, it is best not to feed a captive snake live prey at all. Pythons will go for the dead prey before the live, not only because it's easier – they are highly attracted to the smell of dead prey and may even divert to the dead prey in the midst of attacking a live prey, if they catch the scent of a dead prey in the area. We have no idea if any of these pythons were ever in captivity and what or how they were fed. People find small snakes and keep them until they realize they are going to grow much bigger than they ever imagined. There could be one or two on the loose that are used to eating dead prey. When the python was attempting to consume Stella, its tongue picked up the odor from the dead body under the boat and went for that meat, Spike explained. How else could she have hit it so lucky?"

"This is getting more and more sick, said Noah. How can I eat now."

"Oh come on. Get those ribs out of the oven. The table looks pretty fancy for a guy."

"I have a good teacher."

"By the way, how is Cindy?"

"She is doing well. I don't like her working the three to eleven shift, but she likes it. Maybe she doesn't want to spend evenings with me."

"Why would you think that?"

Noah placed the pan of ribs on the table along with a bowl of salad.

"Dig in big boy!"

"You must get lonely some nights."

"Yes, I do. Cindy should be home in the evening. I have discussed this situation with her numerous times, but she says there are no openings for the day shift. I told her she should look somewhere else for a job, so we can have a normal marriage, be together for dinner and relax in the living room together in the evening. Weekends have been good, but not as good as I want them. She sometimes spends hours on the computer doing her work."

"That must really suck, said Spike. So when you're not with me or the other guys what do you do?"

"I'll rent a movie or go out for dinner or sometimes even stop at a bar for a beer. In fact, Spike, I want to tell you about a conversation I overheard one night in a bar. I was sitting in a booth and the two men sitting behind me were talking about being on the emerald lake and baiting the alligators. One guy was saying he was using chicken for bait and when an alligator jumped for it a python zapped up and attacked the alligator."

"What a fucking sight that must have been. Man, that's like something you see on a television documentary," said Spike.

"It sounds like they were poachers for alligator skin, said Spike. If they were ever caught by the Sheriff, they would be fined. However, I'm not complaining, let them take all the alligators they want. Nevertheless, one downfall is that we don't need alligators that are used to being fed by humans. The dead alligator and python that were found on our property was probably a result of a fight the two reptiles had or maybe it had to do with the poachers," said Spike.

"Could be," said Noah.

"By the way, these ribs are good. I like the sauce. So, did you burn a lot of the leaves back in the forest the other day?" asked Spike.

"You haven't noticed how clean it looks back there?"

"I haven't looked out the back sliders."

"I burned piles and piles of potato vines, so they won't interfere with the photosynthesis of all the trees. The potato vines are native to Brazil. They don't belong here."

"At least they don't eat people," Spike said. But who knows. Nothing would surprise me now!

I can see it now.... "New nightmare in Holly Meadow.... Strangling Potato Vines."

"So, how do you think Lena's bikini ended up in the lake?" asked Spike.

"She probably went skinny dipping with the alligators, Noah said - kidding. She probably just dropped it.

"Do you miss Lena?" asked Spike.

"Of course I do. It's an awful thing that she disappeared. Hey, what is it with all the questions about Lena? By the way, when is the dive team going to search the lake?"

"I had to wait to get the positive DNA on the bikini, so it should be soon. It's a big lake. There's no way they're going to go much further than the immediate area. It would take weeks," said Spike.

"I think I'm going to head up to my place and get some paper work finished. Thanks for the great meal."

"Anytime, Spike."

As soon as Spike walked into his home he called Adam. "Hey, I didn't get any strange vibes from Noah. He acted normal. We'll wait for the tests from his t-shirt. How's Stella doing?"

"She's sleeping. I don't know what's going to happen now. I hope she doesn't tell anybody that she thinks Noah killed Lena. I'll talk to you tomorrow." They hung up.

CHAPTER TWENTY SEVEN

Stella woke up the next morning after Adam had left for work. She felt well rested but still had a little anxiety. She knew Adam would be extremely upset if she discussed her feelings about Noah to anyone. "If only I could get Lena's DNA off Noah's railing where she had to climb over to get onto the porch," she thought. Stella spent the day dazed and confused lying on her sofa twirling her hair.

In his condo below, Spike was busy trying to put pieces of the puzzle together. "I don't believe they'll find any of Noah's DNA on the bikini bottom," he thought. All of a sudden he lifted a chair and threw it against the common wall with Noah's condo. "Fuck you," he yelled with intense anger.

Noah never came over to Spike's condo to find out what the noise was. He must have been out. Lita came home an hour later and saw the damaged wall and broken chair on the floor. "What did you do?" "If I let you know what is currently going on you'll become very upset and depressed. Please give me some time, sweetie. I'll fix the wall tomorrow."

"How can you leave me hanging? You don't seem like yourself. It must be very serious." "Honey, you have your life - taking care of your mother and visiting your sister and brother. Don't let me give you anything right now that will keep you from going on with your good deeds and hobbies. If anything evolves that I feel you should definitely know, I'll tell you. Right now there are issues in the air with nothing solid to validate them."

"If there is anything I can do to help, let me know. I hate to see you this stressed out. I'm meeting Maryann on the tennis court in a few minutes."

Lita went into the bedroom to change into her tennis outfit. Maryann was waiting for Lita on the tennis court. She kept looking at her watch. Finally, she noticed Lita walking toward the court. "Woman, come one. Get your butt in here."

"You serve, said Lita. To me, not the pond." Maryann gave Lita a good serve and they hit the ball back and forth six times before Maryann made an overhead hit over the fence and into the pond. "Simple mistake after six good hits, said Maryann. I found a bunch of new tennis balls at the thrift store." "That doesn't mean you can abuse and pollute the pond, said Lita. Someday we are going to have to go in there and get them all out."

* * *

The next morning, Abe and Maryann laid in their bed and talked about going out on their boat. "How about it, Honey?... let's pack a cooler and spend the day on the lake." "Okay, I'll go in the kitchen and see what I can find." "Do you want any beer?" "Put a couple in there just in case." Abe hopped in the shower and when he was finished and dressed, he felt eager to get started and hurried past his wife in the kitchen. "I'll meet you down on the pier...I have to fill the boat tank with gas." "Okay, see ya in a bit."

Approaching the boat, Abe noticed the ever present droppings of the local Heron birds. He grabbed a rag and tried to remove most of the mess, when he noticed a new tear in the vinyl boat cover. He loved looking at the birds, but not cleaning up after them. "It was probably a racoon that poked the new hole in the cover. A piece of duct tape will mend it," he muttered.

"The hole looks too big for a bird to make," he thought for a second. He folded the cover and jumped onto the boat. As he went to fill the tank, he tripped over the trap door cover on the floor of the boat. "Oh for goodness sakes, looks like the day is not starting too good. Why can't Maryann remember to close the trap door flush to the floor?"

Maryann was at the beginning of the pier on her way to the boat when she smelled a strong odor of bleach. She looked around and noticed Noah washing the railings on his porch. "Good Morning Noah!" "Hi, Maryann. Going out on the lake?" "We sure are." "Beautiful day for it," Noah commented. "I would invite you, but you look busy." "Yeah, I want to scrape off the hornet's nest I found underneath the porch and clean the dirt and spider webs between the spindles. Have a good day out there!" he said. "Thanks," Maryann yelled out as she continued to walk down the pier toward the boat.

Abe heard Maryann's footsteps walking on the pier. Looking refreshed, with her pretty flowered bathing suit, she carried the cooler and picnic basket and a couple of fresh towels draped over her shoulders. Abe's day didn't start out pleasant so as he watched his wife take her last few steps and helped her into the boat, he had a disgusted attitude.

"Why are you so grumpy?" she asked. "Never mind," he grumbled.

Abe started the engine and slowly pulled out of the slip. Maryann sat on the soft leather seats and enjoyed the ride. As they approached the middle of the lake, a strange foul odor drifted up from the inside of the boat.

"What's that odor I smell?" asked Abe.

"Damn, I think I left the hot dogs in the boat the last time we went out. They're in the floor storage."

"Gross. I can't stand it. Feed them to the fish." Maryann pulled the floor door up and stuck her hand down in the storage. "There is a morbid smell down there. They must have rolled into a corner. I can't reach them. I have to clean this storage area out with bleach when we get home."

"Spray some of this window cleaner in there for now, so we can at least tolerate it for the day."

"We'll anchor here. The scenery and breeze is just right." He pulled off his t-shirt and they laid opposite each other on the comfortable leather seats. The rocking of the boat was mellow enough to put a baby to sleep. The warmth of the sun felt like a light blanket against their skin. "I hope heaven is just this good," said Maryann, as her eyes began to close. They both fell asleep.

After about a half hour, Abe was startled and lifted his head. "What was that noise?" he wondered. Maryann did not wake. He looked around and saw a young kid on a jet ski. "He must have blown by us." In a few minutes, Abe was out like a light again.

The trap door to the storage area lifted and made a slam that woke both of them. "What was that?" Maryann woke startled.

"I don't know, honey. Are you getting hungry? Do you want to have a snack or glass of wine?" asked Abe. "Not just yet. I'm really enjoying lying here." His wife responded.

"Okay, I'm going to have a cold drink and sit on the driver's seat."

"Hey, Honey, there are some dark clouds in the distance." Maryann didn't respond. She fell back to sleep. Abe put his earphones on and listened to his collection of soft rock.

The trap door slowly cracked opened and the fork of a tongue wiggled out of the crack. Two wide eyes followed the long slithering sensor as the door slid over the long thick body that was silently making its way out of the storage bin. It raised its head and picked up a scent. Its head turned towards Maryann and opened its jaws while its tongue extended further and waved like a flowing ribbon with a devil's fork. It slid its body with smooth movement as if on air towards her head. Just as it was about to make a grab for her jugular, Maryann turned her head in her sleep and his jaws slammed down on her ponytail. She awoke and tried to turn her neck. She could see its head out of the corner of her eyes and froze like a corpse in a morgue. With her hair entangled in its inverted fangs, it moved its head away from the seat. Her torso remained on the seat while her head dangled from its mouth in midair a few inches from the floor. Some hair released as if on a pulley and her head lay flat on its side. The python made a jolt toward her body swinging her head with it as if to try to make a wrap around her body - but with her long ponytail stuck in its fangs it interfered with its control. Suddenly, the muscular reptile made a sharp jolt forward and back and its jaws broke away, ripping a piece of ponytail from her head. Blood seeped from her skull as the snake made a fast whip around her body.

Feeling like a cleaver was stuck in her head; Maryann struggled with devastating pain and tried to maneuver her neck for air. During the attack, Abe's earphones and distance at the front of the boat blocked him from realizing what was happening to his wife. Fortunately, an ear splitting bang of thunder shook him off his seat. He whipped his earphones off and heard a sudden shriek coming from the cushions where Maryann had been lying. What he saw next was so shocking he hesitated for a moment and thought he was hallucinating; he screamed "Maryann!" and bolted towards his wife. I can't believe what I'm seeing. Abe's brain had trouble grasping the picture in front of him. He slapped his face to make sure he was awake. Maryann was in the midst of struggling to fight off the coils of a huge rock python that was wrapping rapidly around her neck and body. By the gurgling sounds and gasps for air, the snake was quickly cutting off her breathing. She fought, pounding her limbs and twisting her torso fast and hard. Abe grabbed the girth and tugged, but the beast was huge, and its grip was too tight. He was losing his wife. What was he to do, he had no help. He had nothing to stop it. Abe's nerves trembled and jerked so intensely, he was about to lose his mind and considered suicide. His keen eyes suddenly spotted the super sixteen inch newly sharpened boat knife lashed to the mast. He grabbed it and slashed at the coils. It cut into the snake like the finest blade on earth. The python jerked from the wounds and cuts, but the dam coils wrapped tighter. Abe was getting flashbacks but didn't let them get in his way. Quickly, he stabbed at the head of the beast, but missed. Rage rushed through his body. He slashed again with such speed and force the knife hit the head and he sliced into the flesh until the head separated from the body. But what was left of the spastic coils held her neck in a death grip as if they had a life of their own. He pulled at the coil around her neck, and dug his knife in deep while being ever so careful not to cut his wife. A chunk of flesh fell away. Concentrating intensely - his eyesight transformed into that of a dragonfly – to prevent him from cutting Maryann. With careful maneuvers, the sharp blade smoothly sliced into the coil....and soon the snake lay in several pieces, strewn around, and she was free.

Maryann scrambled to a corner of the boat. She had a haunting cough and snake entrails draped her body. Her eyes without movement like frozen ice balls.

Abe's anger surged into a minute of psychotic outrage. He roared like a mad lion and aggressively pulled a piece of python to shreds with his bare hands. Maryann choked and was struggling to get air into her lungs. Panicking with pouring sweat and heavy breathing he said, "*I can't find my frigging cell phone!!*" Abe tried to regain control of himself. He took Maryann in his arms and blew air into her lungs. Can you breath okay? She gave one nod "yes" and choked out "need ice - my head." He gently laid her down on the seat, ran and grabbed ice from the cooler, wrapped it fast in a towel, and placed it on her head. I have to call for emergency and shoot my flairs. You need to go to the hospital. The dark clouds moved over them and there was a downpour with lightning strikes around the boat. Abe rushed to get his flairs but slipped on a puddle of bloody water and snake flesh and banged his head on a hard corner and passed out. Maryann heard her husband fall. She held the ice to her head and forced her weak body to sit up. "Dear God, I need to help Abe. I have to get up, or he's going to die." She began to lift her body but her bare feet slipped on snake flesh and her body slammed against the floor. "My head is throbbing, she cried. Help us please, anybody." She noticed a handle on the side of the seat. The slippery floor should help me maneuver my body to reach the handle, she thought. But large boats that were trying to make it out of the rain kept speeding by and causing high waves. The hard rocking of the boat caused her body to slide back and forth out of control.

The waves finally calmed a bit and she painfully slid her body toward the handle on the side of the seat and grabbed it. She moved one foot forward and then the other and pulled herself into a squatting position. While holding on to the side handle she reached for the rail of the boat and pulled herself to stand. With her drained body and the pouring rain and lightning, she dangerously followed the metal railing with her hands as fast as she could. Abe was making a gurgling sound with his head partially emerged in water. Abe! Abe! Please wake up, she begged. She grabbed Abe's hair and turned his nose and mouth up out of the water. Ferocious thunder rattled the boat. Abe mumbled "My head." "He's alive, thank you God.

"I have to pull the anchor and get this boat started." Maryann pulled the rope on the anchor inch by inch. Her muscles were working as she was sliding in the accumulated rainwater mixed with bloody flesh that was sweeping up and down the boat floor like a tide going in and out. One wave of water on the boat's floor brought the python's floppy head up behind her body - just when her feet skid and her legs slid forward. She weakened and lost some hold of the rope. The python's upper jaw was hanging off loosely away from its head attached by a hair of ligament. She tried to swing away from the sharp fangs, but the movement of the water repeatedly swept the jaw behind her. She lost some strength and her buttocks landed on the python's sharp serrated fangs and they became embedded in her skin. Maryann screeched in agony. She held onto the rope and had no choice but to wiggle her buttocks toward the railing. The pain in her buttocks was excruciating as she moved each hip back and forth and could feel the stabbing force of the fangs in her flesh. She finally grabbed hold of the railing and pulled herself up. The gruesome horror of the snake's fangs in her butt and the blood dripping down her face caused a tremendous surge of adrenaline to rush through her body to fight for her life.

"I am going to pull the rope and bring the anchor into the boat dear lord." She held on to the rope and with all her God given might she brought the anchor up. Her mind was spinning like a twister. Her next thought was, "I have to call for an ambulance to be at the pier

or we're not going to make it. Oh God, my phone is at the back of the boat." Holding on to the metal railing, she struggled in the torrential down pour and gusty winds to make her way toward the back of the boat. A huge wave came and Abe's body swung in the bloody water across her path. She tripped over his leg and slid but was able to keep hold of the railing. She limped, dragging snake flesh stuck between her toes. She struggled stretching one arm into the console feeling all around and grabbed her phone. She tried to call for an ambulance to meet them back at the pier at Holly Meadow. Her connection to 911 dropped repeatedly before she got through - crying, trying to explain where she was - the dispatcher told her "You're going to make it – I have your location. I'm sending a helicopter and ambulance." Feeling hopeful, she made her way to the driver's wheel and started the boat. The rain miraculously stopped just in time to clear her view. Her head was banging and her cleavage held a puddle of blood. But she had a survival mode working in her brain and nature's transmitters pushed her to use her best judgment to drive the boat toward Holly Meadow. With fuzzy vision, she finally could see the pier and E.M.T.'s with some of their friends waiting. She drove through the slow wake signs, feeling very weak and could barely remain in control of boat. As the boat was getting closer to the pier, her body was shutting down and she yelled, "I have to shut the engine." She passed out just as she turned the key. The E.M.T.'s rushed to rescue Maryann and Abe off the boat and to the hospital.

The sounds of the Sirens were fading. Spike, Adam, Nick, and Noah stood on the pier and stared at the boat with astonishment. Tears fell from their eyes.

"This is beyond any nightmare ----- out in the middle of a lake and an extremely aggressive man eating python catches you off guard on your boat!" Adam said harshly with a strong look of shock. All their mouths were dropped to their chest as they glanced at each other in speechless shock...with an "I can't believe it" look on their faces and whispers of "What a tragedy! God had to be with them."

"I wonder why they couldn't see the python before they got on the boat, said Spike. It must have been down in the storage hole."

"Abe did a good job smashing the crap out of this python. He must have been thinking about his ex-wife," said Nick. This is no time to joke, said Spike. He did have experience from the incident with Carolyn. The poor guy had to go through this sick incident again and this time his health could be seriously affected.

"Funny, I smell hot dogs," said Spike. "I do too," said Adam.

"I'll hire someone to clean the boat. We can call the hospital and check on how they're doing in a few hours. Let's head in. I have to report this incident to the Sheriff's Office. I'll give you guys a call later on tonight," said Spike.

CHAPTER TWENTY EIGHT

It was around ten that night, and Spike thought it was time to call the hospital to check how Maryann and Abe were doing. The nurse informed him that Abe had a mild concussion and Maryann had bad scrapes, cuts, contusions, bad black and blue marks, and a hairline fracture on two of her ribs. Spike relayed the information to Adam, Nick, and Noah.

The next morning Spike went to visit Maryann and Abe. He first walked into Abe's hospital room. Feeling a little groggy, he greeted Spike with, "Can you believe there was a python in my frigging boat?"

Abe, "What the heck happened, my man? First, tell me how you are feeling?" "My head hurts, I have a few stitches and black and blues, but other than that, I'm okay. Maryann has a few serious injuries that need to be watched carefully. She says she's in a lot of pain. She had to have thirty stitches in her buttocks. The doctor told me I could go home tomorrow if my blood pressure stays normal. It was sky high when I came in."

"Well, I can understand that. Maybe you shouldn't talk about what happened." "I feel like telling you, Spike." Spike knew the morphine was covering Abe's pain both physically and emotionally. "When I first got to my boat, I noticed a hole in my boat cover. I thought a raccoon might have done it, because

Maryann had left some hot dogs in the storage hole from our last trip out. We didn't notice the smell of the rotten hot dogs until we were in the middle of the lake. I told her to feed them to the fish. She stuck her arm down in the storage hole but couldn't find any hot dogs. I just figured the raccoons took them, because we tend to forget to lock the trap. She sprayed some window cleaner down there and wiped around. The area down there is larger than her arms could reach, but whatever she cleaned seemed to be good enough. We then took a nap. I got up before Maryann and was enjoying a cold drink. I remember I was alarmed by a big bang of thunder and turned around to talk to her and saw a frigging python on her body. I had a mild concussion. I can't remember much after that. The only other thing I can remember right now is that I was lying on the floor of the boat in bloody water and I looked up and saw Maryann soaked with blood. I snapped out of it fully in the middle of the night and asked myself what am I doing here? Maryann told me this morning that I ripped the python to shreds. But I didn't believe it."

"I saw the mess. I hired someone to clean your boat tomorrow. But what's most important is that you guys are okay.

The smell from the rotten hot dogs attracted him to the boat and he somehow made his way in. The trap door to the storage area sometimes doesn't close flush to the floor unless you force it."

"I'm glad you're okay, Abe. I'm going over to say hello to your wife. Take it easy, I'll see you home soon." "Thanks for stopping bye, Spike."

Spike entered Maryann's hospital room. Her head was bandaged like a mummy. She looked at him with surprise. "I'm so happy to see you." "The nurse just gave me pain medication and I'm feeling good right now." Spike hugged her, the best he could. "I apologize for the tragic attack you experienced, sweetheart."

"Spike, it was not your fault. We can only have so much control over nature. By the way, if you happen to wonder what happened to the python's head, it was stuck in my ass. On one of my falls, I landed just right and his fangs became embedded in my cheeks." "My God, that must have been extremely painful." "It was too crazy to even believe that it happened," Maryann said. The doctor told me he had to report the incident to the Sheriff and give the Sheriff the snake's fangs for some type of research in the wildlife laboratory."

"You guys made it through hell, again."

Maryann broke out in tears. "Oh Spike, when is our county going to start taking our problem seriously and offer us some help?"

"The politicians try to play down anything that will effect tourism or keep potential home buyers away from our town. They're not interested in the quality of our lives and the danger that surrounds us. They just figure eventually we'll pay to resolve the problem, even if it means depleting our funds, which I may be forced to do.

I have to go sweetie. Stay strong." He gave Maryann a kiss goodbye. "I'll see you soon," he said. He left the hospital.

* * *

That night while Lita was cooking dinner she had tears in her eyes. "I can't believe what happened to Maryann and Abe."

"I have to talk to the Wildlife Task Force down in the everglades about our problem," Spike told his wife.

"You must have called them a dozen times by now. They won't help us. We're out of their jurisdiction and they're too pre-occupied with their problems with the out-of-control population of Burmese pythons down there. I don't think our own town is taking our problems seriously at all," Lita complained with frustration.

"It's been on the news that the African Rock is overpowering all pythons," Spike commented. "We have to hire a special hunting force to come here and find those monsters and kill as many as they can, said Spike. But since our land is preservation and governed by the state, it would have to go through all kinds of red tape. And I don't see why the association should have to pay for it." "When the heck are you going to talk to the town board again, *in person?*" Lita asked Spike. "Do you know how lucky we have been that no one has actually been killed," Lita strongly spoke out at Spike.

I have to tell you something, Lita. She grabbed the edge of the counter and her knees weakened. Her head hung down. "Don't tell me. What! *What is it that you're going to tell me?* Tell me. Get it over with. Someone died? Someone *did* die! Is that what you are going to tell me?" Spike told Lita in a gentle tone, "Some of us think that Noah killed Lena." "And we are also investigating the possibility that Tom was killed by a python." Lita threw a spatula against the kitchen wall. "You can finish cooking. I'm going to bed." Spike grabbed Lita and hugged her. "I can't take this anymore; she cried and tried to jiggle herself free from his arms. I want to move." She laid her forehead against her husband's chest, pounding her fists on his shoulders. He took a tight gentle hold of his wife and laid his cheeks on the top of her head. "We can't move, he said. We will never be able to sell. The whole county knows about Holly Meadow."

"Someday this will all be history, my dear little wife." "My dear big man, someday soon a few too many people, living here in Holly Meadow, might be history." "*I mean dead!*"

"Why don't you spend some time at your mother's? You could use a break from all this terror."

"Maybe you're right," she responded. "Are you sure you'll understand if I stay at my mother's for a few weeks."

"Yes, honey, you don't have to worry about me and what I'm thinking. I fully understand and I'll feel more at ease that you're away from all these bizarre issues and incidents. I'll visit you often. Don't worry, we'll be back to normal soon," Spike told his wife. Lita knew her husband was trying to be nice and comfort her, but in no way did she believe that things were going to be back to normal soon at Holly Meadow.

The next afternoon Spike received a phone call from the crime lab stating that they found snake scales on Tom Albertson's body. "But we didn't find any internal biological organ residue from a snake on his body. The lab officer explained, a body does decompose at a slower rate when submerged in water, rather than if it was in open air, but the body was in the water for at least eight weeks, that gave plenty of time for a snake to feed on the corpse or just rub up against it. So just because we found snake scales on the body does not tell us that this person was killed by a snake."

Spike asked, "Does this mean it's possible that we may never know the cause of death on Mr. Albertson?"

"It is a possibility. If you want intensive skeletal and flesh research it will cost thousands of dollars. The state will pay for all costs pertaining to standard procedures in forensic, but extensive tests that will only show possible animal intervention of a corpse found in a lake will not be covered by the state. We have found no evidence of foul play on the body, partially because it was over fifty percent decomposed. It will remain in the possible murder victim category until the case is closed. Cases like this are sometimes never closed."

"Okay, thank you Sir, for all your help."

"I haven't finished yet," the officer said.

"What do you mean?"

"We are very interested in the t-shirt."

"Why is that?"

"Because the same DNA found on the t-shirt you brought in, was also found on the black bikini bottom, which you stated, was found in Emerald Lake."

"*What!*" Spike said in major shock. His heart palpitated.

"You will have to meet with a detective in our department so we can discuss anything more you know about the missing female resident in Holly Meadow."

"Excuse me Sir, but I'm intensely shocked about this. Is it definitely a positive match?" asked Spike.

"Yes it is. We are very interested in compiling some information about the owner of the t-shirt. Can you come to the station on Monday?" asked the officer.

"Yeah, sure."

"See you at ten."

"Okay Sir."

Spike went to the bar and decided he needed a drop of tequila in his soda to calm him down. Soda is not strong enough this time, he thought. The smell of the tequila made him more furious at Noah. He could feel the blood rushing through his veins as anger built up inside. "How could that bastard do anything to that cute little woman." The tequila fragrance, though not pleasant, brought back memories of adorable Lena, as if it were a pleasant perfume she wore. "I'm supposed to repair the wall tonight, but I would rather throw the sofa through it. Maybe it will knock his head off." He couldn't relax –his gut felt full of charged wires that could light up.

Spike tried hard to keep himself from throwing an outrageous fit. I have to call Adam, Abe, and Nick and let them know. He took another drop of tequila and began pacing and sweating, cuffing and opening his hands. He could taste the salt from his sweat. Perfect timing for the after taste of tequila. His mind was racing. "Where's the body?" he thought. "That frigging dive team better show up soon." He caught his flushed face in the dining room mirror. His gut boiled. His anger was getting more intense. His face was getting redder. "I have a murderer living next door to me," he mumbled. His anger surged and he became emotionally agitated to the point of loss of self-control. He whipped his glass at the mirror - it hit the wide wooden frame and fell to the floor without a break. The phone rang. "Hi honey, how are you doing?" His mind went blank. He couldn't recognize the voice. "Honey, are you there?" asked Lita. "I'm sorry sweetheart. You got me at a bad time. Can we talk in the morning?" Spike asked his wife. "I'm sorry, honey, let me call you in the morning and I'll explain everything." "Okay, I understand. I hope you'll feel better," said Lita- feeling concerned.

Spike felt hot and paced back and forth in his living room. "I have to take a cold shower," he thought aloud. He went into the bathroom, pulled off his clothes, and turned on the cold water. He was just about to hop in the shower, when the phone rang again. He ran and looked at the caller I.D. It was Noah. He ran back to the shower and got in. The water was not as cold as he wished.

The shower calmed him a bit. He called Adam, Abe, and Nick and asked them to come over. Adam responded, "I'm a little out of breath right now, but I gut ya. I'll be over in an hour." Spike then called Nick. "Nick, I need you to come over in an hour." "Okay, I understand. I'll be there." Abe also agreed to come.

Adam, Abe, and Nick showed up at Spike's at the same time. Spike told them to grab a drink and sit on the sofa. "You guys need to be comfortable for this one. I got a call today from the crime lab officer and he told me Noah's DNA was on the black bikini bottom."

"You're kidding us you asshole. That's not funny," said Adam.

"No, I'm not kidding you, you asshole," said Spike.

"What the hell is going on around here?" Nick shouted.

"I'm beside myself, said Spike. I'm struggling to stay in control. With no *body* - there will be no charge against Noah unless we have some sort of overwhelming circumstantial evidence. The divers are supposed to be here next Wednesday morning. If they don't find anything we'll have to search the forest again, but this time for a grave. I hope it was just an affair and Noah has nothing to do with Lena's disappearance."

"He was probably just lonely at night and they had a fling now and then," Nick commented.

"That's what I'm hoping, said Spike. Because if the residents here find out he did kill her, you know it could trigger one of them to snap and kill *him*. Like maybe me," said Spike.

"Until we have more evidence we have to act friendly toward him," said Nick.

"Yes, you're right, we're even going to continue to invite him to all our meetings," said Spike.

"We have to, said Nick, or he'll become suspicious."

CHAPTER TWENTY NINE

The Florida criminal investigation underwater dive team arrived the following Wednesday morning to search Emerald Lake for the sad but realistic possibility of finding Lena's body. There were six divers. They searched the lake within a three-mile perimeter of Holly Meadow and did not find any trace of human remains. There was the possibility that the skeleton of a petite woman would be too small and discolored to notice, especially if it is snagged in the thick black brush at the bottom of the lake. Emerald Lake is a very difficult lake to search. It's extremely murky and has a dense undergrowth of weeds which makes it very difficult for the divers to see, even with their powerful lighting. After a twelve-hour mission of exerting great physical and mental strength, the divers ended the search for the day.

Spike sat at his desk that late afternoon and wrote the good, but discouraging, news to all the residents. The lack of closure was causing Spike and the Holly Meadow residents lots of frustration.

* * *

While the divers were working that day, they used most of the area near the lake for their equipment. Jack walked the front grounds and noticed there were numerous tennis balls in the front pond near the tennis court. I better get a rake and try to retrieve some of this rubber out of the pond, he thought. He found the longest rake he had and stood on the grass, throwing it forward across the water in a sweeping motion. "This is strenuous on my arm. Maybe I'll put on my high rubber boots and just walk in and grab the balls." He went to his shed and grabbed his boots. "A pair of high rubber gloves won't hurt either," he thought. Now looking quite protected, he walked back to the pond and stepped into the water slowly toward the neon green tennis balls...some floating and some soiled half-sunk. "Damn, I forgot a bucket. I'll just throw them on the grass for now." As he continued to walk in the black water, he felt his boots sink in the sludge deeper and deeper. "I'm bringing myself too close to the middle of the pond. Damn it! My boot is stuck in this mush."

Jack moved his way close to the middle of the pond where the waterfall was connected. He became trapped and unable to move one of his legs up, to step further on. He pulled and pulled but his foot would not budge. Jack heard a big splash and looked around. He noticed movement in the water in front of him about ten feet away. "Oh God, don't let it be." Two eyes began moving slowly along the surface of the pond directly toward him. "Holy Crap! He's huge. Damn!" He tried to pull his leg again but lost his balance and fell forward. Drenched and full of mud, he knew his life was in danger if he didn't work hard to move away from the alligator and make a run for the grass. Jack reached his hand down into the water and felt around his boot hoping to rip away the trapping debris. He felt a pipe and a rope. The toe area of the boot was lodged under the fountain pipe and the rope was entangled around the ankle of the boot. He couldn't get the boot loose from the bottom of the pond. The two eyes gliding above the water were getting closer to him. He kicked his leg back and forth to loosen it, but had no luck. "I have to take my leg out of the boot." He wiggled his leg to let loose of the boot but his toes would not give and release his foot. The alligator was smoothly moving his way directly toward Jack. "I have to trust this sucker." Jack stood still and lowered his breath. The alligator was getting closer and closer. Now, the monster was just inches away with what looked like a twenty-inch head facing his belly. Jack held his breath. "Come on pal, you're not hungry." The alligator stopped. It seemed like an hour, but it was only a few seconds. He could not hold his breath any longer. Jack slowly let out some air and inhaled while the alligator's mouth was at his belt buckle. "Should I scream? Should I move? Is it lunch time? Am I just in your way?"....his confused mind thought. Jack kept his body frozen. The alligator was in charge. "Decide what you want to do you son of a bitch!" The alligator moved his head to the left of Jack's body and swam on by him. Jack let out a gush of air. "Wow! That was close. Now if I can get this stupid boot loose." Suddenly, he was startled and heard a loud snort behind him and fell backwards into the pond. Jack's head became covered with mud and weeds at the bottom of the pond and he lost his sight. He fought to bring himself up and get some air. Only his forehead reached the top of the water when he lost control of his mouth and the dark dirty water poured in. He struggled fast and hard with his arms and one leg and as he stood up his trapped boot let loose. Jack swung his head around looking for the gator through his muddy eyes as he gagged and coughed the dirty water out. He saw the alligator heading up a bank on the grass. He then sneezed mud and pebbles from his nose. More than ready to escape the pond as fast as possible, he attempted to walk out of the water but felt a heavy pull on his boot. He was dragging something. Jack wobbled and limped and started to make it to the grass, dragging the entanglement on one boot. The lower the water got, the harder the pull got, but he kept walking. What was only a few feet seemed like a mile. A few more steps and his foot hit the grass. He bent his knee and pulled his other booted foot out of the water. He turned and sat on the grass and saw a few feet of rope wrapped and stuck around his boot extending into the water. Jack disentangled the rope and let it go. "The heck with those tennis balls. Fuck. That was almost worse than being in Vietnam. I'm over my work time. I'm going home to shower."

CHAPTER THIRTY

During the coming week, Spike felt a board meeting was due. He posted the date on the bulletin near the mailboxes for all residents to see. Surprisingly there was a large turnout. Residents were becoming increasingly concerned about their community and began to show some respect for the board members. Spike was very thankful. Some residents asked if they could help in any way. Adam made a list of names of volunteers. The very sensitive and potentially criminal issues could not be disclosed or made public. The community was stressed and any further information concerning Lena and Tom would cause a major uproar. After an intense review of the budget and talk about new allocations, someone stood up and shouted, "What are you going to do about the killer pythons?" Adam took over and explained. "Right now, we are on our own. I apologize for the uncomfortable atmosphere here at Holly Meadow - but the county doesn't seem to think two or three snakes pose a lethal threat to our community." One resident yelled, "It's been four snakes! Get your snakes straight!" A few found that statement funny and laughed. Spike continued - "Abe, Adam, Nick, Noah, and myself are doing all we can without the help of the county or state. As you all know, there were three very devastating attacks involving four of our residents and they're lucky to be alive. Walk with caution and be aware of your surroundings at all times. Hopefully, there are not any more around. And if there are - we will do everything we can to try and eliminate them." Another resident raised his hand. "Did you find out what happened to Lena?" "Unfortunately, no we haven't. But we may have some leads." Noah asked, "What leads are you talking about? I wasn't notified of any leads." Spike turned to Noah and told him, there wasn't anything that could be discussed at this point.

Sophia raised her hand and asked, "Has the body, found in the lake, been identified?" Spike cleared his throat. "I'm sorry to have to let everyone know that the body in the lake has been identified as being our former maintenance man, Tom Albertson. A sad *aaawww...* came from the crowd. It's been very hard for me to let this information out and I apologize for the delay." Everyone became silent, then questions began to slowly dart out; *"Was he, was he murdered?" "Did he kill himself?" "Was it a python?"....* came from all corners of the room. *A python!* An elderly woman cried hysterically at length. *I'm so scared!*

"We had lab studies done on the corpse and because of the decomposition of the body they could not prove a particular cause of death." A few women broke down. "Tom was a great guy." A cute aged face elderly woman stood up and darted her finger at the board. *"I think his wife killed him! As soon as I heard there was a man found in the lake, I knew it was Tom."* Everyone became quiet. "Why do you think it was his wife, Mrs. Calucci?" asked Spike. "Because I saw his wife on the pier with Tom a few months ago. They were having a bad fight. She told him - if he didn't give her the money to pay her car payment he would be sorry." The whole board looked at each other. "Did you ever see Carrie here again after that particular fight Mrs. Calucci?" "Why yes. As usual they would sneak down the pier so no one could hear them. I was usually sitting down at the umbrella table near the boats with my camera and binoculars - I guess they didn't consider me a person. It was always early in the morning. One morning I heard a big splash. I turned around and all I saw was Carrie walking down the pier toward the exit." "Why didn't you tell us this information earlier?"

"I'm a bird. I flew up north the next day. Sometimes I fly back and forth from New York every three or four months. I had to get my new hearing aids at my doctor in New York. I just recently came down and was shocked to find out all the terrible things that have been happening here. The snakes scare me. I don't like snakes. Even the ones that men have attached to their bodies." Everyone remained quiet. "Please continue, Mrs. Calucci," said Spike with his ears glued to her voice.

"I thought the splash I heard was an alligator and that Tom might have been in the men's room, but now after I heard of a man's body that was found and that a new maintenance man was hired, I thought she might have done something terrible."

"You obviously didn't see Tom floating in the water?"

"No, I didn't. However, what I did notice is that the Holly Boat was wobbling and it was a few feet further down the pier than when I came to take my pictures that morning. I remember that, because there was a beautiful Heron Bird standing on the seat and I took a picture of it."

"Can we have a copy of that picture?"

"Yes, you can."

"Mrs. Calucci, do you really think Carrie could overtake Tom?"-a resident asked.

"Hell, she's bigger than him. She could just sit on him and shoot him."

"But you didn't hear a gun shot."

"No, but if I had a gun in my stomach and was told to jump in the lake or else - I might not be so afraid of the alligators after all." "She drowned him. I know she did." "Hey! This is starting to sound like a court room," came from across the room. "Can we get out of here?" "Of course, anyone is free to leave at any time." Some left - some stayed. "This is quite a truck load of information, Mrs. Calucci. Would you come down to the police station and make out a report?" "Like hell, I will. I'm eighty two years old. If they want information they can come to me." "I don't understand," some women cried. "There are a lot of things in life that we are finding very hard to understand right now. I'm glad that you all showed up. We all need each other's support at this time. I hope we can all learn to get along and help each other," Spike urged. "We will inform the police of Mrs. Calucci's observations and we will keep you all updated. Thank you everybody for attending. This meeting is adjourned."

Stella went to bed that night thinking about the meeting. She turned to Adam and told him she thought they should have had a moment of silence for Tom and a prayer for Lena. "I guess there is just *too* much to remember. Now we have additional information to work on." "Do you think Mrs. Calucci is telling the truth, Adam?" "I don't think she would make up a story like that, Stella. These will be never ending open issues until they are figured out or solved."

"In between researching Mrs. Calucci's story, we might start looking in the forest for a grave."

"*A grave!*" Stella's jaws dropped. Have a good night's sleep honey," said Adam. "Oh sure, you say that as if it's so easy. I feel like I'm a character stuck in the middle of a horror story." "I'm sorry to say, you are." Adam responded.

CHAPTER THIRTY ONE

Spike called the Sheriff's office and reported Mrs. Calucci's story. The Sheriff's office sent a detective to Holly Meadow to investigate the crime scene once again.

Before the detective had arrived, Spike, Abe, Adam, Nick, and Noah got together and went down the pier to look around. Spike looked down off the side of the pier and saw a rope tied to one of the poles that hold the pier up. He took his buck knife out of his belt and cut the rope. He went to the next pole and saw another rope. He pulled at it and it was stuck. He lay his body down on the wood planks and looked underneath the pier. The rope was snagged in a pile of weeds. Directly under the pier there was a dirty white sock. He told the other guys to watch for alligators while he yanked at the rope and reached his arm down under to get the sock. Spike couldn't reach the sock. He told Adam to reach under the other side of the pier and tell him if he can see where the rope is. Adam said, "It's caught on a root."

"Can you grab it?"

"First and most important - watch close for alligators and pythons."

"Okay guys, we're watching. I'm holding my machete, said Nick. This area still stinks of the rotten corpse."

Adam reached down in the murky water, grabbed the root of the plant and pulled it up with the rope. The sock was caught on the rope with weeds entangled around it.

"Wait, I see a cell phone." Adam reached down and grabbed a rusted out cell phone.

"I'll call Mrs. Calucci and tell her to call me when the detective arrives - so we can give him these articles," said Spike.

A detective came to Mrs. Calucci's house that night and filled out a report with all her information. Before she finished her report she called Spike and he brought the articles they had found to her home and gave them to the detective.

After Spike left, Mrs. Calucci continued, "now that I remember detective, Tom was holding a can of soda in his hand if that's any help." "Anything will help, Mrs. Calucci. Do you remember the color of the can?" "Why yes, it was bright red. I remember saying - that fat slob shouldn't be drinking that junk."

"Thanks for your time." The detective left.

* * *

Spike had to wait for Mrs. Albertson to be notified of the DNA findings first - and then *he* would be notified.

The lab called Spike four days later and told him there was DNA from Tom Albertson on the sock and on the rope. Spike was not surprised.

The detective went to Mrs. Albertson and asked if she had ever been on the pier with her husband, Tom. She told him, "She had never been on the pier."

"Do you own a gun, Mrs. Albertson?"

"Why, yes I do. For my personal protection. Why are you asking me these questions?"

"Carrie, do you remember, any time at all, being on the pier and asking your husband for money to make your car payment." "Yeah, I always asked him for my car payment." "But you just told me you have never been on the pier." "I was when I had to chase him around the grounds to ask him for my car payment." "I thought you meant for recreational reasons. Little did he know my car was paid off two years ago. But I needed the extra money for my collection of pickles, if you know what I mean detective." "You must have quite a large collection."

"Would you mind if we took a sample of your DNA down to the lab. We would like to close this case - but we need one last thing. We need to find out if your DNA is on a sock and rope that was found around a couple of poles on the pier."

"Now what would my DNA be doing on those items?"

"DNA simply falls off your skin or body. There are traces of people's DNA everywhere. It's part of the closing procedure, so we don't leave any part of this case unfinished."

"Do they have to take my blood? I don't like needles, they give me nightmares." *"Nightmares!"* The detective was trying hard to remain as patient as possible. "No, the technician can simply swipe your skin."

"I'll pick you up in the morning and we'll go together." "What if I don't wanna go?" "Well, we would have to get a special demand from the courts." "Courts? What do they have to do with this?" "I'll beep outside about ten a.m. tomorrow, Carrie. It won't take long."

"Well, I guess. If you say it'll close the case. All cases should be closed, to keep stuff from falling out. See you then detective." The detective shook his head and smiled. He was happy to leave.

A few days later, Spike heard from the lab and they told him they did not find any of Carrie's DNA on the rope or sock. Spike felt relieved and called his buddies. "Guess this case will have to remain open forever, said Spike. Mrs. Calucci's story is not enough evidence. *Even if it is true.*"

CHAPTER THIRTY TWO

On a Saturday afternoon before Jack left Holly Meadow for his day off, he stopped by Spike's and told him he did try to clear out all the tennis balls from the front pond, but it ended up being a very challenging disaster.

"Well, at least you made an effort, Jack."

"There's a long rope connected to the pipe that runs the waterfall. My boot got tangled in it. I think the rope should be removed. There's no use for it being there, unless you know what it's used for, Spike."

"Ah no, I have no idea, Jack."

"Well maybe I'll give it another shot one of these days and try to cut the rope out. I'll just have to make sure there are no gators around."

"Okay Jack, keep me updated."

In the middle of his living room, Spike sat on his sofa trying to make sense of it all. The phone rang. It was Lita. "Hi, honey. I'm ready to come home, I miss you," she said. "How is your mother doing?" Spike asked. "She really has enjoyed my company and seems to have more life in her, but I can't stay here forever. I'll be home Friday," she told him.

"Okay, honey, if that's how you feel, that's fine with me. Just prepare yourself to be strong minded about what is going on around here. Nothing is solved yet."

"I will." They hung up.

* * *

Not knowing that Jack had already made an attempt to retrieve the tennis balls, Maryann called Lita that Saturday night and asked her if she wouldn't mind helping her get all those balls out of the pond tomorrow.

"You silly woman. Why should I have to help you? You put them there on purpose and now I have to get myself all muddy and wet....Oh, okay. I'll meet you there around ten tomorrow morning."

"Make sure you wear old shabby clothes that you want to throw away," said Maryann.

Maryann arrived at the pond and was checking to see if there were any alligators around. Lita snuck up behind, "Boo!" Maryann shook. "Oh, don't do that." "Are we just walking right in the pond and grabbing the balls?" asked Maryann.

"Yeah," Lita smirked.

"I overheard someone in the parking lot complain about them, that's why I called you last night," said Maryann. "I'll step in first and tell you how it feels."

Maryann began to walk in, hesitantly.

"Oh, it feels so mushy and gross."

"Keep going and grab those two on the left."

"Okay boss. Aren't you going to help me?"

"Maybe, huh! I got *you* in the pond."

"You *what!* Catch!" said Maryann.

"Ouch, you hit my head."

"There are some more over there on the right of the fountain," said Lita.

Maryann was waist deep in the midst of eerie creepy water… surely paying for her fun. "I can't stand this," she said. "Gross!"

"What's the matter?"

"I stepped on something round and smooth."

"Maybe it's a turtle. Just hurry and grab the balls."

"Here, catch."

"There are five more over there."

"Oh, brother!"

She continued to walk as her feet sunk down to her ankles in the mud.

"I'll never do this again."

"Hurry, throw me the balls."

"Give me a chance, this is real gruesome, and scary ya know."

"Oh my God, there's a python right behind you." "*Aaahhhhh!*" Maryann jumped, tripped, and fell in the water.

"Just kidding. *Huh!* We'll see how many balls you whip over the fence from now on."

"Oh shut up! I'm coming out….I don't see any more balls. How many did I get?"

"I think twenty."

"Oh my God, my foot is stuck in something."

"What is it stuck in?"

"My toes are in two slots like a ballerina position."

"Well slide them out and get out of there."

"Okay, I'm coming." "Oh damn!"

"What's the matter now?"

"The turtle must have moved, or this is another one. I'm trying to maintain my balance. My right foot slipped and sunk deeper in the mud. One of my toes is lodged in a whole again." She gave Lita a startled look.

"Help me, Lita!"

"You can do it girl, come on, try hard and reach for my hand."

"I can't, my toe won't release."

"Shake it. Pull it"

"It feels like it's stuck in a finger hole of a bowling ball."

"Shake harder."

After several shakes and pulls, her toe set free. She had a few feet before she could reach the grass area. She slowly stepped forward when her body encountered an obstruction of entangled rope hidden in the black water. Her feet slipped backwards and her head fell forward. On the bottom of the pond, dark dirty water stirred in front of her eyes. She held her breath and placed one hand in front of the other. Sharp pieces of gravel gouged her hands and knees. The thick deep mud only allowed for a slow crawl. Lita became nervous and ran into the pond to help her. She reached in and grabbed Maryann's arms and brought her up. Maryann made a grueling gasp for air. Draped with mud, she held on to Lita for dear life. Lita led her to the grass and they fell to the dry ground and broke out in a cry. Lita reached and hugged Maryann, "I'm so sorry, honey. Let's throw these balls in the dumpster and go home and take a long shower."

* * *

That whole afternoon, Adam was working overtime at the bank. Stella and Spike sat in their home offices, both minds generating enough electricity to set off sparks. Stella thought about the card she found in the mail and how closely related it was to Noah. Then she recalled Tina Hardy's comment in the parking lot that day when she was getting in her car. Tina yelled something like, there was a rumor that Jack was having an affair with an "Ally."

"Could she have meant, "Lena," Stella thought. She stepped off the couch and paced. "I wonder if she meant "Lena?" Stella shuffled through her paperwork and looked for Tina's number.

Hi Tina, "This is Stella. We met for lunch." "Yes, of course. What's up?" "When we were leaving that day, I remember while we were just about to get into our cars, you yelled something across the parking lot about a rumor that Jack was having an affair." "Oh Yeah, I remember, said Tina." "Can you please tell me the name of the woman again?" "He had a bookkeeper named Ally, and as the divorce was nearing, a few acquaintances told me they were having an affair." "Are you sure her name was Ally?" "From what I remember that's what it sounded like to me. I never had a chance to meet her." "Is there a way you could verify her name?" "Listen, Stella, I don't mean to be rude, but do you really think I have time to track down people I knew years ago? I guess your little Lena friend is still missing and you're trying to put some pieces together. I'm sorry I can't help you." Tina hung up. "What a bitch," Stella thought. "I would like to check the circumstances of Tina and Jack's divorce on file in the courts. I'm not ready to eliminate Jack from my list of possible suspects. After Adam leaves for work tomorrow, I'll drive down to Coller County and read the recordings."

Stella got out of bed as soon as Adam left, put some dressy clothes on, and began her drive down to the Capri Island area to find the County Courthouse. She told Adam she would be late getting home because she joined the Glitzy Blitzy Girly Group. After three hours of driving, she finally arrived at the Coller County Courthouse. She went to the divorce records department and entered "Hardy" in the computer. With intense concentration, her eyes scrolled through the numerous pages in the divorce decree and saw that Jack's friend had filed charges against Tina. It was a simple sentence with no details. This made Stella frustrated. Who was the friend, she nervously thought. The information continued about irreconcilable differences and the financial aspect. Nothing much different from most divorce records, unless there is major violence of course.

"I have to head back home and pump Jack for more information," she thought. She left the courthouse and began her long journey back home.

She arrived home around six. Adam was relaxed on the sofa watching television... ... "Hi honey, did you have fun with the new group?" he asked.

"Yeah, it was fun to meet new women."

"Did you make yourself some dinner, Adam?"

"Oh don't worry, I took care of myself," he said.

"I'm going up to change," Stella told him.

She unzipped the back of her dress and let it fall to the floor. Adam silently crept up the stairs and peeked as she took off her bra. She faced the closet looking for a nightgown and could not see him. He snuck up behind her and began kissing the back of her neck. He sucked gently on her shoulders and wrapped his arms around her front and while she lifted her arms and placed them behind her around his neck, he gently played with her protruding nipples. She leaned her head back on his shoulder and pressed her body against his warm pulsating wand. The stimulation was getting intense. She turned and kissed him all over his face and down the front of his body. The pleasure she wanted to give was out of control. She went back and forth with expertise all over. She couldn't get enough of his well-endowed lollipop. Knowing she turned him on to a point where he reached a euphoric feeling of heaven - made her feel beautiful. She wanted more, more, and more. She totally consumed him until he was far above the clouds. His body was hers, and as she led him to his divine universe, he released his burst of stars with gratifying sounds.

He then took her on the floor, slithered his saliva all over her soft little flesh, until rushes ran up and down her body and forced her legs to butterfly. Her vocal cords went into spastic mode with beautiful sounds of release. They laid on the old bedroom rug as if in paradise. It was heavenly, she whispered.

* * *

The next morning, Stella called Carolyn and told her she went down to Capri Island and looked at the records. "I'm wondering what Tina did to cause Jack's friend to file charges against her. This is going to bug me until I find out." "You are going to have to get to know Jack better, so he opens up to you more, said Carolyn. When you see him on the grounds, act very friendly and invite him over to the pool for a beer. Spike won't notice. Be discreet."

"I'll try, but it will be difficult to get that deep into his past. Jack doesn't spend much time doing nothing around here. He is a pretty good worker. I'll let you know if I get any more information out of him. Talk later."

Stella put on her bathing suit and beach wrap and headed down to the pool. Jack was nowhere in sight. She went to lay on a lounge chair and the plastic bands ripped and she fell through and scraped her butt on the pavement. "My God, can't this place keep these chairs repaired properly?" A hand held out to help her up. It was Jack.

"Oh Jack, I didn't see you here."

"I just came down the pier. Are you alright?" he asked.

"Yeah, I'm fine. I just have a nice scrape on my butt." She tied her beach wrap around her waist.

"I have a guy coming to fix these chairs tomorrow. I apologize that I didn't place the worn ones aside. I was just on my way to inform Spike there's a couple of large mutilated turtles on the pier. They actually look like they were attacked, swallowed, and regurgitated."

Stella started hyperventilating. "I didn't take my pill this morning," she said.

"I'm surprised you have the courage to lie down here," said Jack.

I'm fighting it, Jack. This is my home."

"Yeah, but until things are resolved and it feels comfortable around here, you really shouldn't take any chances," he said.

"Do you really think so, Jack? You are always all over the property. Do you ever see any pythons?"

"No, but it doesn't mean they're not here. They blend well with the scenery and there's not much food for them around here. The poison kills any rats that may be around and from what I've heard, there have never been many rabbits or raccoons in this area. There's plenty of food in the everglades where they should be living.

"Oh God help us," said Stella.

"Take it easy Stella, try to relax."

"Jack, don't you ever feel lonely? I always see you working so hard around here and then I think the poor guy has no one to go home to."

"Believe me, like I told you before, my ex-wife drained that part out of me. I don't long to be with a woman anymore. Heck, she almost killed my bookkeeper. Some jerk told her I was having an affair with Lena."

"Lena! Her name was Lena?"

"Yeah, why? asked Jack.

"Oh nothing," said Stella.

"Oh you mean you are shocked because the woman that's missing here is named Lena?" asked Jack.

"No! I mean Yes!" said Stella.

"It was getting close to our divorce and I think Tina was feeling a little guilty so she thought she would place the blame on someone else. I never had anything to do with Lena."

"When you said she almost killed Lena....what did she actually do to her?" asked Stella.

"She waited in the parking lot until Lena left her office and she grabbed the woman by the throat with a rope and forced her in the trunk of her car. She brought her home in the trunk and was trying to force me to admit that Lena and I were having an affair. I had to agree or she wouldn't give me the keys to the trunk. I ran to the trunk and got her out and I called the police and Lena pressed charges against Tina for kidnapping. I was involved because my wife committed a felony and the truth was right in front of the officers and detectives that showed up. The car was under my name. Rope was wrapped around Lena's neck. She had scrape marks all over her and her DNA was in the trunk and all, so I had to testify against my soon not-to-be wife. They handcuffed Tina and brought her to jail for the night. I left her there all night. I had no desire to bail her out. That caused more tension between us. Even though it was a felony, she had political connections and only received probation and community service. It was her first offense.

"After the divorce was finalized, I moved up here with the little money I had, to start a new life. I have been much more relaxed and more like myself since it ended."

"That's quite a story. I can see why you moved away from that area."

"Basically, I never thought Tina had it in her to do such a crime. The divorce must have pushed her over the edge. She is a well-educated successful woman. Deep inside she must have still loved me. Sometimes I feel she still does. You know - when you get that feeling that someone is thinking about you."

"Yeah, I do and usually the phone rings and it's that person."

"Well I haven't spoken to her since and don't plan to. The past is the past in this case. I better clean that mess of turtles before the stench starts to travel. I'll talk to you later."

Stella walked back up to her condo. She cleaned herself off with alcohol.

Now, she knew there were two sides to Tina and Jack's story. But who was telling the truth? "Maybe I should try and get in touch with this woman, Lena? She may still be at the Transportation Department down in Coller County." Stella called the company and asked for a bookkeeper named Lena. The operator said, there was not a Lena working for the company."

"Is there anyone that has been around for the past five years that might have known her?" she asked the operator."

"Possibly. Who did she work for?"

"Jack Hardy."

"Oh Jack! I know whom I can connect you with. Wait one moment please." Stella heard ringing. She was getting impatient. Eight rings now. Finally, someone picked up. "Suzanne Baker, can I help you?"

"Yes, I'm looking for an old friend, Lena, who worked as a bookkeeper in your department approximately five years ago."

"Oh, you must mean Lena Cawta. She worked for a man named Jack Hardy. She left a few years ago, took her pension and moved up north somewhere." "Can you please tell me if you can remember where she moved to? I really would love to get in touch with her...we were high school friends." "Give me a moment. Let me think. It was in the Springwater area. Something like Palm Town."

"Palm Town? Do you mean Palm Harbour?" "Yeah, that could be it. It was so long ago, I really don't know for sure."

Stella's heart was palpitating. She hung up. "My God, this is getting freakier by the minute. After all this time, no one has talked about Lena's last name." She ran to her desk and grabbed the Holly Meadow Directory, drew her finger down the pages, Lena, Lena, come on where are you. Here it is....Lena - Kotta! If I don't die from anxiety now, I never will.

"Spike, pick up the phone. Hurry, pick up the phone." Spike picked up - all he could hear was heavy breathing.... Hello?...

"Spike it's me Stella...please come up quick."

"Sit down, I have to explain."

"Calm down Stella. You're not breathing right." "You wouldn't be either. JaJa Jack had an affair with Lena back in Capri Island around the time of his divorce. Before his divorce, after divorce, oh, I don't know....but he was having one. I haven't told you, but I have been researching Jack Hardy's background. I even met with his ex-wife."

"You've been spying on Jack? I thought you were onto Noah?" "I haven't ruled him out. Listen to me, this is too creepy. Jack was married to this woman, Tina, who Jack claims kidnapped a Lena

Kotta, who was his bookkeeper at the time, because there were rumors he was having an affair with Lena Kotta."

Stella told Spike, "I called Jack's former company and talked to a lady who remembers an employee Lena who worked with Jack, that may have moved to Palm Harbour."

"So what are you saying, Stella?"

"Don't you get it?"

"I don't know how Jack managed to get the luck to work here, but his goal was to be in the area that Lena was living in because they are or were lovers. Lena might have told him about the job opening here."

"But if they had been lovers for *that long*, wouldn't Jack be devastated that she is gone or hasn't been around, or dead?" asked Spike.

"I don't know. I just don't know. You're right, he has been acting normal. Maybe he knows where she is. If he knows she is safe, why would he be worried? One point is, he claims he has not even met her," said Stella.

"What would be the purpose of the set up? I mean, him hiding her?" asked Spike.

"The other day when I was down at the pool, I had a conversation with Jack and he mentioned that even though it's been five years he said he sometimes felt that his ex, Tina, still thought about him or loved him."

"I don't know, but this might be the reason he had to hide Lena; Jack told me Tina kidnapped his friend, Lena, in the past. Who knows what else she is capable of doing, even if it has been five years. Tina could feel Lena was the culprit that ruined their marriage and she could have been carrying all this built up anger for the past five years and then suddenly snapped. Maybe Tina has been making threats against Lena so he had to move her in with him."

"Stella, you actually think Lena would leave her condo and her job for *Jack!*"

"If it meant her life!"

"Stella, you might be onto something but it is damn difficult to believe. Some people do have the same names. Did you check the spelling of the bookkeeper's last name? It could be different."

"I thought about a similarity of names and that it could be a coincidence," said Stella.

"And what about Noah, his love card and ladder?" asked Spike.

"That's our second scenario," said Stella.

"I think it's our first to be honest with you, said Spike. After all, Noah's DNA *was* found on the black bikini bottom."

"Maybe the lab made a mistake. They do make mistakes," said Stella.

"I doubt it. Do you think it's easy for me to sleep at night thinking I might be living next to a psycho? He is one of our best friends. We all work together around here. Now…Abe, Adam, Nick and I don't know how to handle him. We should be the ones on sedatives."

"Let's all get together by the pool this weekend," Stella suggested. We have to invite Noah. We'll act like we usually do toward him. I'm interested to see if we can pick up on anything unusual about him when he's around all of us in a social situation. Just have a small glass of healthy red wine before you go to the pool and you'll feel relaxed," Stella told Spike.

CHAPTER THIRTY THREE

It was Saturday morning and Maryann and Abe began walking toward the beginning of the pier by Noah's porch when they bumped into Spike, Lita, Stella and Adam.

The smell of fresh leaves was in the air and the water ruffled with the breeze. Maryann commented how soothing the atmosphere was as they began their walk down the beautiful sun lit canal draped with tropical ornaments.

"When Abe and I were out on our boat that day we were attacked, as I approached this pier, I now remember there was a terrible odor of bleach," said Maryann. I looked over and Noah was cleaning his railing and spindles."

"*With Bleach?*" Stella asked with surprise."

"Yes, straight bleach. He said he was getting rid of the hornet nests and spider webs and stuff."

"*Spike?*"..... said Stella.

"We'll talk about it later Stella," he responded.

Nick and Bernice were sitting under an umbrella table by the pool.

"Hi guys!" They all said as they walked into the pool area.

Bernice noticed everyone avoided the lounge chairs and sat at tables.

"No lounging?" Bernice asked aloud.

"Guess not," said Spike. "Who the heck would lounge around here? Everyone laughed. "I dare any one of you to lay on a lounge by the pier where Carolyn was."

"You can dare all you want, but I'm not lying anywhere around here, said Stella. I didn't take my tranquilizer this morning because I wanted to enjoy a glass of wine today."

Suddenly, Noah came in through the gate with his wife Cindy. "*Cindy*, what a surprise! We never see you." The women greeted her happily.

"Hey, Cindy, how are you?" The guys all said.

"Jack just had the lounge chairs re-strapped, they should be comfortable," Spike told them.

"Yeah, the ones near the pier are the best," said Stella.

"Thanks guys," said Noah.

Noah and Cindy went to lay on the lounges.

"That's where he belongs," Stella whispered to Adam.

"Cool it, babe."

"Seems like we all brought wine," Stella commented.

"Yeah, I'm not a drinker, but sometimes if I have a little wine it does relax me, especially red wine," Spike mentioned.

"I get a major headache from red wine," Cindy yelled from across the pool.

"It's getting hot, anyone ready for a dip?" asked Nick.

"Sure!" said the rest of the men.

While the men were cooling off in the pool talking about sports, Stella finished her glass of wine and her eyes became watery.

"I have been forcing myself to come down here and lay on a lounge, but today with everyone here, I feel sensitive about the fact that we can't all relax together anymore and have a good time like we used to. I have to go home. Sorry girls."

"We understand, said Maryann. I'm feeling sort of uncomfortable myself. Every noise I hear I have to look to see where it's coming from."

* * *

In the morning, dressed in his sharp suit, Adam kissed his wife good-bye while she was having her coffee at the kitchen table. He mentioned he had a busy day ahead of him at the bank.

"Sorry about leaving the pool so fast yesterday, honey."

"That's okay, we all understood. We had a good time. I guess you're going food shopping this morning babe, you got up before me." Adam commented.

It was rare that Stella was up and about before Adam left for work, unless she went food shopping to beat the crowd. But this morning she was anxious.

Today, Stella's mission was to find Jack's home and look for traces of Lena. She got the address from Spike, put it in her GPS, and was on her way. Jack was already at Holly Meadow, so she didn't have to worry about him - while she was checking out his house. She pulled into his driveway and got out of the car. She peeked through some windows.

"Can I help you, Maam?" Came a voice from behind. Stella jumped.

"Oh, excuse me, Sir. I was wondering if this house was for sale. I saw this address in the paper but I think I wrote down the wrong house number."

"I don't think Jack has any plans on moving Maam. It must be the Ranch, down the street, you saw in the newspaper. It's been for sale for over six months and only a handful of people have looked at it. It's a good deal, but the way the economy is now, as you know, things are tough. I can tell you exactly where it is," the man said.

"Oh thank you Sir. Just give me the number and I'm sure I'll find it."

"Okay Maam, it's down around the corner on the right, number seventy one."

"Thanks again Sir. No problem."

Stella walked to her car and left. "These fifty-five plus communities watch out for each other like hawks. I'll never get further with this case unless I come up with better evidence. Maybe I should just give up."

CHAPTER THIRTY FOUR

Jack decided he would get the trashy rotten rope out of the front pond. He noticed Stella pulling into the parking lot during his walk over to the pond.

"Hey Stella, How are you doing?" he yelled over to her as she got out of her car. She put on a fake smile and felt a little jittery. "I'm fine. How about you? Jack." "I'm getting myself ready to cut that old rope out of the front pond, wanna help?" "Maybe I should, what the hell, why not?" she responded.

"I was only kidding," said Jack.

"No, actually I could use some exercise."

"Okay, if you say so."

"The last time I went into that pond to take the tennis balls out, I had an alligator staring at my belt buckle. I have to observe the whole area - and the water - very carefully before I start working in it again."

"Yeah, I don't want any alligators around, said Stella. I'll go up and change and meet you at the pond."

"I'm ready, Jack."

"Okay, I'll go in just far enough to grab the rope and you can hold it above the water while you're standing on the grass. As you're holding it, I'll slowly walk into the water and follow the rope to where it's tangled and try to cut it with my buck knife. I might need to get a machete. Here goes, stand right here just at the edge of the water. I left it in this area after I disentangled it from my boot." He stepped into the pond a couple of feet and didn't see the rope.

Jack walked deeper into the water and began penetrating the eerie muddy sludge with his hands hoping to feel the rope. The uncomfortable feeling of having his hands deep down on the mysterious floor sent a chill up his spine. He swished his hands in the murky water in between a bunch of rotten weeds and felt nothing but lots of broken branches and a couple of long thick sticks that were jammed somewhere. His hand swept over what felt like a mossy turtle shell. I remember it was near the pipe. It might be attached to it. He felt all around the pipe and the bottom of the ornamental fountain and didn't feel the rope or anything that felt like it could be a rope. "I don't understand. It was a thick long brown rope all knotted up in big loops. I can't find it. All I'm feeling is sludge and slippery branches. I'm giving up. I don't even see any of those tennis balls I left behind the other day." "Maybe someone else cleaned them out," said Stella. Jack turned his head and gave a blank stare. "Someone is watching us, Stella." "A hundred people could be watching us, Jack. We are in a condominium complex." "No, I mean someone is closely observing what we are doing." "How can you know that? Did you see someone in a window?" No, I got a chill and a strange feeling for just a second that someone's eyes were mysteriously fixed on us." "It was an alligator. You better hurry out." "I'm serious," said Stella. "Stella, I'm sure you must have experienced the feeling of someone watching you, at least once in your life." Jack walked out of the pond. "I'm going to the shower by the pool to wash this crud off. Thanks for trying to help me. We'll talk later."

On the way back to her condo, Stella felt a creepiness about what Jack had said. She could not help roll her eyes up and down all the condo windows as she past the buildings. But was it a *condo* window? It could have been someone in a car. The thought of someone sitting in a car watching her, gave her a scary feeling. She walked faster and was happy to get into her home.

A few minutes later, there was a knock on Stella's door. It was Joe, who lived in the building near the pond.

"Hi Stella, I was wondering what you and Jack were looking for in the pond. I was watching you two and hoping you weren't looking to remove the rope - because I took it out yesterday."

"Oh yes, we were looking for the rope, Joe."

"I apologize. I didn't know anyone else knew about it. I was sitting on the bench by the pond and noticed the trashy rope just floating there, so I yanked it and cut it out piece by piece. It was quite a long rope. I threw it in the dumpster. I'm sorry that you guys went through all that trouble today," Joe told Stella.

"It's okay, thanks for removing it. I'll let Jack know."

A couple of days went by and some residents noticed that Jack hadn't been around. A few called Spike and asked if he knew where he was. Spike didn't notice he wasn't around. He gave him a call but Jack didn't answer his phone. He figured he was just busy.

CHAPTER THIRTY FIVE

Spike was sitting in his office when suddenly it entered his mind that, strangely, he had not received any phone calls within the past few weeks from residents complaining about their clothes dryers not working properly. He was supposed to get back to five of the residents many weeks ago, but with all that had evolved since then, it totally slipped his mind. In addition, the residents never called again to complain, except for today. Mr. Mel Thompson who lived in the same building as Spike and Noah called. He yelled, that he was fed up with all the lint backing up into his laundry room. Mr. Thompson told Spike he had paid a commercial technician to clean out his outgoing air hose a couple of months ago but it became blocked again. "The buildup is causing a moldy stench," Mr. Thompson complained. Spike said, "I'll have an industrial technician check the outgoing vent. Too much lint back-up could cause a fire, so don't leave the dryer running when you go out," Spike told Mr. Thompson.

A couple of days later, a dryer technician came over to Mr. Thompson's condo and unclogged his outgoing vent in the floor with his industrial vacuum. The technician told Mr. Thompson - "There was quite a lot of lint and some leaves that blew up from the bottom that I vacuumed out, so your dryer should be working much better now. The moldy stench should dissipate in a couple of days." "You can spray some disinfectant on a wet cloth and dry it. That might help. I never smelled mold or mildew like this before," said the technician. "It must be wet rotten leaves with lots of dead bugs and maybe even a dead coon down around there. It should dry out, now that there is more air flowing through."

CHAPTER THIRTY SIX

Spike called Abe, Adam and Nick and invited them to his place so they could discuss the situation with Noah. Stella told Adam to make sure he reminded Spike about the fact that Noah washed his railings with bleach.

They all grabbed themselves a drink from Spike's bar and sat around the dining room table. Spike first asked Abe - what he thought about Noah? Abe said, "The fact that Noah was cleaning his railings with bleach could just be a coincidence. People here at Holly Meadow have to clean their railings often because of all the bugs and hornet nests." Spike took notes as he asked each one what they thought. Next, he asked Adam's opinion. Adam said, "That he felt that just because Lena's bikini bottom was in the lake means nothing." Nick spoke next. "I think the fact that Noah's DNA was found on Lena's bikini bottom means something. Noah is a married man. If he was fooling around with Lena, that's a major concern."

"What if we are making a mistake and the bikini bottom belongs to Cindy?" asked Nick.

"A bikini on Cindy? You gotta be kidding me... and what would Lena's DNA be doing on Cindy's bathing suit?" asked Spike.

"Actually, the fact that my wife saw him burning his ladder should be something of concern, said Adam. The love note my wife found could be just coincidental but the words "when you step up into my Ark" is just *too* coincidental. I personally don't feel he wanted to burn leaves that day. His goal was to burn the ladder and make us think he wanted to burn leaves."

Spike said, "The only thing I have on Noah was when we were at a meeting, Noah reacted nervously surprised when I mentioned I had some private information about Lena's disappearance that could not be disclosed. In addition, there have been a few little surprised expressions he has been making all along when Lena's name is mentioned. We just don't have enough solid evidence to bring to the police. We are going to have to ask Noah to join us at our meetings. If anything more suspicious turns up as time goes on, we'll take it from there. I did want to do another search of the forest for a possible grave. How do you guys feel about it? asked Spike. It would be just us. We can tell anyone who's curious that we are searching for pythons. We'll also have to ask Noah to join us." "We're doing an awful lot of work that the county should be doing. Don't you think so, guys?" said Adam.

Yeah, but this isn't New York, said Nick. If you want a feeling of thoroughness, you have to do it yourself. As serious as this issue is, it seems that if the police don't have a lot of leads or evidence, they slow down. And when you think about it, they have no leads or evidence concerning Lena. Noah's DNA on her bathing suit was not a good enough lead for them.

"It would be taken very serious in New Jersey," said Abe. "I think it's a good lead."

"I think it's a good lead too. They could have at least questioned him or performed one search of the forest with cadaver dogs, said Spike.

"True. Not to offer one search of the forest was careless on their part," said Abe.

"Is everyone in on the search?" "I'm in," they all said. "Okay. Is Saturday morning at ten good?" They looked at each other and nodded yes. "Looks like it's fine with us," said Nick. "See ya then," said Spike.

Abe, Adam, and Nick got up and left. Spike wasn't feeling any better about Noah. It was going to be very hard for him to be his friend until Lena's disappearance was resolved.

* * *

Stella heard Adam walk through the door.

"How did it go?"

"As good as it could. We just don't have enough evidence on Noah."

"I know we don't, Adam. We don't have enough evidence on anybody."

"What do you mean, Stella? What the hell are you hiding from me? Are you still playing detective?"

"Calm down. I'm giving up. I tried all I could and I got nowhere."

"Spike, Abe, Nick, Noah, and I are going into the forest to search for a grave next Saturday. Don't mention anything about it to anyone. If anyone asks, tell them we're looking for pythons."

A few more days went by and residents showed more concern that Jack hadn't been around. A few called Spike and asked if he knew where he was. Spike was so pre-occupied with all that was going on; he still hadn't noticed that Jack wasn't around. He gave him a call but Jack didn't answer his phone. Again, he figured he was just busy.

Saturday came and the guys prepared themselves well - bringing along machetes, water, bug repellent, cell phones and a rifle. They synchronized their watches and each assigned themselves a different path and planned a time and meeting point when they were finished.

Spike led himself into blinding thick brush and had to whack his machete constantly. After about fifty feet into the forest, he looked ahead and noticed a pole of sunlight shining on what looked like a pile of white eggs nestled in the ground. He stood still, sweating in a wide bar of sun shining through some tall trees; his face covered with dirt and crumbled leaves all over his t-shirt and jeans. A chipmunk scurried under some underbrush on his left and Spike's head made a quick turn. The forest was fully alive with pleasant noises of mother nature. However, underneath all the beauty, was an eerie feeling of terror. On guard, with his machete held in the air for a quick strike, he scoped around and very carefully approached the eggs. He glanced down and saw what looked like hundreds of little snakes coming out of their shells, pecking aggressively into the air with their little pointed mouths. You frigging little murderers he said, as he took a chance and bent over and slashed at the baby snakes and eggs as if he was chopping celery. "I have to make sure I kill every one of you little frigging bastards," he said aloud as he slashed away. "This means there's an aggressive mother python around close by," he thought.

He heard a shuffle in the leaves and jumped. It was two squirrels playing. He bent back down and before he made his next chop, he heard a movement behind him. Spike flew his tight muscular body up with a fast turn of his back and swung his machete like a hard whip, matching the expertise of a black belt. A few squirrels scooted away. He cleared some branches around him. He brushed the sweat off his forehead with his arm. He only had to make a few more chops to make sure the job was completely done. "I'll be damned, if I leave one of you bastards alive." He noticed all flesh and only a milky substance. "You little twisted dicks operate with no red blood. How do you fuel those deranged brains? Looks like I'll have to do some more research on you African Rock psychopaths." When he was finished, Spike slashed his way into the forest another fifty feet. The brush was so thick; he would not see a grave if there was one. His arms were scratched and bleeding to a point where he felt he should start heading back. He turned his body around to follow his path back. As he stepped over the broken branches, he tripped and fell to the ground. Spike lifted his head and faced the wide-open jaws of a python. "Hi Mom! Pissed about your kids?" He suddenly gained a major life saving rush of adrenaline and with his extra sharp machete, he lifted his arm, swung, and cut the python's head off so fast it flew in mid-air and he didn't hear it land. "I don't know where that energy came from, but thank you almighty God! He gasped. While barely able to catch his breath, he lay on his back and looked at the sky with praying hands. He then got up and walked aimlessly, trying to burn off what was left of his adrenaline.

He called his friends on his cell and told them he was on his way back. They all said they were ready to head back also, except for Adam. He did not answer his phone. Adam attempted his walk back, but lost his path inward to follow. One thing they all forgot was a compass. He followed the sun westward toward his building.

Adam had to work hard again, slashing the bushes to make way. He came to an area where there was nothing but cypress trees and piles of potato vines. He found a machete on the ground and figured someone was cutting the vines and forgot to take it back with them. He bent down to grab the machete and noticed a boot under a pile of cut up vines. He moved some of the pile and shockingly saw the tail of a python. Not knowing if the python was alive or dead, he began slicing at the vines and as he got closer to the floor of the pile, what he saw was so repulsive he threw his guts up. Adam keeled over and heaved. He fell to the ground, grabbed his cell phone, and tried to talk to Spike. Spike recognized his number. "What is it? Adam. Are you okay? I tried calling you but you didn't answer." Adam babbled, incoherently." Adam, what's going on? Tell me where you are." He gagged and heaved. "I think, a few feet back of second building." Spike bolted towards behind the building.

"Adam, make a sound." Spike could hear a heaving sound. He followed the sound. Spike found Adam on the ground in the fetal position. Adam pointed to the pile of vines. Spike walked over to the pile and let out a fierce mad growl, *Nooo!* He saw Jack's boots sticking out of a python's mouth. He called 911. The python was still alive and making contractions. The Task Force, Ambulances, Sheriffs, and Local News Reporters flooded the parking lot and ran into the woods. There were so many flashing lights it was impossible to see. A couple of gunshots were heard. Residents cried and screamed from their balconies. The flashing lights blinded them and made them dizzy. *"What now? "Help us, Dear God!"* They yelled. The other men returned from the forest and Spike called them and told them to stay in the parking lot. Their wives ran into Stella's condo and wept uncontrollably. The officials cut the python open and removed Jack. Without thought, they knew he would be dead. He suffocated. There was a large bruise on his head. The python struck him, he passed out, and there was the python's meal, lying flat out, and ready to consume. Exactly the way scientists described the danger of the African Rock.

Spike was feeling dizzy and nauseous and slowly paced his weak legs home. The officials tried to keep everyone calm but the small community was out of control. There was major hysteria. Their confused minds spun as if inside the eye of a hurricane.

After all the officials left, Spike's friends went to check on Spike. They entered his condo, stumbled into the living room and collapsed on the couch. They all threw away their male egos and cried hard. Noah asked Nick how he got the black and blue mark on his forehead. "I got hit by something that flew at me."

Spike asked, "Was it the head of a python?" "Yeah right. You're funny Spike." "I'm not kidding. I killed about a hundred fucking snake eggs and the mother. I chopped those little fucking murderers like I was chopping celery. I fucking sliced the mother's head off so fast it flew high in the air and I didn't hear it land."

"Did any of you guys see any snakes?"

"No. No graves either. How the heck could you see a grave in all that jungle brush?" said Nick.

"Maybe I hit it lucky guys and killed the only female on the property." "Hopefully, the one that got Jack, was the last fucking python around," said Nick. "Poor Jack. He was a good honest worker and a real nice man. There is nothing that can describe the emotional journey of horror we are all going through," said Noah.

CHAPTER THIRTY SEVEN

Later that night, Noah sat in his living room and waited for his wife Cindy to come home from work. He was crying about Jack and Lena. It was time to let out his deep hidden feelings of guilt. He thought about the night he and Spike had dinner and how Spike questioned him about how he felt about Cindy working nights.

Cindy entered through the door and saw Noah sitting on the sofa with his hands folded on his thighs and his tearful eyes looking downward like a deeply sad little boy.

"What's the matter honey?" she asked.

"Jack is dead. A python got him."

"Oh my God! How *Sick! Oh how awful.* I never had the chance to get to know him, in a personal way, but what a bizarre tragic accident. And it happened right here on our property. I heard he was a good man and was willing to help everyone with anything. I have never mentioned anything about what has been going on in our community to anyone at work. It's too unbelievable. They might think I'm a fruitcake. Tears rolled down Cindy's cheeks. Noah, the tension here at Holly Meadow is unbearable. And we are all stuck here."

"Condos are still not selling anywhere - unless you give them away. And we wouldn't even be able to give them away. Word has got out about the pythons. And Lena is still in the news as missing. We are living a nightmare, Noah." "Nightmare at Holly Meadow," how's that Noah?

"I could write a book." "It would definitely be a best seller. This is real stuff that is unheard of. The African Rock python is here in Florida, the state of paradise and DisneyWorld."

"Cindy, all these years that you have been working nights - there have been many times when I have felt very lonely. Let's face it, you have worked many hours of overtime - leaving early in the afternoon and working until sometimes one in the morning. Did you ever think that maybe you're a workaholic? Did you ever feel bad about leaving me alone all those hours? I've had dinner in pubs and pizza places more than I've had dinner with you!

"I'm so sorry Noah, but there haven't been any openings for the nine to five shift."

"I have to confess something to you, Cindy."

"What do you have confess?"

She placed her briefcase down and sat next to her husband on the sofa.

"A few months ago I uh...."

"You what?"

"I had a fling."

"What do you mean? Noah!...you had an affair?"

"No, just a fling. It was a fast few minute fling down on the pier."

"How could you Noah! How could you do that to me?"

"I regret it tremendously."

"Who was this "few minute fling with?"

"I'm sorry to say, it was with Lena. She and I were drinking and sitting on the pier and it just happened. I was lonely, honey!

I know it was a very indecent and disrespectful act. It will never happen again."

"Yeah, no kidding. She's dead."

"Don't say that Cindy! We don't know for sure."

"I can see how you can get lonely, Noah, but that's no reason to cheat on me. How can I trust you from now on?"

"You'll have to have faith in me. It was just two silly drunk people who made a mistake. Will you forgive me?"

"Forgiveness won't take away the damage and allow me to trust you. I need time. You hurt me. I'm too hurt. Maybe in a few days, when I get over the shock we can start working on a bridge of reconciliation. Cindy broke out in a cry. "We can try and work on how to communicate better."

"Hopefully, if we work hard enough, the road ahead will take me to a miracle of fully restored trust in you, Noah."

"I know these next few weeks will be tough for you, Cindy. Please don't let the anger and pain prevent you from forgiving me."

"Now I have to tell you something very important, I mean important in a different way. Lena threw her black bikini bottom in the lake, after we were together, and a black bikini bottom has been found in the lake and my DNA could be on it. I know Lena had numerous black bikinis. We all would jokingly compliment her bathing suit, because it was always black and she would respond "Oh thanks, I just bought it."

But the fact is, she had a black bikini on the day she disappeared and it could be the one she wore when she was with me."

Cindy's stomach churned. "You could be accused of her disappearance. *Or are you responsible for her disappearance? Maybe there was an accident you're not telling me about, Noah? Tell me the truth, Noah!*"

"How could you possibly think that? I would never hurt that little woman."

"At least I'll never have to worry about you fooling around with her again. Thank goodness she's gone."

"Stop it! We don't know if she's gone. Moreover, it wasn't all her fault. I came on to her. I told you, I was lonely."

Cindy said with a guilty tone, "Well, I mean, I do hope the woman is safe and does show up somewhere alive, one of these days, but it's highly unlikely. If you told me you were with a woman other than Lena, I would leave you."

"If it happens again, I'll file for a divorce." "We have to keep this so-called fling of yours a secret. It's too risky. Even if it happened a few weeks before her disappearance, you could be criminally investigated."

"I agree," Noah responded.

CHAPTER THIRTY EIGHT

The next day, after a long cool shower, Adam stepped out and smelled smoke. He rushed outside and could see smoke coming from one of the other condos on his floor. Nervously, he ran for his phone and called 911. The firemen ripped the door down and there were flames coming out of the laundry room in Mel Thompson's condo. There was chaos and confusion in the parking lot.

The men extinguished the fire rapidly with extreme professionalism and efficiency. The tragedy caused massive fire and water damage to the upper, lower and side condos. Three fire inspectors came in with masks and gloves to do their investigation. They dissected the damaged area of the condo looking for the cause of the fire. "Looks pretty definite to me, the fire began in the laundry room," Inspector Luigi Caboni pointed out. "No, ya kiddin, Luigi," said Sal. Inspector Sal Lorenzo stuck a long snake with a mechanical clutch device down the outgoing air vent behind the clothes dryer. Sal pulled out a bunch of leaves that had such a putrid smell he gagged through his mask. "Sal, dida you hava to bring up the leaves," Luigi complained. Sal scattered the leaves and pulled out a few pieces of small bony like material. Sal pushed the snake device back down the vent hole and it became stuck. He jiggled it a few times and brought it up with a broken piece of jaw bone. "Looka what I found fellas. Something wasa dead in that vent for quite a while, maybe months. I only hava piece of jaw bone." "It wasa squirrel," said Luigi. "You stupida sona of bitch, thisa no squirrel. Ahhh, you wouldn't hava this job if it wasn't for your Uncle. Wait, let mia a pulla this dirty rag offa the teeth." Inspector Lorenzo pulled a tiny shredded black bikini top off the teeth and threw the top in a trash can. "This was very big male racoon. The racoon climbed into the venta from the bottom of the building." "That doesn't look like a raccoon jaw to me, said Antonio. It looks more like a big snake." "Thera no big snake around here. Snake in the everglades, Antonio." "Okay, if you say so boss." Sal threw the jaws in the trash. "That's it guys. We solved this case. There wasa problem deep down in the outgoing dryer vent thata caused this fire. We hava seen this many times. It was clogged with a big deada racoon which caused leaves and lint to accumulate deep down neara the outside vent atta the bottom of the building. Alright let's getta outa here fellas, we hava more work to do."

Unfortunately, Inspector Lorenzo didn't believe Antonio. Mr. Lorenzo never heard of pythons being anywhere but in the everglades. The python had disintegrated and all that was left were its jaws with a black bikini top caught on its teeth. Now that the bathing suit top was thrown in the trash and taken away, how would anyone at Holly Meadow know that what the Inspectors found might help with Lena's disappearance.

Spike was furious with Mel Thompson. "I told you not to leave the condo with the dryer on," he told Mel. "Spike, that was before I had the lower vent cleaned. The commercial technicians don't clean the vents all the way to the ground level. Then when I told you I began to have a problem again, you sent an industrial technician over. However, he also must not have cleaned the vent thoroughly. He obviously just cleaned enough to let good airflow out for a short period, before the lint began to trap and accumulate again. Don't worry, I have enough insurance to cover the damage to the other condos," Mel told Spike.

For the next few weeks, there were constant sounds of banging and chain saws and the parking lot was full of trucks and building materials.

After the damaged condos were fully rehabbed, their residents were relieved. And the neighbors more than appreciated that peace and quiet was restored.

The weather was getting cooler and the residents were feeling more comfortable and less fearful the longer time went by without incident. After a few months, the fear of pythons had diminished. They finally could get together, lay by the pool, and enjoy the beautiful sun and clear blue sky over Emerald Lake.

"I finished my therapy sessions, Adam, and I'm weaning myself off the medication. In the early morning when all is calm and I'm alone, I feel a soothing contentment and totally at one with the universe. It took many hours of training but I am at peace with myself and at times feel joyful. "That's wonderful honey." Adam rejoiced.

Carolyn announced, "I'll have you all know that Dean and I are engaged." Everyone smiled. "We are all so happy for you," Bernice said with great joy.

"My wife changed her work shift to nine to five, so we can have dinner together every night," said Noah.

"I'm glad the attendance at the board meetings picked up," Spike mentioned.

"I suggested we have a moment of silence for Lena, Tom and Jack at every meeting and everyone agreed. Sometimes we even have a full house and the residents actually have come to their senses and show some appreciation for the board and their hard work," said Adam.

"One more thing everyone, Dean and I are thinking about having our wedding here - by the pool - in the Summer."

"Oh, Carolyn, that would be such an enjoyable event for all of us. Let me know when you want to start the preparations," said Stella.

"I'm excited. I love weddings," said Bernice. "We will have to buy new lounge chairs and paint the pier."

"Well, I have to say it looks like things are finally looking better and close to normal here at Holly Meadow, said Stella. I hope to God there are no more pythons. Of course it will never be completely normal without finding out what happened to our dear Lena."

Spike mentioned, "Sometimes I find that what has happened in this community, so unbelievable, I don't grasp it very well. I think I see a glimpse of it all and then all the bizarre terror and loss that I feel seems to rise up and tell me that what I experienced just couldn't be true."

"Fortunately, there hasn't been a python sighting since we lost our dear Jack, which was the same day Spike killed all those snake eggs and the mother. The lab mentioned in the report that the snake that attacked our dear Jack was a male. Maybe it was the father of those eggs and that is the end of the pythons, said Stella.

"Or was it the mother? It's close to dry season when pythons become dormant," Spike mysteriously thought. His eyes bulged as he looked to the side. The inside of his stomach rumbled with pain. He decided to remain silent.

"Why ruin a great day!"

CHAPTER THIRTY NINE

Everyone left their pleasant day at the pool with a long awaited feeling of happiness and contentment in their lovely Holly Meadow community.

Cindy and Noah held hands walking down the pier and were just about to step in their door, when Cindy remembered she had a bag of potatoes she had to get out of the car. She said, "I'll get them honey, the car is right here. I left it open. Go ahead in and freshen up. I'll start boiling the water for home-made mashed potatoes tonight."

Noah felt a contentment he hadn't felt in a long time. His wife was well rested and was making a nice dinner. He went into the master bedroom, put on his comfortable jogging pants, and then went into the bathroom to wash up. He turned on the sink water, soaped his hands and face, and moved his face down to rinse it off in the sink bowl. After he was finished, he could not help notice the sun reflect off a shiny gold necklace, on the vanity, that read "Lena" in a carved signature as the pendant. He picked up the necklace, lifted it closer to his eyes toward the light above the sink, and saw Cindy in the mirror holding her thirty-eight caliber pistol straight at him.

"You don't need to look closer. I'll tell you what it says, you no good frigging liar," she said with a devilish hundred watt smile.

"Nice jewelry, I found under my nightstand. Too bad it wasn't mine and belonged to that dead bitch you were having an affair with. Noah turned around with his hands up, *"You killed Lena? What the heck is wrong with you, Cindy? Do you realize your facing life in prison. Was she worth throwing your life away? Was she worth giving up paradise for a cold dark cell. Because that's where you're going. Put the gun down."*

"No, I won't, she responded."

"Why didn't you let me know, a long time ago, you knew Lena and I were having an affair? Why did you want to stay?" asked Noah.

"Because I kept hoping. I kept hoping she would move or it would end, Noah. I tried so hard to get the day shift, but it didn't work out, until now. And now I realize I can't be your wife any longer. It's too late. I'm too hurt."

"I'll have you know, I didn't think those small snakes I captured down in the everglades were going to cause such a disaster. I hadn't seen them since I let them loose over two years ago. All of a sudden, they began migrating away from the deep forest where I left them, and they had grown two hundred times their original size."

Cindy's eyes filled up as she held her gun tight and a little jittery.

Noah sensed her arm was getting tired. *"You* brought those snakes here? Cindy, there are a lot of wonderful people here."

"And you're not one of them, my dearly beloved Noah. I came home early one night and heard giggling in our bedroom. I peeked through the bedroom door hinge space and saw your little tramp bouncing up and down on your obviously rock hard dick - Cindy let out in distress with teary eyes, struggling to keep the gun pointing sharply at him. Did she suck to impress a married man?

Did she make oooh sounds while it got caught between her tonsils to make you feel you had a big lollipop? I can hear it – Oh suck harder, suck harder. It wasn't one of my favorite romantic things, Noah! She sucked all right! She was a no good tramp!

"You murderer! How many snakes did you capture?" Noah asked with steaming anger. How many you bitch?

"I think seven. They were small. They looked a little over a foot long."

"So that means they're all gone. Carolyn is one. The Ape is two. Abe's boat incident is three. Spike killed one – that's four. Jack is five. The one found near the front pond is six. Is Lena seven? Is that snake gone, Cindy? Tell me, you bitch. I don't want anyone else here *to die!*" He yelled, even though he was facing a loaded barrel. "You made this community a living hell!"

Cindy was shaking as she explained - "Yes, her snake is gone. I fed it rat poison indirectly. It was the best way to kill it. You had just put some poison out on the rat traps. I thought, perfect, there would be no suspicion if the python was brought to the lab. I had to confirm that it was dead for peace of mind. One late night shortly after Lena was consumed or should I say, after I gave the cute starving python, Lena for dinner - I took a powerful flashlight and looked and looked relentlessly under the building. I didn't give up because there was a strange stench under one of the condo's to the side of ours. I dragged my body under the building a few feet and observed a long python skin hanging out of a dryer vent with a piece of black material that looked like a bra cup. I could barely reach the snakeskin, but after many tries, I finally got hold of it and pulled it from the vent. It didn't have the black bra attached to it and I couldn't reach any further so I gave up. I figured the black bra or bikini top must be snagged in the vent and would never be found. The hibiscus flowers were beginning to bloom so I sprayed the area with multiple cans of hibiscus scent so no one would smell the foul odor on their rear balconies. I shoved a bunch of potato vine leaves under the building. My goal was accomplished. Lena was gone and so was the snake."

"Do you know what it was like, every time I had to drive by your little Ms. Muffit in the parking lot, knowing you two were having an affair?"

"I kept one snake in a box under the porch and had a plan to have it bite that little slut of yours, but it got away before my mission was accomplished. I figured one little bite to your little slut would do the job and then everyone else in the complex would know there were venomous snakes on the property and if they saw one they would know enough to kill it and it would take any suspicion away that she was intentionally bitten. It was the cleverest way of killing her. Obviously, I didn't know they were constrictors....poor Carolyn...I did feel bad about what happened to her and all the others."

"I stopped by a pet store near the everglades to ask some questions, but the sales clerk told me he couldn't help me because taking the snakes from the everglades was illegal. The only thing he told me was that one was a female."

"I hope it was the one Spike killed in the forest," thought Noah.

Dismayed and jittery, she continued. "One day when I noticed a big python staying under our porch, I thought I would invite your little Ms. Muffit over for her favorite drink. Low and behold, it was a Sunday afternoon when I noticed her slowly walking from the pier looking sad. You know how misery loves company. I yelled over to her and she climbed up the little ladder. I took a glass that you had drunk out of that morning which contained some water with your saliva. I then placed a pulverized tranquilizer and some rat poison into your glass and filled it with her favorite gold tequila. Was I lucky she loves tequila because that stuff is so strong and disgusting it hides the taste of chemicals. I made sure we would end up sitting on the railing admiring the beautiful forest. I watched a big furry wolf spider crawl up a spindle and sit next to her. I said to myself, this might do it. It scared her, but she jumped off and ran inside. I brushed it off the railing and convinced her it was harmless and she sat back up on the railing. After her first yawn, I knew it would be very easy to bump her off the railing onto the forest floor. However, I found it was much easier than I could ever imagine. The pollen was bothering me. All I did was let out a big sneeze and when I turned around she had fallen and her head was lying close to the python's body. She was out of it. Her eyes were closed and she didn't respond when I yelled to help her. I don't have to tell you what happened after that," Cindy said with a wise look.

"You're a very sick woman," said Noah, trying to keep from showing any emotion for Lena."

"Listen, you asshole, you never invited me to the Sunday gatherings in the clubhouse, because you always said you didn't want me around the guys when they were swearing and talking obnoxious. You said I was much better than that. Nevertheless, every Sunday I would watch all the wives walk down the pier laughing. When I asked you why the other men didn't mind *their wives* being there...you told me their wives were closet drinkers and always drank themselves into oblivion before they got to the clubhouse. And me being the naïve computer geek that I was, believed you, until I began watching all those Lifetime movies on Sunday afternoons and smartened up. Those women on Lifetime were clever and they knew how to take a deceptive path to figure out their husbands. They were masters at manipulating them and getting revenge. Boy, were they good," said Cindy.

"What did you tell everyone when they asked you where I was, Noah? Did you say - I don't want that fat bitch here….is that what you told them? You made a fool out of me, didn't you? And they all knew you were banging little Ms. Muffit on my clean sheets, while I was at work. Didn't they? They did. Didn't they, you asshole?"

Noah's arms were weak, he brought them down. "Don't move again, my finger is right on the trigger - ready to pull. If you think you can pull a fast one, it's not worth the chance, is it Noah?"

"I never said anything bad about you, Cindy. I swear I never spoke bad about you. "She was slight and could sneak up the ladder at night with no problem. No one ever saw her," claimed Noah.

"Yes, she surely was slight. Like I said, that's all I did was sneeze and she fell off the railing. My original plan fell through. No pun intended. I dreamed for weeks pushing her off that railing. It felt so good. That was going to be my climax of gratification, like eating a box of good chocolates. But it failed, just because I sneezed."

"Well, then you didn't push her, did you? Maybe we can get you off - if you just say she fell off. You have no prior record. We'll get a good lawyer," Noah sweated out.

"Come on Cindy, you're not serious, honey….give me the gun."

"Don't you…honey me…you sleaze bag. Get on the floor. *Get on the floor!* I'm not your honey anymore.

"I don't need a lawyer. There's no body, smartass. With no body, the circumstantial evidence has to be incredibly overwhelming and convincing. Try to outsmart me on that one."

"They would just have to find some miniscule flesh or the python's jawbone with Lena's DNA, and residual evidence of the narcotic and rat poison," said Noah.

Noah was trying hard to scrape up anything they could get on her. He wanted her to feel that she needed him and therefore had to keep him alive.

"Most of the snakes are non-existent. The snakes are either dead and disposed of or partially to fully decomposed and full of someone else's DNA. I made sure of that! I accumulated many of your left over glasses filled with water, leaned over the railing, and poured every one of them all over Lena's body and the python's body so they would be full of your DNA," said Cindy.

"Do you want to try again, Noah?"

"What do you want? Cindy."

"I'm not finished with my revenge. I want a divorce and all our assets. I want to leave you sleeping in a tent, and you can't tell anyone what I just told you about Lena." "If you do, I'll go looking for you in your tent and I *will* kill you."

"Fine, let me get up and we can talk about the arrangements."

The phone rang.

"Let's not answer it," she said.

The caller didn't leave a message.

"Get up, we'll sit in the dining room."

"Are you going to have that gun in my face?"

"No, I don't think we are going to kill each other at this point. I don't want to spend the rest of my life in a dark cell, and neither do you," she said.

The phone rang again. Cindy walked fast to the machine and tried to turn it off with her left hand but she had trouble figuring out how to do it. She spoke loud and nervous in a mad voice. "This dam machine won't shut up!" Noah heard a few fuzzy words come from the machine. She banged the machine and turned it over while her right arm hung down with the gun in her hand. Noah walked very slowly toward her, and very lovingly asked, "Honey, why are you so nervous about a message being left?" He then dashed fast behind her, grabbed her arm and the gun. He moved fast away a few feet and held the gun straight at Cindy.

What are you doing? I thought we were going to talk?" she asked.

"Why don't you return your boyfriend's call, Cindy," he wants to know, *if I heard correctly*, "How is it going?" She shook shocked and her eyeballs pranced with paranoia.

"There were eight pythons, Cindy. The python that attacked Stella in the Holly Boat disappeared and we are not sure if it was involved in any of the other attacks. At this moment there is an African Rock python, alive and under our porch. When we were all coming back from the pool this afternoon, and walking down the pier, I saw a huge python coiled up by a bush underneath our porch. I didn't want to scare anyone, since we all had such a pleasant day."

"I was going to shoot it quietly through a pillow and bury it tonight. But now that you told me without certainty that you planted seven pythons here at Holly Meadow, hoping one would kill Lena, I would bet on it you remembered wrong. It was eight pythons you had taken from the everglades," said Noah.

"You were right. I don't want to spend the rest of my life in a dark cell. I have decided that I will not kill the eighth python until it has a good last dinner. I hope that your fat butt won't cause the thirty footer with a girth the size of a tire to regurgitate. I wouldn't want to disappoint it."

Cindy was sweating profusely. Her knees fell to the floor while she held her hands in prayer.

"I will confess my unfaithfulness to all my friends in a few days, after you're gone," he told her.

"Noah, what do you mean, gone? Okay, okay, I will be the one to agree to leave. You can have everything. I promise Noah. Noah, please don't," begged Cindy.

"It was okay for you to hold a gun at me and threaten *my life,* but now that it's the other way, you're scared out of your mind, you selfish cold geek! You never felt guilty about not spending any time with me. I confessed my infidelity and you had the nerve to want to kill me, when you were doing the same thing, screwing the janitor on your desk. How many desks did you cave in, Cindy? This was all planned, so you and your degenerate boyfriend could have a good life - with the retirement money that we inherited from my hard working father. Death is a very scary thing isn't it, Cindy? It's mysterious because we don't know what really happens when we die. There are all kinds of beliefs out there, but there is no definite proof of what really happens. If you knew you were going to a beautiful place, you might not be so scared. Just think of how high the suicide rate would be. The human race would be extinct. At times, I felt my life wasn't worth living. The mystery of not knowing if death was worse is what kept me alive. I had a lot of questions with no answers. I wanted a wife that appreciated me and respected me. However, I didn't sense any of that coming from you. Time is too short to waste being unhappy. My friends are always there for me but Lena made me feel a secret happiness that was exciting. We weren't in love, but we did love each other and whenever I needed someone to listen she was there. She never brushed me off like you did."

"They will understand why you left me. And I will too." Goodbye, *my sweet wife.* Noah was shaking and sweating while he held the gun at Cindy with his right hand and used his left hand to shuffle through the nearby draws looking for string to tie Cindy's hands. He finally found some old twine.

"Put your body face forward against the wall," he told his wife. "You pushed me into doing this Cindy, I really don't want to do this, but you had to be a bitch, you couldn't understand why I acted the way I did. You killed the woman that was making me happy. You could have left me, you sick bitch," he told her, as he wrapped the twine around her wrists.

"Walk out through the sliders and onto the porch," he demanded. Cindy walked out. "Sit on the railing." He grabbed a pillow and shoved it against Cindy's face. Her head slammed against the corner column. As he held the pillow, he dug the loaded gun into her stomach waiting for her to pass out. She held on to the railing as hard as she could but was losing oxygen fast. Finally, she fell over onto the forest floor. Noah looked over the railing and observed her lifeless body. He ran into the condo, grabbed a flashlight, ran back onto the porch and jumped over the railing to look for the python. The python was coiled under the porch behind a bush. Thank goodness, it's still here, he thought, with sweat pouring down his face. In the darkness, he could see the glowing green eyes of the creepy African Rock reptile. He moved his flashlight to judge its distance and it quickly moved its head and slicked its tongue out toward him and Cindy's body. "It's sensing the smell of flesh. I'd better leave." Noah struggled with his thoughts. He knew deep in his mind he lowered himself to the demented sick person that Cindy had become. However, the devastating pain and overwhelming anger drove him with force beyond his control. His heart was pounding and his breath was heavy. He quickly dragged Cindy's body closer to the python behind a bush and then hurried back into his condo and slammed the slider shut. He went upstairs to wash up and broke out in a wild cry. After a tiring fight with his feelings, he went to bed. His body was numb as if it didn't exist. He couldn't feel the sheets. A cold chill passed through him and he imagined he was a corpse. Maybe in his guilty subconscious, he was hoping.

Noah thought the devil overpowered his divine soul.

"She murdered my precious little Lena?" His mind repeated as he fell in and out of sleep. A ray of morning sunlight streamed through the side of the blind and hit his face. His eyes squinted open and adjusted to the light, as he hoped it was all just a nightmare. He felt terrified and exhausted. He pushed himself up to a sitting position with his legs off the side of the bed. His eyes became teary. Immense guilt over came him and severe emotional turmoil rumbled in his gut. He threw his arms up in the air and yelled, *"What the heck did I do?" God, please forgive me. I wasn't thinking rational.*

Hysterically crying, he choked and his turned down lips scratched out, *I realize what I did was a terrible sin. Please forgive me, God! Please! I beg you!*

He pushed his tired lead heavy body to a standing position and was loosely banging back and forth against the sidewalls while trying to bring himself down the stairs to make some coffee. "I murdered my wife and I'm looking forward to a cup of coffee. I guess it's the world's most comforting pacifier *in all* circumstances."

Noah sat at his kitchen table ridden with fear that the python could be found with evidence of Cindy's gruesome death.

A few days went by and there was no sign of the eighth python. Noah searched the forest and under the building as often as he could, without his friends noticing, but it was becoming too risky. If he were caught red-handed near the bulky python, there would be too much curiosity and suspicion.

He had to let it go, forget the past, and let destiny takes its path.

Noah forced himself to go about his life in a normal manner.

CHAPTER FORTY

The temperatures in Florida became slightly cooler and the holidays were approaching. A few weeks passed and Lita and Spike were planning their neighborhood Christmas party. They found three of the tallest and most beautiful evergreen trees down at the corner lot and placed them elegantly in their condo for their friends to enjoy. Noah pushed himself to attend the party. As he walked into Spike's place and was greeted - he couldn't steer his body fast enough to the bottle of Jack Daniels sitting on the bar, to warm him up, both physically and emotionally. All his old buddies were there. It was nice to be with everyone.

Stella wobbled with her martini glass and sat next to Noah on the sofa. Spike and Abe were standing in a corner laughing about their stupid idea of building a snake trap. Maryann was laughing with Bernice about the snake fang scars she had on her ass. Adam was busy talking to Nick. Stella put her arm around Noah and happily slurred "What a year this has been, wouldn't you say, Noah? "It surely has been a unique and difficult year," he slurred back. Suddenly, Noah's cell phone rang its fancy Godfather tune. "Excuse me Stella, I have to reach into my pocket." Stella removed her loosely hanging arm from around Noah's neck. Noah looked at his caller I.D. and it read "Lena Kotta." His eyes bulged as big as soccer balls. "What's the matter Noah, you look like you saw a ghost?" Noah couldn't answer Stella. Nor could he answer his phone. He sat frozen. "Hey boy, how come you didn't answer your phone?" Stella asked. "Oh, I don't answer numbers I don't recognize," he responded. "Oh well, then I guess it's time for another drink. I'll surprise you," she said. She got up and went into the kitchen to fix her and Noah a drink. Noah stood up and looked at his caller I.D. again while his vision focused in and out. The walls seemed like they were moving and his stomach felt nauseous. He wobbled into another room, out of sight from his friends, pulled up the number, and tried to direct his jittery finger over the keypad until it hit and could press the talk button...Lena answered. He trembled. Before he could say one word, she asked, "What's the problem Noah, you can't believe it's me?" "That demented wife of yours tried to kill me." Sweat poured down Noah's face. "I played dead and managed to get away. Dawn was approaching and Jack came to work before the sun had risen. I ran to him and begged him to help me. I've been staying at his house, but now his family is ready to take over his estate and I have to leave. I am moving to Ohio to live with my sister. I'm sorry it turned out this way." Lena hung up. Noah wiped his face and neck with his handkerchief and struggled to compose himself. His heart was racing and he felt faint. He sat back down on the sofa, took some deep breaths, and waited for Stella to return with their drinks. Suddenly the front door bell rang. He could hear the anxious footsteps of a few friends walking down the front hallway to greet the next guest. As the door squeaked open, Noah overheard Stella say, "Cindy, we never see you, we're so glad you were able to find time to join us.

Interesting information for my readers made to the public on website:

"VOICE OF AMERICA"

Pythons Unlock Human Heart Health Secrets.

-+ALL CREDIT GOES TO:
Shelley Schlender with permission.

Last updated on: October 30, 2011 8:00 PM

Studying snakes might seem like an unlikely way to help people with heart disease, but a python's remarkable ability to quickly enlarge its heart during digestion has Colorado medical researchers looking toward surprising new therapies to treat human heart conditions.

Young Burmese coil in plastic boxes at a science lab at the University of Colorado in Boulder. Each one is well over a meter long, but they can grow to seven meters.

The snakes' "extreme" physiology is why molecular biologist Leslie Leinwand studies them. For instance, she says, even a big python never needs a mid-day dinner or even a weekly meal.

"They can go for months and months without eating anything, and nothing terrible happens to them."

When these giant serpents do finally show up for supper, they prefer rats, pigs or even a deer. And, unlike people, pythons never nibble. They swallow their prey whole, in one gulp. After that, Leinwand says, things get even stranger.

"Right after they eat a meal, the bulk of their organs in the body get bigger."

To speed digestion after that monstrous meal, the python's heart also gets bigger - 40 percent larger than normal - and it can take two weeks for a python to finish digesting its dinner. After that, the heart and digestive organs gradually return to their normal size.

Dramatic changes:

The key to this unusual process appears to be the python's blood. When scientists filter out the red blood cells of a resting python, the remaining plasma is clear, like human plasma.
However, python plasma changes dramatically during the first days of digestion.

"Their blood is actually milky white, and what's making it white, is actually the fat in the blood," CU student Ryan Doptis explains.

That fat gives the python energy to digest its meal, says Leinwand, just as blood fats fuel our bodies. However, she says, the strange, milky blood coursing through a python's body during the digestion process contains 50 times more fat than normal. In people, high blood fat can increase the risk of heart attack, but that's not the case for these snakes.

Impact on mammals

Post-graduate student, lead researcher Cecilia Riquelme, wondered if the fatty snake blood could produce similar changes to a mammal's heart. So she followed a hunch.

"There has to be a factor in the blood that was inducing all the organs to grow in a concerted manner. So how can we prove that?" Riquelme says. "I decided maybe I can just try the python blood on cardiac cells in the laboratory."

So Riquelme bathed heart cells from a rat in python plasma. The cells grew bigger and stronger.

The results, published on line in Science, astonished Leinwand. "That was the first eureka moment of this project. Because, it still would be of academic interest if this was something specific to snakes. But when she showed that you could promote this type of cellular growth in the heart cells of a mammal, that motivated us to really push on this project."
Heart drug for humans?

The researchers zeroed in on three key fatty acids in the python's milky blood, fats which are also found in foods such as coconut oil, animal fat and butter.

"So it's myristic, palmitic and palmitoleic," Leinwand says. "I want to emphasize it needs to be those three and in a particular combination that's found in the python."

These fatty acids are only a fraction of the many fats in a python's blood. Still, in the right proportions, even small amounts of them have proven powerful at strengthening the heart of a healthy, live mouse.

If further testing shows that these fatty acids can also strengthen a sick mammalian heart - possibly a diseased human heart, Leinwand envisions a new drug for treating heart disease.

"Those three fatty acids would be the drug," she says.

Please support a longer hunting season and an increase in hunting permits for foreign pythons in Florida's everglades and the surrounding area. These reptiles are disrupting the natural ecology system in the everglades.

In recent years, the python population has grown substantially and the man-eating African Rock pythons are migrating out of their natural habitat and into residential areas where they are a dangerous threat to children and humans in general.

Printed in the United States
By Bookmasters